JEWELS TO KILL FOR

Jack Dillon Dublin Tale 15

Second Edition

JEWELS TO KILL FOR

Jack Dillon Dublin Tale 15
Second Edition

Mike Faricy

Library of Congress Control Number: 2023920568
paperback ISBN: 978-1-962080-89-7
e-Book ISBN: 978-1-962080-90-3

MJF Publishing books may be purchased for education, Business, or promotional use. For information on bulk purchases, please contact the author directly at mikefaricyauthor@gmail.com

Published by

MJF Publishing
https://www.mikefaricybooks.com

Acknowledgments

I would like to thank the following people for their help & support: Special thanks to Nick, Roy, Julie, Mittie, and Toui for their hard work, cheerful patience and positive feedback. I would like to thank family and friends for their encouragement and unqualified support. Special thanks to Maggie, Jed, Schatz, Pat, Av, Emily and Pat, for not rolling their eyes, at least when I was there. Most of all, to my wife, Teresa, whose belief, support and inspiration has, from day one, never waned.

To Teresa
"An absolute bunch of knackers. Did you ever?"

PROLOGUE

Suel groaned as he slid out of his car. It wasn't quite 8:00 on a Monday morning, and he happened to park next to Dillon. "Oh, for God's sake, it's fecking freezing out. Of course, it wouldn't be Irish weather without some rain to make it completely miserable," he said as he hurried into the building.

Dillon grew up in Minnesota. He'd checked the weather report over there this morning like he did every day. The forecasted high temperature for this February day was fifteen degrees below zero on the Fahrenheit scale. That was minus twenty-six in Celsius, not to mention the three feet of snow on the Minnesota ground, with more on the way. He looked around the parking lot and glanced up at the gray sky. There was a light drizzle, but it wasn't lashing rain. *Yeah, it's a hell of a lot better than Minnesota at the moment*, he thought and followed Suel into the building.

"I don't know how you can stand it. There's something wrong with you, Dillon. The more miserable the weather, the more you like it," Suel said as they stepped onto the elevator.

"What can I tell you? I grew up in worse. It would get so cold I've seen dogs lifting their legs and getting stuck to fire hydrants."

"Really?" Suel asked. He gave Dillon a look and shook his head. They stepped out of the elevator and headed down the hall to Special Branch. Dillon input the code on the keypad next to the door. The door buzzed.

Suel pushed it open and headed for the breakroom. "I'm grabbing a hot tea. You want anything?"

"I'll see you in there," Dillon said.

The door to DCI McCabe's office suddenly opened, and McCabe stepped out. "Oh, Dillon, Suel, perfect. A moment of your time, please. Might as well leave your jackets on."

Suel waited until McCabe stepped back into his office and then looked over at Dillon and mouthed a rather foul invective. When they stepped into the office, McCabe was standing at the printer behind his desk. He took the two pages coming out of the printer, tapped them twice on the credenza, stapled them together, and handed them to Suel.

"This just came across from Finglas Station. Another shooting. The third in as many days. Victim is a male, no ID yet."

"Was he homeless, someone living on the street?" Suel asked.

"Slim chance. He was found in the driver's seat of a Mercedes parked in front of a council housing residence in Finglas."

"Did they think to run the license plate?"

"I'm presuming they have by now. The request came through around four a.m. Anyway, he was apparently shot sometime in the early morning hours. Finglas Station is asking for help. It's their third shooting in as many days. They're seeing a pattern and hoping to stop a gang war before it gets any worse. They're still on site. I'd like you to check it out and let me know. Any questions?"

Dillon shook his head. Suel said, "We're on it, sir."

"Good, close the door on your way out," McCabe said.

They headed out of the office. Suel gave a longing look at the breakroom as they made their way back to the elevator. "I'll drive," Dillon said.

Suel didn't respond. Once back in the car, he sat in the passenger seat with his arms crossed and looking anything but happy. Dillon input the Finglas address into the GPS and then pulled out of the parking lot. Instead of following the GPS directions and turning left to head out of Phoenix Park, he turned right and headed up Chesterfield Avenue, the main road in the park. He took the second turn in the roundabout and then pulled into the parking lot at the Phoenix Park Tea Room. "You stay here and see if you can find a smile. I'll grab a tea and a coffee."

Suel gave a slight nod. Dillon left the car running and hurried up the asphalt path to the Tea Room, a white octagonal structure surrounded by picnic tables. Given the weather, no one was seated outside. When he stepped inside, there were only four customers in the place, all quietly sipping tea. Dillon ordered tea, black coffee, and two chocolate brownies. He was back at the car four minutes later. He knocked on Suel's window, handed him the tea and the bag of brownies, and hurried over to the driver's side. He settled in behind the wheel, took a sip of his coffee, and set his cup in the console.

"You didn't have to do this, Dillon. Thanks. Sorry if I'm a bit of a pain this morning."

"You're not a bit of a bit of a pain, Paddy. You're a major pain in the ass. What's up? And before you say anything, let me just guess, Kira, again?"

"She said she didn't want to see me any more. Said it just wasn't working out."

Dillon had a number of different comments on the tip of his tongue. Not the least of which was this wasn't the first time Kira had expressed her unhappiness. Instead, he just said, "I'm sorry to hear that. Been there a number of times, and it's not fun. If there's anything I can do to help, let me know. I got us each a brownie in that bag. Figured you could use some sweetening."

Suel smiled and said, "Thanks. I take back some of the things the lads have been saying about you."

"That's more like it," Dillon said. They headed out of Phoenix Park and up to the Finglas section of Dublin.

ONE

They were headed over to Plunkett Avenue in Finglas. The crime scene was in the front parking lot of a two-story council housing structure, probably built in the mid to late 50s or early 60s. There were twenty attached units in the brick building, all with an outside entrance and a set of exposed stairs leading to the ten units on the second floor. A parking lot was at the front of the building where, at the moment, there were three Gardaí vehicles and a van from Dublin City Mortuary.

Dillon parked out on the street since both entrances to the parking lot were taped off by white plastic tape with blue letters that read '**GARDA NO ENTRY**' and then below that in smaller letters **CONFIDENTIAL TEL NO** with the **1 800 666111** number to report any information one might have. Two officers in raincoats and looking very cold stood at entrances on either end of the parking lot in the event someone decided the 'No Entry' didn't apply to them.

Dillon and Suel climbed out of the car and walked over to the nearest entry. Their IDs dangled from lanyards around their necks. The officer at the entrance took one look and nodded in the direction of the squad cars, then sneezed and sniffled. Dillon and Suel headed toward the black Mercedes surrounded by the squad cars. As they approached, Suel asked, "Who's in charge?"

"That would be me, DI Suel, and it's about damn time. How are you doing?" a voice called from the front of the Mercedes.

Suel glanced over the roof of the car and said, "God deliver me, Tully Egan. Who did you piss off to be put in charge of this investigation?"

"The list is long, Paddy, very long. It's good to have you with us. We've been more than a little busy," Egan said as he walked to the rear of the Mercedes and shook hands with Suel. "We can use all the help we can get, even if it's from the likes of you."

"Before you go too far down that road, I don't believe you've met my partner, US Marshal Jack Dillon."

Egan held out his hand and shook with Dillon. "No, we've not met, but I've heard about you and always wanted to meet the legend. You've been with Special Branch for a bit. You were involved in that situation out at Terminal Two a few years back, weren't you?"

Dillon nodded and said, "We heard you've been busy. Unfortunately, DCI McCabe mentioned this isn't the first incident."

Egan shook his head. "The third in as many days. No ID on your man, but I'm guessing it's somehow related to the other two. We're thinking maybe there's a bit of a flare-up between some locals and perhaps a Russian group."

"No idea who your man is? Have you thought about running the car license?" Suel said.

"Well, now, there you go. Why didn't we think of that? Great advice from Special Branch. Dillon, my condolences. You've got a lot of work to do bringing your partner up to speed, but you probably know that already. Yeah, Paddy, we've been waiting on the information. A new system, and if you can believe it, it's temporarily down. Take a look at him. I'm guessing mid to late thirties. No billfold. The insurance and license information was torn off the windscreen. It's beyond strange. We'll find out who he is soon enough. You can see where they tore the holder off the inside of the windshield."

Dillon glanced over at the passenger side of the car. In Ireland, there was a cardboard strip called a disc holder attached to the inside of the windshield. Usually provided by the insurance company, it has pockets that hold an insurance disc, a tax disc, and an NCT (National Car Testing) disc. Now just the remnants of the strip were stuck to the windshield. *Definitely torn off*, Dillon thought.

"Is there a weapon on your man?" Suel asked just as two men wheeled a gurney over.

Egan shook his head.

Dillon glanced over at the gurney, recognized Noel Leonard from Dublin City Morgue, and said, "Oh, hey, Noel, good to see you."

"Dillon, always a pleasure. How you been keeping?"

"Good, good, thanks for asking. And you?"

"The same, not a bother. Getting up close and personal with DI Egan here over the last few days." Leonard looked over at Egan and said, "Okay with you if we take your man? We've got photographs and stats."

Egan nodded and said, "Yeah, go ahead. We've taken his prints but wouldn't mind if you run them, too."

"Standard procedure," Leonard said.

The body was leaning forward with the right shoulder against the steering wheel, partially holding the man up. The victim's hair was black, cut close on the side and longer on top, partially covering what little of the face Dillon could see. The head was down and turned slightly, with the face more or less hidden either by the long black hair or the console.

Leonard and his partner wore blue latex gloves. They opened the driver's door, lowered the gurney, and quickly stretched out and opened the black plastic body bag.

Leonard took hold of the collar on the victim's jacket and pulled him up and back into a sitting position. As he did so, the long black hair fell away from his face exposing the entry wound on the right side of his skull and the exit wound that was just above the left eye. Leonard reached beneath the arms of the body and began to pull him partially out of the vehicle. As soon as he took a step back, his assistant reached in, grabbed the body by the belt buckle, and then angled the body back and forth, gradually working the legs over the seat and out of the car.

They laid the body on the gurney, and just as they took hold of the sides of the body bag, Suel shouted, "Wait a damn minute. I, I know this knacker."

"Suel, are you sure?" Egan asked and shot a look at Suel.

"Jesus Christ, and no surprise. Neil Kinan. I'm sure of it. I know the family. Grew up with them. Pull the jacket up on his right arm. There should be a tattoo on his forearm, a Celtic cross with the flag draped over it."

Leonard reached down and began to inch up the sleeve of the black leather jacket, and suddenly, there it was, the base of a Celtic cross. He hiked the sleeve up further until both ends of the Irish flag appeared, one side green, the other orange.

"That's good enough for me," Suel said. "I haven't seen him in years. I know he did two or three years in Mountjoy. That was probably six or eight years ago. He was a good kid who took a number of bad turns. Damn it."

"No weapon," Noel Leonard said and then looked up at DI Egan. "Okay to close the bag?"

"Yeah, go ahead." Egan looked over at Suel and Dillon. "Thus far, none of the residents we contacted saw or heard anything. In other words, no one's talking."

"Any idea why he was here?"

Egan shook his head. "Could be anything from meeting someone in the parking lot to paying one of the residents for a night of pleasure. At this stage, no idea, and, like I said, no one is talking, yet."

TWO

As they climbed into Dillon's car, Suel said, "I've got the address here." They'd spent the last two hours in the Finglas Police Station, filing reports and reviewing records on Neil Kinan. Suel had been correct. Kinan had been sentenced to four years in Mountjoy Prison for drug trafficking but was released after two years and served the last two years in the community on license, a process that was pretty standard.

The address listed for Kinan turned out to be his mother's home. Suel recognized it because he'd grown up on the next street over. He'd offered to inform the family of Kinan's death, and he read the address off to Dillon, who input it into his GPS, although Suel knew exactly how to get there.

Dillon backed out of the parking place at Finglas Station, and they headed over to 52 Maryfield Cres. Suel had lived nearby at 110 Ardlea Road, in the area of Dublin known as Artane. Along the way, Suel described the Kinan family, five children. Neil was the second oldest and one of two boys. His older brother, Eoin, was a bricklayer and, as far as Suel knew, lived somewhere in Dublin. Of the three girls, Suel could only remember the name of one, Shannon. She was two or three years younger than him, and he lost track of her once he left school.

They drove out of Finglas along Glasnevin Avenue, which eventually turned into Collins Avenue once they entered Glasnevin. They drove all the way to Malahide Road, where they turned left and, a few minutes later, entered Artane and pulled onto Maryfield Cres.

"That's the place up ahead, the third one in, with that red car parked in the drive," Suel said and shook his head. "Amazing. It looks pretty much the same. Well, except that's a nicer car than I recall ever being in the area." The home was one of eight attached, two-story stucco units. The housing was the same up and down the street and no doubt on all the other streets in the area, including the next street over where Suel had grown up.

Dillon had been in enough of the homes to know the floor plan just by looking at the front windows. Three bedrooms upstairs, in this case, one for the parents, one for the boys, and one for the girls. A bathroom would be at the end of the hall on the second floor next to the staircase and across from the third bedroom. With any luck, the bathroom would now have a shower rather than the original cast iron tub. The bedrooms on either exterior wall would have been built with coal-burning fireplaces for heat, although now all the units would have radiators and gas-fueled furnaces. The first floor would have a sitting room with a coal-burning fireplace and a kitchen with a dining area and another larger, coal-burning fire-place originally meant for cooking.

Dillon pulled to a stop in front of number 52 and glanced over at Suel. "You want me to come in with you? Happy to sit in the car and wait if you'd prefer."

"No, come on in. Wouldn't want you to miss out on the fun. Actually, I could use your support. I haven't seen Mrs. Kinan for twenty-plus years. I doubt she'll remember me, and after I tell her what happened, she sure as hell will never want to see me again. Damn it, come on, we might as well get this over with."

They climbed out of the car, walked through the front gate, and headed for the door. A sign just above the mail slot on the front door said, 'Please. No Solicitors.' Suel rang the doorbell, and they heard it chime inside. A moment later, the door opened, and an attractive blonde woman dressed in jeans and a red sweater answered the door.

She looked at the two of them and was about to say something when Suel said, "Shannon? Shannon Kinan?"

"Yes, I'm sorry. Do I know you?"

"Yeah, from a hundred years back, I'm Paddy Suel. I grew up behind you on Ardlea Road."

She seemed to think for a moment and then smiled and said, "Yes, yes, now I remember, and didn't you join An Garda Síochána?"

"Yes, I did. Still there, umm, as a matter of fact, that's why we're here. I'm afraid—"

"Oh, for the love of God. Don't tell me. No, wait, on second thought, do tell me. What stupid thing has my idiot brother Neil done now? Is he back to selling drugs? Did he rob a bank and leave his credit card there?"

"Actually, no. May we come inside and talk to you?"

After standing back to let them enter, Shannon asked again what was going on.

"I'm sorry to tell you this, but he was shot early this morning. Shot in his car."

She just stared for a long minute, trying to process what Suel had just said. "Shot? Where? When? Is he okay? What hospital is he—"

"Shannon, he was killed. We're part of the investigative team. Right now, we're just beginning to look into the situation. Because I knew Neil and your mother, well, and you, I wanted to be the one to tell you this unfortunate news. Is your mother home, and could we talk to her?"

She suddenly looked past Suel and extended her hand. "I'm sorry we've not met. Nothing like a first impression, eh? I'm Shannon Kinan."

Dillon stepped forward and said, "Shannon, it's nice to meet you. I'm sorry it's under this circumstance. And I—"

"No. You know what. In a way, this is good news, and it's not a surprise. This was bound to happen sooner or later. Neil just never caught on. You'd think his two years in the Joy would wake him up, but as soon as they let him out, he was back with the same crowd, doing the same dumb ass things. Oh my God, what a waste. What a stupid, stupid—" Tears started running down both cheeks, and she brought her hands up to her face as she cried, "Neil. Oh, Neil, why? Why?"

Dillon wasn't sure what to do, and he automatically wrapped his arms around her. She leaned into him and sobbed on his shoulder for a good long minute before she pulled back and wiped the tears from her face as best she could. "Oh, look at me. Sorry. We've some tea going in the kitchen and—"

"Shannon? Shannon?" An older voice suddenly called from the kitchen.

They followed Shannon into the kitchen. Lizzy Kinan was seated at an oak table with a mug of tea and a plate with a half-dozen chocolate-covered biscuits in front of her.

"Mum, you remember Paddy Suel. He grew up behind us on Ardlea Road."

"Suel? Paddy Suel? Are you the lad that broke the neighbor's window playing hurling in the back garden?" she laughed.

Suel hung his head and said, "Aw, Mrs. Kinan, I was hoping you'd forget that day."

"Forget it? Hardly, I loved it. They were dreadful neighbors."

"I'll get yous both a tea," Shannon said.

"And some more biscuits," Mrs. Kinan said. "You lads would eat an entire package."

"Mrs. Kinan, this is my partner, US Marshal Jack Dillon. He's attached to An Garda Síochána."

"Oh, so you're with the Guards, are you?"

"Yes, ma'am, we are," Suel said as they each took a chair opposite Mrs. Kinan. Once they were settled in, Shannon arrived with two mugs of tea. She set a mug in front of Suel and Dillon and then took a seat opposite them and next to her mother. Suel took a spoonful of sugar from the bowl on the table and stirred it into his tea. Dillon took a long sip and tried not to make a face.

"I'm afraid I have some bad news, ma'am," Suel said.

She looked at him and shook her head. "And you're with the Guards, so I would guess this is about Neil. God save us. What has he done this time?"

"I'm afraid he was killed earlier this morning over in Finglas."

"What? Killed? Neil? But how? What happened?"

"We don't have much information at this stage, just that he was killed in his car, and he—"

"Oh, that fancy black thing. Why am I not surprised? Was it a car crash? I suppose he was on the piss and driving too fast."

"Actually, no, ma'am. He was parked in front of a council house, and he was shot. Apparently, he died instantly. So, he didn't feel any pain."

"Shot? Did you say shot?"

"Yes, ma'am."

She took a deep breath and shook her head. "Good lord, the work we've done. The time we've spent, and he just never ever copped on. I gave him a room here. Can you imagine? He's thirty-five years old and—"

"Thirty-six, mum," Shannon said.

"Oh, even better, thirty-six and still living here. Never had a job he could hold for more than ninety days. Always going for the next big idea, which never, ever seemed to work. Honest to God," she said and shook her head. "Well, if you'll excuse me. I'm going to take some quiet time," she said as she got up from the table and left the room.

"Shannon, I'm sorry. I didn't mean to—"

Shannon raised a hand. "Don't say another word. In many ways, it's the logical end. He just never, ever copped on to life. Always with a plan to be a millionaire. Always knew more than anyone else. Thought he knew more than everyone who worked hard. And now this. I've no doubt whatever he was doing there, he was up to no good. Damn it. So much to offer, and he just always threw it away and messed up. Thirty-six years old, still living with his mum, and never even offered to pay a bill."

"We'll leave you to it, and we should probably get going," Suel said. "Your mother will be contacted by Finglas Station in the next day or two. They'll want to go through his belongings, looking for clues and—"

"The two of yas are not going anywhere until you finish your tea and eat a couple of those biscuits," she said.

THREE

They chatted with Shannon for another forty minutes, exchanged phone numbers, and promised to stay in touch. On their way out the door, they looked in on Mrs. Kinan. She was seated in a wingback chair in the sitting room, quietly saying the rosary. Suel didn't want to interrupt, and after they both said yet another 'goodbye' to Shannon, they headed out to the car.

Once in the car, Suel lifted the bag with the remaining brownie and said, "You going to eat this thing?"

Dillon shook his head and said, "No, you go ahead."

Suel crammed half the brownie into his mouth and said, "I'm thinking of calling Tully Egan at Finglas Station and volunteering the two of us to search through Neil's room and anything else he may have. It might make it easier on Mrs. Kinan if we showed up rather than someone she didn't know."

"Yeah, that's probably a good idea. I found it interesting that although they were both upset, I mean, who wouldn't be, but at the end of the day, they didn't seem to be all that surprised. It was like his death was the logical outcome of the life he led, and if it hadn't happened now, well, then it probably would next month or the month after."

"You think they may know what, exactly, he was up to?"

Dillon shook his head. "I didn't get that feeling. I just had the sense they weren't completely surprised because he was always involved with other idiots doing stupid things."

"Just incredible," Suel said and shoved the rest of the brownie into his mouth.

Once back in the office, Dillon met with DCI McCabe and brought him up to date. Suel phoned DI Tully Egan and suggested he and Dillon search Neil Kinan's personal items looking for something that might lead to a clue to whoever shot him. Egan thanked him and said he expected the warrant to arrive later that afternoon.

Dillon and Suel were having lunch in the breakroom when Suel got a call.

"Tully?" was how he answered. "Mmm, okay. Yeah, about thirty or forty-five minutes," he said and then disconnected.

"Did the warrant arrive?" Dillon asked.

Suel took a bite of his sandwich, nodded, and said, "Yeah."

This time, Suel drove to Finglas Station, a contemporary building on Mellows Road. They pulled into the parking lot and entered the front lobby. As they approached the front desk, the sergeant seated behind the counter looked up. "DI Suel?"

Suel nodded.

"I have an envelope for you, and I'll need a signature." He handed a form to Suel.

Suel signed the form and handed it back to the sergeant, then opened the envelope and checked the warrant. "Yeah, this will do. Thank you," he said, and they headed back to the car.

As they pulled out of the parking lot, Dillon was on his cell phone, placing a call to Shannon Kinan. She answered on the fourth ring. "Hello?"

"Hi Shannon, this is Jack Dillon."

"Oh, hi, umm, is everything okay?"

"Yes, it is. Say, we were able to get in touch with the powers that be over at Finglas Garda Station. They were going to do a search of Neil's personal items at your mother's house. We took the search warrant. Paddy and I would like to do the search ourselves, just to keep things a little more private, if that would be okay with you."

Suel looked over and shook his head.

"So, they're going to go through mom's house?"

"No, they won't because we told them we could do it, and that way, we can keep things focused just on Neil's things."

"When were you thinking of coming over?"

"Well, we could do it today if that works for you. The sooner we get it done, the less problem I think it will be for you and your mum."

"Would you be able to come over right now? That would work the best. My mum is at church talking to the priest, and she's liable to be there for a while. It would be wonderful if you could do this while she's gone."

"We'll head over right now. Thanks, Shannon, see you shortly."

"Smooth, Dillon, very smooth," Suel said and chuckled.

"This will work. Mrs. Kinan is up at the church visiting the priest. Hopefully, we can get in and out before she's back. I don't want to stress her out any more than she already is. At the end of the day, even though he was an idiot, she lost a son to a violent event."

"Yeah, I hear you."

Suel pulled in front of the Kinan house ten minutes later. Shannon opened the front door as they stepped through the gate. "Oh, thanks for coming right away. Mum will be at the church for another hour or two. They've arranged a prayer service, and Father White will be distributing communion."

"Thanks for helping out, Shannon," Suel said. "I felt so sorry for your mum and you this morning. There's just no easy way to let a family know what happened, and at the end of the day, it's a heartbreak for everyone."

Shannon nodded and said, "Come in and follow me upstairs. I'll show you Neil's room."

"Did he keep things anywhere else besides his room?"

She shook her head and said, "Not that I'm aware of. We have a garden shed in the back, and you could certainly take a look. I don't think he was ever in there. One of us had to cut the grass here. Neil was always too busy," she said and rolled her eyes. "Mick, our older brother, was ready to kill him. Oh, God, I probably shouldn't have said that," she said as they climbed the stairs.

"Not to worry," Suel replied.

She walked down the hall and opened the door to the third bedroom, just across from the bathroom. "Here it is, would yous like a tea or anything?"

"No, thank you. We'll be just fine," Suel said.

"All right then, I'll leave you to it," she said and headed back downstairs.

They stepped into the bedroom. A small fireplace, originally coal-burning, was on the wall to the left. A potted plastic plant was centered in the fireplace, and a wooden armoire of stained pine was next to it. A single bed was up against the radiator on the back wall, just below the windows looking out over the back garden. There was a sleeping bag on the bed, no sheets, and a very thin pillow. A worn wooden dresser with four drawers and the initials 'MK' carved on top of the dresser was next to the bed. A framed mirror with a crack running across the bottom was hanging above the dresser.

Dillon opened the door on the armoire. Four wrinkled shirts were on hangers, along with three pairs of jeans. Two pairs of scuffed shoes, both needing a shine, and a pair of well-worn walking boots were on the floor of the armoire. A cardboard box for a case of wine was filled with a stack of papers and envelopes in the back, just behind the walking boots. "I'm getting the feeling his mother didn't want to make things too comfortable for him," Dillon said.

"Who could blame her?" Suel said and pulled the top drawer open on the dresser.

Dillon took out his cell phone and took two photographs of the armoire. He ran his hand over the wrinkled shirts and checked the pockets on the jeans in case there might be something hidden. He stepped over to the bed, unzipped and opened the sleeping bag. A few long blonde hairs lay inside. An apparently used prophylactic was down towards the bottom of the sleeping bag. Dillon took two more pictures and then partially rolled up the sleeping bag, clearing the lower half of the single bed. He reached into the armoire, pulled out the wine box with the papers and envelopes, and set them on the bed.

"Hey, Paddy, take pictures of the drawers just to cover our ass in case we come up with something."

"You finding anything?" Suel asked.

"Not so far, but I'll start on this stack of mail and papers now."

Suel looked over, shook his head, and then pulled his cell phone out and took a photograph of the top drawer.

Dillon started going through the envelopes and papers. After a couple of minutes, he pulled up the disc holder that had apparently been on the inside of the windshield of the Mercedes Neil Kinan was found in. He pulled out the vehicle title. The name on the title for the 2021 Mercedes was listed as a gentleman named Robert O'Shea.

"What do you think about this?" Dillon asked and passed the title over to Suel.

Suel read through the title and looked up at Dillon. "My first thought is that Kinan didn't own the car he was found in, followed by the thought that he probably stole it."

"All this information was in the disc holder that was torn off the windshield of that Mercedes. The car had Dublin plates. I wonder if they were legit or if they'd been taken from another vehicle and placed on the Mercedes."

"Probably one of a number of scams we're liable to find here. All those papers are Kinan's?"

Dillon shook his head. "They're just in his possession, or rather were. A fair amount of mail from different homes on the street. It's like he was going through people's mailboxes looking for information. Well, plus the disc holder from the Mercedes. The guy had no legal source of income, at least that we know of. For the love of God, he was still living in his mother's house. Sleeping in a sleeping bag. Oh, by the way, evidence of a friend joining him in the sleeping bag."

"What? Don't tell me you found a thong."

"No, a prophylactic."

"You mean a used rubber? For God's sake, go wash your hands."

"Relax, I didn't touch it," Dillon said and started to wipe his hand on Suel's shirt until Suel slapped it away.

It took the better part of an hour, at which point Dillon had gone through the wine box full of papers and envelopes from various neighborhood addresses, plus the documents for the Mercedes. Suel had added a Christmas card from the dresser with the photo of a naked blonde woman wearing a Santa hat and a pleasant smile. The card was signed with the name Gemma, and below the name, a heart was drawn with an arrow through it. They headed downstairs, spoke to Shannon in the kitchen for a few minutes, and then left.

FOUR

As Suel pulled around the corner and headed back to Finglas Station, Dillon asked, "You think she was glad to see us go?"

Suel shook his head. "That might be too strong a term. I think she was just happy to have us out of there before her mother returned. It's gotta be tough. Regardless of what a worthless piece of shite her brother was, in the end, he was still the woman's son and Shannon's brother. I'm sure his mother is probably thinking back and wondering what she could or should have done differently."

"Was the father in the picture?"

Suel nodded and said, "Oh, yeah. Nice enough lad, if I remember. Died some years ago. Worked for Dublin County in the parks department. I think he died of a heart attack in his early fifties, but don't hold me to that."

"Do you like Shannon?"

Suel glanced over. "Shannon? Yeah, she seemed very nice. But if you're asking would I like to bed her? I got enough trouble on my hands just trying to get Kira back to being the lovely thing she was when we first met.

The last thing I need to do is bring another woman into the picture. Help yourself if that's what you're asking."

"Thanks, I just might do that."

Suel pulled into the Finglas Station parking lot, and they headed into the building. Dillon carried the wine box filled with papers. They set the box on DI Egan's desk and explained what they thought they might have found, which, with the exception of the Mercedes information, wasn't all that much.

Egan closely examined the photo of the naked woman on the Christmas card and set it off to the side. "Interesting info on the Mercedes. We finally got the response on the license plates a couple of hours ago. The Department of Transport's system is back up and running. The license plates on the Mercedes are actually for a 2020 Volkswagen Golf. I'm guessing Kinan was worried about having the Mercedes spotted and hoping the different license plate might stop him from getting pulled over."

"Yeah, unless they ran a check on that license plate and found it was for a Volkswagen instead of a Mercedes."

"And if the department's system was up and running," Egan said.

"There is that. So, what do you want us to do with all these envelopes and papers obviously taken from neighbors' mailboxes?" Suel said.

"Did you find anything in there like bank statements or insurance papers?"

Dillon shook his head and said, "Nothing like that, but my sense is that's the sort of thing Kinan was looking for. You think this could have been an attempt to find a way into people's accounts? You know, the way someone who isn't necessarily tech-savvy would go about it. Or, did he just gather this information up, the names and addresses, and pass it on to someone who was a lot more tech-savvy?"

"Based on what you have in the box, it would seem technology was not his strong suit," Egan said.

"Yeah, his sister told us not only did he not have a computer, but he hated the things and would do almost anything to avoid having to use one."

"I know the feeling," Egan said. "Okay, I'll pass this on to some underlings. In the meantime, try and find out who Kinan was in contact with. He had to be up to something. Just driving around in that stolen Mercedes seems to point to more than one individual. See if you can find out how, exactly, he acquired that vehicle."

"I'll start by giving this Robert O'Shea a call," Dillon said.

"Good, and Paddy," Egan said, "with any luck, we'll have a number of names from the fingerprints we recovered from the Mercedes. There's an outside chance our shooter may be among them. See if you can find that needle in the haystack."

By the time they were back in Special Branch, it was almost five. They got a couple things organized for the morning and left the office together. "You got plans for tonight?" Dillon asked.

"Herself canceled them. What about you?"

"I'm planning on taking Lucifer for a walk, grabbing a leftover meal from the refrigerator, and going to bed at a decent hour."

"You interested in stopping for a pint?" Suel asked.

"Yeah, I could probably do that. But one's my limit, and I'll buy."

That brought a smile to Suel's face, and he said, "How 'bout we stop at the Autobahn?"

"That would be perfect. I'll see you there," Dillon said. Since they had parked next to each other, Dillon followed Suel all the way to the Autobahn pub. He parked just behind Suel on Collins Avenue, and they headed into the pub together.

"See if you can search out a table, and I'll get the pints. You having a Guinness?"

"Do bears shite in the woods?" Suel replied and looked around for a table.

Dillon happened to catch the barman in between groups and ordered two pints of Guinness. The barman poured the pints, then topped them up after the prescribed two minutes, and shoved the glasses across the bar to Dillon.

Dillon caught Suel's wave from a table in the back of the pub. He took a healthy sip from one of the glasses so it wouldn't spill as he headed for their table. Once he arrived, he set his glass on the table.

"Well, done, you didn't spill so much as a drop," Suel said.

"That's because I took a big sip from both glasses," Dillon said and then took a sip from Suel's glass before he set it down in front of him.

"Oh, Jaysus, but you're a right plonker, Dillon," Suel said as he laughed and raised his glass across the table. They clinked glasses, and each took a big gulp. "Oh, just what the doctor ordered," Suel said. He took another large sip and looked around the place. "Pretty crowded for a Monday night. I guess everyone's in need of some relaxation."

"Yeah, I guess. Hey, you don't have to go into any detail, but I hope things work out for the best with you and Kira, whichever way it goes."

Suel took another sip and nodded. "Yeah, I'm starting to get to that place where I'm thinking I can only do so much, and if it's not making her happy, there's feck all I can do to change things."

"Well, believe me, I know how that works. Anyway, I hope things work out. If there's anything I can do, let me know."

"Thanks. Oh, and by the way, I'd say Shannon Kinan seemed to have a bit of an eye for you today."

"Shannon? Oh, thanks, do you really think so? She was too—"

"Dillon, you weren't paying attention, again. She was offering you tea and biscuits while we were looking through that depressing jail cell her brother lived in. She wasn't the least bit interested in the likes of me."

"What?"

"Did you notice how she was looking at you? Studying you?"

"No, I guess I didn't pick up on that."

"Typical. You were too interested in going through the contents of your man's Mercedes disc holder."

"Yeah, Robert O'Shea. Say, I wonder if Finglas Station ever contacted him to let him know his car has been recovered."

"Yeah, recovered with a body in it. I'd guess, right now, it's probably being put through the paces in the Tech Department. They'll be getting fingerprints, hair samples, the works. It could be weeks before your man gets it back. Then I don't know, if you're well-heeled enough to drive a Mercedes, would you want one that someone was murdered in?"

Dillon thought for a moment and said, "I think the world is just crazy enough that there's some nut case out there who would pay extra to have a car someone had been murdered in."

Suel thought for a moment and slowly nodded. A waitress stopped at the table and said, "Can I get yous another round?"

"Yes, please, two pints of Guinness," Suel said and pulled a twenty euro note from his pocket.

"Oh, I don't know, Paddy. I should—"

"That's right, Dillon, you don't know. So shut your trap and let me buy. We'll take the two pints, love," Suel said, and the waitress headed toward the bar.

They'd finished the second round, and Dillon said, "Thanks, Paddy. Much appreciated. I'll see you in the morning."

"Thanks for the warning, Dillon. Hopefully, I can get one of those wretched cups of tea from the break-room tomorrow before we head off tracking down another murder."

"With any luck, tonight will be a quiet night in Finglas," Dillon said, and they walked out together.

FIVE

When Dillon opened his front door, Lucifer, his irreverent black dog, was standing about ten inches away. The dog didn't bother to look and simply leaped out of the house, hurried over to the driver's door, turned to face Dillon, and proceeded to leave a rather large deposit.

Serves me right, Dillon thought. He picked up the three pieces of mail just inside the door and walked into the kitchen. He tossed the envelopes on the counter, grabbed a dog biscuit from the cookie jar, and walked back to the entry. He pulled the leash from the hook on the wall, opened the front door, and tossed the dog biscuit in Lucifer's direction. He snatched it in midair and quickly gobbled it so he wouldn't have to share.

Dillon locked the door behind him and clipped the leash onto Lucifer's collar. They headed out through the front gate and up the lane. They passed Tara's home two doors up and across the lane. She and Dillon seemed to have developed an 'occasional' relationship, taking turns on which one would suggest a get-together. At present, he reasoned it was Tara's turn to initiate, but based on the gray Mazda MX-5 parked in front of her house and the closed drapes on the sitting room window, that might be awhile.

They took a right turn at the top of the lane, walked down St. Pappins Road past the retail corner, then took a right and headed down Ballymun Road. As they walked down the road, they passed St. Albert Park just across the way, but at this time of year, the gates were locked at 6:00 in the evening. Dillon took them on the long route, down to Griffith Avenue and then up Ballygall Road, eventually weaving the way back down their lane. He noted that, after the two-mile walk, the drapes were still drawn, and the gray Mazda MX-5 was still parked in front of Tara's.

Once back in the house, he unclipped the leash, tossed another biscuit to Lucifer and opened the refrigerator to see what his options were. The pickings were slim. Half a sausage pizza with extra cheese or the remains of a fish and chips order from sometime last week. He tossed the pizza on a plate and headed for the sitting room. No sooner had he sat down and turned on the TV than his phone rang.

The number was unidentified, yet it looked familiar, and he decided to answer, "Jack Dillon."

"Oh, hi, umm, Officer Dillon. This is Shannon Kinan. I just got a call from my mum. Two men wanted to look at Neil's room. They told her they loaned him some tools. She didn't let them in, but she's afraid they may come back and—"

"Are you there now?"

"No, I was just going to head over, and I—"

"Don't go over. Let me make a phone call, get someone there, and I'll call you once I get there and make sure your mum's okay."

"Are you sure? I'm sorry to cause a problem."

"It's not a problem, Shannon. I'm heading out the door now," Dillon said as he hurried toward the door.

"Oh, I'm sorry. I didn't know who to call and—"

"I'll be there shortly," Dillon said and disconnected. He phoned Garda Central.

"Garda Central," was the answer after two rings.

"This is Marshal Jack Dillon with Dublin Special Branch. I just received a report of two individuals attempting to enter the residence of a murder victim at 52 Maryfield Cres in Artane. Can you dispatch a squad car, please? I'm headed there driving from Glasnevin, so I'm ten minutes away."

"ID number please?"

Fortunately, Dillon's ID was still hanging around his neck, and he read the number into the phone.

"Address is 52 Maryfield Cres in Artane?"

"Yes," Dillon said as he closed the front door behind him and hurried to his car.

"Squad is being dispatched."

"Thank you," Dillon said. He disconnected and had just shoved his cell phone back into his pocket as he stepped around the front of his car and slipped. "What the—" There it was, Lucifer's recent, relatively fresh deposit, now nothing more than a foot-and-a-half-long skid mark.

"Damn it," Dillon seethed and hurried out to the street curb. He scrapped the sole of his shoe against the curb a half-dozen times. Then stepped onto the lawn and dragged his foot across the grass in the front garden for a good ten feet before he hurried back to the car. He carefully stepped around the skid mark, climbed in, and backed into the lane.

Along the way, he phoned Suel and ended up leaving a message. "Paddy, it's Dillon. Call me when you get this." It became apparent from the smell in the car that his shoe hadn't been completely cleaned. But time was of the essence, and he drove on. He pulled in front of the Kinan home in just over seven minutes after running a red light and barely slowing for two stop signs.

There wasn't a squad car in sight. He walked up to the door and rang the doorbell. Once again, he heard the bell chiming inside. After a long minute, he rang the bell again and then heard what sounded like a door inside the house closing.

"I told you to go away. Now I've called the Garda, so you'd better leave."

"Mrs. Kinan, it's Marshal Jack Dillon with Special Branch. I got a call from Shannon, and I—"

"Oh, yes, just a moment," she said. Dillon heard a chain lock being removed from the door, and then the doorknob clicked, and the door opened. "Oh, thank you for coming. They were here not twenty minutes ago. Told me Neil had something of theirs up in his room."

"Did they tell you what it was?"

She shook her head. "No, and I told them you had been here this morning and taken everything, but they said they had to check."

"Do you know who they were?"

She shook her head again. "No, I'd never seen them before, but I'd told Neil if he was going to stay here, the home was off limits to his no-count friends."

"You're okay?"

"Yes, thanks for asking."

"I've called for the Garda to stop by. I'll wait until they come."

"Would you like to come in? I can make us tea."

Fortunately, Dillon remembered the condition of his shoe and said, "I'll just wait for the Garda out here. Go back to whatever you were doing."

"Mmm, I was just watching the news, as if things weren't bad enough," she said and closed the door.

Dillon stepped onto the lawn, gave a quick glance around, and then dragged the sole of his shoe down the length of the lawn, back up and down once more.

SIX

Dillon waited for another ten or fifteen minutes and was about to ring the doorbell and tell Mrs. Kinan everything seemed to be quiet. Suddenly, a pair of headlights came around a distant corner, and he stepped off the lawn and onto the drive. The image of a squad car appeared as the headlights rounded the curve in the road. Dillon stepped out of the front garden, stood on the curb behind his car, and gave a wave.

The squad car pulled over, and the driver's window was lowered. The officer driving was the only one in the car.

"Good evening. Are you Special Branch?" the driver asked.

"Yeah, Jack Dillon," Dillon said and held out the ID hanging from his neck.

"What seems to be the problem?"

"Murder victim shot in Finglas early this morning lived here with his mother. Two men stopped here tonight and wanted to go through his bedroom. I was part of a team that went through the place today. We took anything remotely looking like it might hold some information. She didn't let them in, and hopefully, they won't be back. You're working third shift?"

"Yeah, till 7:00 tomorrow morning."

"Would you be able to drive past the place a couple of times? She doesn't have a car, so anyone parked here might suggest a problem."

"Yeah, I can do that, as long as things remain quiet."

Dillon thought for a moment and said, "Her daughter has a nice-looking red car. If that's parked in the drive, there's no need to worry."

"You know the make or the license number?"

Dillon shook his head. "No, sorry, but I don't."

"Okay, I'll keep an eye out."

"You out of Clontarf Station?" Dillon asked.

"No, Santry."

"Oh, yeah, say hi to DI Mullen next time you see him."

"You know Billy?"

"We worked a case a while back. Couple of guys getting into the ATMs attached to the front of the banks."

He nodded and smiled. "College lads, if I remember correctly."

"Yeah, well, they've each got a year sentence to study up on the finer points of their activities."

He laughed at that and said, "I'll drive by every so often tonight."

"Thanks. Oh, I didn't catch your name."

"McHugh, Marty McHugh," he said and held his hand out.

"Nice to meet you, Marty. I appreciate the help." They shook hands. Dillon watched as the squad car slowly disappeared down the road. He started to head back to the front door when another pair of lights came up the road. He waited next to his car just in case it happened to be the earlier visitors. He watched as the vehicle slowed and then pulled alongside, and the window lowered on the red car.

"Oh, Dillon, thank you for being here," Shannon said as she leaned out of the window.

"Hi, Shannon. You just missed the squad car. He's going to check on your mom's place every so often throughout the night. She said she told whoever it was that we took everything away earlier today. Hopefully, they got the message."

"Oh, God, I'm sorry to put you through this. Let me just pull into the drive," she said, then turned in front of Dillon's car, missing it by less than a half-inch as she drove in and parked. She climbed out of the car wearing a short black skirt, a white leather jacket, and stiletto heels. Dillon wondered if she'd been on a date.

"Thank you so much for rushing over at the drop of a hat. That's so kind of you," she said, leaning forward and kissing him on the cheek. She remained in the position for a second or two longer, and then he wasn't sure but thought, *did she just rub the tip of her tongue on my cheek?*

"Happy to check on your mum," he said as she looked up at him with her gorgeous brown eyes and smiled. "She said she told whoever it was that we'd taken everything earlier today."

"Yeah, that's what you just told me. Hopefully, they got the message. Let me just run in there for a minute," she said and hurried up to the door. As she did, she glanced at the lawn where Dillon had dragged his foot up and down and seemed to do a bit of a double take before stepping up to the door. She inserted a key in the lock and called, "Mum, it's Shannon. Mum?" she said as she closed the door behind her.

Dillon leaned against the three-foot wall for the next ten minutes until Shannon stepped outside. She called, "Goodbye, Mum," and locked the door behind her.

"God bless, it never ends. She wants me to take her grocery shopping tomorrow. I checked, and the refrigerator and the cupboards are full. Oh, I could use a drink, and I certainly owe you one. Would you mind joining me in a pub? The Ardlea Inn is just a minute or two away. That is unless you've something else scheduled."

"No, no, that would work. Yeah, I'd, I'd like that. I'll have to follow you."

"Perfect. Let's go," she said. Dillon opened the driver's door for her. She climbed in, flashed a smile, and started her car. He hurried back to his car, turned it on, and quickly backed up as she pulled out of the drive and over the curb, narrowly missing his car again.

The Ardlea Inn was a neighborhood pub. A two-story structure with large windows and black trim on the first floor and a white stucco exterior on the second-floor, housing what appeared to be a couple of residential units. There were two doors, one for the lounge and one for the bar.

They parked in the parking lot. Based on the little he'd seen of Shannon's driving, he purposely pulled in, leaving an open spot between them. As he climbed out of his car, he noticed she was a couple of inches over the white line designating the parking spot but decided not to mention it. "Lounge or bar?" he asked.

"Oh, let's do the bar. The lounge has a local group playing tonight, and we won't be able to hear a word the other is saying."

Dillon thought *it was more than a little strange a group would be playing live somewhere on a Monday night*, but then, what did he know? He held the door for her and followed her into the bar. It was definitely quiet, just a handful of tables and half of them empty. Shannon headed to a table in a distant corner. A padded bench formed a right angle on two sides of the table. Shannon slid onto the padded bench on the right side of the table. Dillon slid in on the left side and settled in no more than an inch or two from Shannon.

A waitress approached fifteen seconds later. "Hi, Shannon. What can I get for yous?"

Shannon glanced over at Dillon and raised an eye-brow.

"Oh, I'll have a pint of Guinness," Dillon said.

"Your usual?" the waitress asked Shannon.

"Yeah, thanks, Christy." Once the waitress left, Shannon said, "Now, no argument. I'm buying tonight. Besides, I want to know more about you. How in God's name did you ever end up all the way over here and in An Garda Síochána?"

"Oh, a bit of a long story," Dillon said and went on to give a much shorter version. He left out the shootings at the airport and finished up with, "So, that's my story. Tell me about yourself. What do you do when you're not looking after your mum?"

The waitress suddenly appeared and set Dillon's pint of Guinness in front of him and then a half-glass of Guinness in front of Shannon. "Anything else you'd like?"

Shannon glanced at Dillon and seemed to flare her eyes.

"No, this is fine, thank you," Dillon said, then turned to Shannon. "I believe you were about to tell me all sorts of personal information."

She raised her glass in a toast, they clinked glasses, and each took a hearty sip. "Well, I'm an accountant, which means I'm boring, and I work eternally. When I'm not working with clients, I mind my mum. God love her. There are days it drives me crazy, but we're blessed to still have her. All I have to do is look out the window, and I'll see someone who has it much worse. So, are you seeing anyone? Have you fallen for an Irish girl yet?"

Dillon smiled and shook his head. "I've fallen for a number of them, but eventually, they all seem to come to their senses and move on."

"Sounds like you just haven't found the right one."

They chatted on, and much like meeting up with Suel two hours earlier, they ordered a second round. "Interested in another?" Shannon said as she nodded at Dillon's nearly empty second glass, and he suddenly felt her foot stroking his leg.

"Oh, thank you, but I'd better take a pass. I've got an early day tomorrow and should probably head home. Thank you, though. I'll drive past your mum's home just to check on things. Now, next time, it's my turn to pay, and no argument. I'll give you a call."

"I'll look forward to that. Thank you again for dropping everything and checking on my mum."

"Happy to do so," he said and drained his glass.

"I really enjoyed this. You're very kind," she said, then grabbed her purse and slid off the padded bench. When Dillon stood, she leaned over and gave him a lingering kiss on the cheek, squeezing his forearm as she did so.

"After you," Dillon said and extended his hand. Shannon headed toward the door, and Dillon admired the view as he followed her out of the bar. He held the driver's door for her and got a kiss on the lips in return. Once he was settled in his car, he started it and quickly backed out of the parking spot, placing the car in drive and hurrying out of the lot as Shannon began to back up.

He drove past her mother's house. Everything appeared to be quiet, and he headed home.

He parked in his drive, stepped in the front door, and closed it behind him. He peeked into the sitting room. He'd been in such a hurry to leave he'd left the TV on and apparently left the plate with half the pizza sitting on the couch. Now the plate was upside down on the floor, and there was no sign of the pizza or, for that matter, Lucifer, who, apparently, was already asleep upstairs.

SEVEN

ucifer was asleep on the bed, and Dillon was too tired to move him. He slept until his alarm went off. Two pints of Guinness would do that, then he remembered he'd actually had four pints over the course of the evening. He wandered into the bathroom, looked at himself in the mirror, and focused for a moment on the two lipstick smudges on his cheek. He shaved, showered, and was downstairs eating breakfast when Lucifer made his appearance. He let him out into the front garden, placed his dishes in the dishwasher, and filled Lucifer's food and water dishes.

He was back in Special Branch going through the file on Neil Kinan and the other two shooting victims in Finglas while sipping a large coffee from one of the vending trucks in Phoenix Park. All three men had been small-time criminals with records beginning as teenagers. They'd all served time, two years as a matter of fact, but with today's sentencing guidelines, that wasn't particularly unusual. They'd served at different times and in different facilities, so they hadn't met in prison. They were from different areas in Dublin, and Dillon couldn't find any real connection between the three. That still didn't mean they hadn't known one another. It simply meant there was no particular connection on the books.

Suel arrived forty-five minutes later. He picked up the empty mug from his desk and headed toward the breakroom. He gave Dillon a 'follow me' nod along the way. "How'd your night go?" Suel asked as Dillon walked in.

"Interesting. I got a call from Shannon Kinan," Dillon said and went on to tell him about the evening, talking most about his time with Shannon at the Ardlea Inn.

"I'm not surprised. Now you've got me wondering if there really was anyone wanting to look through the room. I bet she just wanted to get you to herself and investigate you. See if you'd match up to whatever her current needs are."

"No, I talked to Mrs. Kinan, and she told me about the two guys. In fact, she had the door locked and chained when I rang her doorbell. I've been going over the files on the three shooting victims. Similar idiots but nothing in the files suggesting they knew one another. All three served time but not together and not at the same time or place. That said, I'm having a tough time thinking they're random targets. There's gotta be something there. We just haven't found it yet."

Suel tossed his tea bag into the trash and took his first sip. He winced and shook his head. "God, but that's desperate."

"You ever think of bringing your own tea in and just keeping it locked in your desk instead of torturing yourself every day?"

Suel thought about that for a moment and then shook his head. He was about to take a second sip when DCI McCabe appeared in the doorway and said, "Dillon, Suel, a moment of your time, please."

"Oh, shite, I knew it was too good to be true," Suel said. He set his mug on the counter and followed Dillon into McCabe's office.

McCabe stepped behind his desk, pulled three pages from the printer, tapped them a couple of times on the credenza, stapled a corner, and handed them to Dillon. "Unfortunately, there's been another shooting in Finglas."

"Someone in their car at three or four in the morning?" Suel asked.

"No, this time, your man was waiting at a bus stop on Seamus Ennis Avenue."

"Someone with a record?" Dillon questioned.

McCabe smiled and said, "That will be for you to determine. It occurred barely two hours ago. Actually, on the corner of Seamus Ennis and McKee Avenues. They've set up a perimeter."

"That's just a block or two from Finglas Station," Dillon said.

"Yes, and as I said, not more than two hours ago, so it happened in broad daylight. Check it out and keep me posted. I think it might be a good idea to add a second team. Four murders in as many days. We need to get on top of this and fast."

"On it, sir," Suel said, and they hurried out of the office.

"I'll drive," Dillon said.

Suel hurried into the breakroom and grabbed his tea mug. He stood at his desk, took a sip, grimaced, and shook his head. "Oh, why the hell do I even bother?"

They took the elevator down to the ground floor, went out the rear door, and into the secure parking lot. Dillon drove to Finglas while Suel read the brief description of the incident.

"Victim is a man named Thomas Davy. Waiting for a bus, suspected to have been shot from a passing vehicle."

"Anyone else around?" Dillon asked. "We have anything like a license number, a description of the vehicle, or God forbid, the shooter?"

"Doesn't appear to be anything like that. But then this is the initial report. You'd think at that hour someone, somewhere, would be around. That's a busy intersection. There's a traffic light. People would be heading to work."

"I'm surprised he's the only person at the bus stop. There had to be other folks waiting for the bus at that hour, heading into the city center for their job. Damn it," Dillon said. "I wonder if he's got a record. Was this a random drive-by, or was he an intentional target?"

As they approached, traffic was becoming more backed up. It was twenty minutes past 9:00. Theoretically, rush hour had ended, but this was a busy intersection even on the quietest of holidays, and today was a normal working Tuesday. Dillon pulled into the Molloys Liquor store parking lot. The store wasn't open for another hour. Right now, the lot was largely filled with police squads, an emergency vehicle, and the Dublin Morgue van.

EIGHT

They climbed out of the car and headed over to DI Tully Egan, who was busy talking to two officers next to the bus stop. A white tent had been erected to secure the immediate scene and hide the victim's body from curious passersby. A gurney had an empty body bag stretched out on it and was positioned next to the entrance to the tent, more or less hiding it from vehicles driving past.

A very tired looking DI Egan nodded toward Dillon and Suel and held up an index finger, suggesting they wait for a minute. A moment later, Noel Leonard, from the Dublin Morgue, stepped out of the white tent and nodded at Egan, who stepped over to the tent. They had a brief conversation. As they spoke, another man stepped out of the tent and wheeled the gurney inside. Leonard said something else to Egan, who nodded, and then Leonard stepped back into the tent.

Egan gave Dillon and Suel a wave, and they walked over to him.

"Sorry to keep you waiting, lads. Thanks for joining us. You get the info on the victim, Thomas Davy?"

"Only that he was shot here at the bus stop. Besides his name and an approximate time, really nothing else," Suel said.

"You think this is related to the other three shootings?" Dillon asked.

"I'm pretty sure it will be. Like everywhere, we're understaffed and overwhelmed. The other three have been linked by the use of the same weapon, a nine-millimeter Glock. I suspect this will be the fourth."

"The other three all had prior records. Anything on Davy?"

Egan shook his head. "Not at the moment, but I suspect that will change."

"Witnesses?" Dillon asked.

"A woman and a man, they were just over there, at the entrance to the parking lot, heading toward the bus stop. They saw Davy seeming to jerk, and then he fell backward. They never heard a shot being fired, which may suggest a silencer but could also mean a horn honking, an engine roaring, or even a motorcycle. They placed their 999 call almost immediately. Your man was shot in the chest. I've three officers canvasing the shops in the area, but so far, nothing. Most of them were still closed at that early hour."

The flap covering the entrance to the tent was suddenly pushed back, and Noel Leonard and another individual emerged with the gurney. They wheeled it toward the Dublin Morgue van back in the parking lot and stopped for a moment next to Egan.

"Once we load this in the van, we'll be back to pick up our cases. We've got photos and an estimated time of death. Obviously just an educated guess at this point, but I'm betting on this being related to the other three. Give us a minute, and I'll be back to answer questions," Leonard said. They wheeled the gurney along the sidewalk and back into the parking lot.

Egan watched them for a moment, then said, "Murdered with the same weapon and each with a record are the only things that link them thus far. Still, I'm having a tough time thinking these are random."

"You have any sense they may have been scamming people or coming up with some computer hacking plan?" Dillon asked.

Both Egan and Suel looked at Dillon.

"Where are you getting that?" Egan asked.

"We went through Kinan's room at his mother's. Other than a used rubber in the bottom of his sleeping bag, the only other thing we found was a box full of envelopes and papers that appeared to be stolen from neighbors' mailboxes."

Egan made a face. "That sounds like something from the last century. Mail? Stolen mail? Everything's done on computer in today's world. Who writes a check? It's all automatic payments online. Good Lord, even I'm using my credit card for something that only costs five euros, and I'm one of the least technical people out there. I'm constantly asking one of my daughters for help on the computer."

"Oh, the poor things, having to deal with the likes of you," Suel said, and they all laughed.

"You're telling me. Thank God they're as patient as their mother."

Leonard hurried back, nodded at Dillon and Suel, and said, "Sorry to keep you waiting. Cause of death is a chest wound. Death appears to have been virtually instant."

"Shot in the heart?" Suel asked.

"Possibly, I'm leaning more toward the aortic arch, the brachiocephalic trunk. I'll know more this afternoon. We have a team being assembled now for the autopsy. I'm still thinking this will be either the same weapon as the previous three or one very similar. We'll hopefully be able to recover the round and send it over to Ballistics today. Your witnesses see anyone?"

Egan shook his head. "They didn't see anyone and didn't hear anything," he said. A driver suddenly leaned on the horn as a tow truck dragging a car pulled in front of him.

"Something like that could have covered the noise," Leonard said. "Anything else? If not, I'd like to get back and get things moving."

Egan looked at Dillon and Suel, then nodded and said, "Don't let us hold you up."

Leonard gave a quick nod and hurried back to the Dublin Morgue van.

"You've got the cell phones of the earlier victims?" Dillon asked.

"We do, nothing out of the ordinary. We've had two people going through text messages. They came up empty-handed," Egan said.

"I'd like to run those cell phones through our Tech Lab if that's okay."

"I don't see a problem with that. Let me make a call, and I can have them transferred unless you want to pick them up."

"We might as well get them. We're just a few minutes away from the station. We'd be happy to transfer them."

"You thinking of anything in particular?"

"No, just trying to cover all the bases, or probably more like I'm grasping at straws. There just has to be something out there we're missing."

"God bless if you lads can find whatever it is," Egan said and pulled out his phone.

NINE

An officer was waiting for them at the front desk when they stepped into the Finglas Station. "Suel and Dillon with Special Branch?" he asked. They nodded, held out their IDs, and he handed them a handful of papers requiring signatures and ID numbers. Once they were finished, he reached over the counter and took hold of a plastic evidence bag. Inside the evidence bag were three separate evidence bags, each holding a cell phone from the previous murder victims, one of whom was Neil Kinan.

"Thanks," Dillon said.

The officer shrugged and said, "Good luck. Hope you're able to find something."

"We'll see," Suel said, and they headed out to the parking lot.

Suel set the bag on his lap as Dillon drove back to Special Branch. "One can only hope they come up with something," Suel muttered, then seemed to make an uncomfortable movement.

Dillon caught the look on Suel's face out of the corner of his eye but didn't mention it. "Yeah, well, if anyone can, my money's on Emily."

"Yeah," Suel said and then made another unhappy face.

"You know, while we're down there in the Tech Department, I'd like to stop in Ballistics. Did anyone other than Egan happen to mention to you that the first three victims were shot with a nine-millimeter Glock?"

"No, that was the first I'd heard of it. I'm guessing Egan's so busy going out on murder scene calls he hasn't had time to really think about getting the information out. He looks like he's slept about six hours total over the last four days," Suel said as he adjusted his position in the passenger seat.

"Yeah, he's pretty beat," Dillon said. He waited for an oncoming car to pass, then turned into the secured Special Branch parking lot. Both Dillon and Suel lifted the IDs hanging around their necks. They got a wave from the officer in the guard house as he pressed the button that raised the security barrier so they could enter. Dillon found a parking spot just one lane over from the rear entrance to the building and pulled in. By the time he turned off the car and climbed out, Suel was halfway to the building. He punched in the security code and then hurried inside. Dillon caught the door just before it closed.

"You anxious to get those cell phones to the Tech Lab?" Dillon said as he caught up to Suel in the hallway.

"No, my body has been giving me a warning it's going to do something very unpleasant, my choice where. I got about ninety seconds left to decide," Suel said. He handed the evidence bag with the phones and the paperwork to Dillon and hurried toward the men's room in the opposite direction.

"Don't forget to wash your hands," Dillon called after him. He wound his way through the halls to the Tech Lab and pushed the intercom button next to the door. A moment later, a pleasant female voice said, "Tech Lab."

"Hi, Emily, Jack Dillon with a project for you."

"Oh, Dillon, what's the password?"

"Password?" he asked.

"That's it," she laughed, and the door opened.

Dillon walked past three long white counters with stacks of boxes and evidence bags. Emily was standing at the fourth counter, tapping on a keyboard and staring at a computer screen mounted on the wall.

"Hi, Dillon. What do you have?" she said, still focused on the wall screen.

"You hear about the shootings over in Finglas?" Dillon said.

"Yeah, three of them. I heard Ballistics determined all three were from the same weapon."

"Yeah, looks like there was a fourth one there this morning."

She looked over at him and took her hands off the keyboard. "A fourth one. In Finglas?"

Dillon nodded. "Yeah, around 7:00 this morning. Some guy named Thomas Davy at a bus stop."

She glanced at the evidence bag with the phones. "Those have anything to do with the shootings?"

"Yeah, we're not finding many similarities in the first three victims. A two-year sentence served by each of them but, other than that, no real connection. They were in different facilities at different times, so the particular sentence doesn't seem to be a connection. I've got their cell phones and was hoping you could see if there are any common links in the phone history. We've been unable to come up with anything substantial thus far. But we're having a hard time thinking these are random, and it's just a coincidence the first three served time."

"Were they employed?"

"The only one I know about is the third victim, Neil Kinan. He was doing occasional odd jobs. Hired a few times but never seemed to last in a job more than a hundred and twenty days." She nodded, suggesting she was familiar with the situation.

Dillon glanced over at the counter lined with evidence bags and boxes. "Looks like you're jammed. Any idea on a time frame?"

"You're dealing with four murders in the past four days?"

"Yes, the first three, all with the same weapon, a nine-millimeter Glock. Noel Leonard at Dublin Morgue said this morning's killing looked similar, and it wouldn't surprise him if it turned out to be the same nine-millimeter."

She shook her head and glanced at the clock on the wall. "No promises, but let me see what I can do. You got some paperwork for me?"

Dillon set the papers on the counter and then laid the evidence bag with the three phones on top. "Here you go. Thanks in advance, Emily. We're really at a loss as far as coming up with anything concrete."

"Like I said, no promises, but keep your fingers crossed," she said.

"Thanks, I'll get out of your hair."

"I'll call you if and when," she said as Dillon headed for the door.

He turned to give her a wave when he got to the door, but she was back on the keyboard and focused on the screen, now displaying a series of graphs. He took the elevator up to Special Branch, punched in the key code, and headed for his desk. The lights were off in DCI McCabe's office, and the door was closed. After leaving the phones with Emily, he actually felt some stress relief and hoped he wouldn't have to worry about yet another murder in Finglas in the next twenty-four hours. He headed into the breakroom and poured himself a coffee.

TEN

At no surprise, the coffee hadn't improved over the course of the morning. Suel stepped into the office about twenty minutes later and headed toward Dillon's desk.

"Wow, Paddy, everything okay? You look about twenty pounds lighter," Dillon said and then chuckled.

"Yeah, so much for having mustard-encrusted salmon for dinner last night. I gave Kira a call on my way home after meeting you at the Autobahn. Probably the two pints of Guinness that made me think I'd have a chance."

"So, you didn't go over to her place?"

"I only wish. No, we met for a late dinner at some fancy place she wanted to go to. I figured if it got me back in her good graces, it would be worth it. We had dinner with a bottle of wine. The damn night cost me a hundred and forty euros for dinner, the wine, oh, and she had some custard thing for dessert that was hard on the top."

"Crème brûlée?"

"Yeah, that's what it was, and she didn't even think about sharing. At that point, I was about ready to suggest we head back to my place and enjoy ourselves when she suddenly picked up her purse, gave me a peck on the cheek, and headed out the door. She told me she had a busy day coming up. I'm left thinking, you got a busy day? I gotta work with f'ing Dillon," Suel said and then laughed.

"Did she really leave you in the restaurant?"

"Yeah, it's almost like she timed it. I'm waiting for the server to bring my credit card back, and she gets up, kisses me on the cheek, and hurries out the door."

"You must have done something to piss her off if she's treating you like this. How long has this been going on?"

"At least a couple of weeks. I'm thinking, come on. I mean, if I did something that pissed her off, which is entirely possible, the least she could do would be to tell me what I did. You know, bitch me out, and then we can make up in bed. But this? Man, I can't figure it out, and I'm not getting anything."

"Wish I could help you, but I'm just another oblivious guy."

"God, I don't know. Anyway, did you drop the phones off with your friend down in the Tech Lab?"

"Yeah, she had a counter full of things lined up to go through, evidence bags, boxes. Looked like she was jammed, just like the rest of us. I told her the phones were from the Finglas murders, and that seemed to register. Said she'd see what she could do. With a murder every day for the past four days, I think the phones might be moved up close to the front of the line."

Suel nodded and said, "Well, at least something seems to be going right."

"In the meantime, I'm going to go through the files on those first three victims again and see if something comes up. I don't know what it is, but I have to believe we're missing something."

"I'll start in on the Thomas Davy file," Suel said.

"If there even is one. Didn't Egan say Davy didn't have a record?" Dillon asked.

"Still doesn't hurt to check. He may have tended bar at a place the other three went to. I'll try to find out," Suel said and headed back to his desk.

Two hours later, Dillon pulled on his jacket and walked over to Suel's desk. It was a little after 1:00. "I'm thinking of stepping outside and grabbing a shepherd's pie at the food truck. You want one?"

"Yeah, that sounds great. Here," Suel said, pulling a ten euro note from his pocket. "I'll expect the change."

"We'll see," Dillon said as he snatched the note from Suel's hand and headed out of the office. He took the elevator down to the ground floor and stepped outside. The temp was four degrees Celsius, about forty on the Fahrenheit scale. It was sunny, there wasn't any snow or ice, and for the second week in February, Dillon thought of it as a heat wave.

The food truck he was looking for was parked down the road. Barely a five-minute walk away, which was just perfect. There were three people in line when he arrived, and while he waited, he watched the half-dozen deer in the field across the way. A car stopped, and a woman stepped out, took pictures of the deer with her cell phone, and then drove off.

"Sir?" the man in the food truck said.

"Oh, sorry. I was watching the deer over in the field. I need two shepherd's pies, please."

"Anything else?" the man asked.

Dillon thought for a moment and said, "Yes, a medium tea and coffee. No cream or sugar."

"Coming right up."

Dillon was heading back to the office a minute later, carrying a cardboard tray. A guy leaving the building held the door for him as he entered.

"Thanks," Dillon said and hurried inside. The two men at the security station smiled, gave him a nod, and waved him through. He took the elevator up to Special Branch, and just as he approached the door, a woman stepped out and held the door for him.

His first thought was his luck seemed to be changing, and perhaps he should buy a lottery ticket. He called, "Dinner is served," as he walked past Suel's desk, heading for the breakroom. Suel was right behind him, and they settled into a table toward the back of the room.

Dillon passed a Styrofoam box with the shepherd's pie, along with the tea, a plastic fork, and a paper napkin, over to Suel. He opened up the box with his pie and dug in. "Mmm-mmm, delicious," he said over a mouthful.

"Thanks for the tea. Do I owe you anything?" Suel asked.

Dillon reached into his pocket and handed a two-euro coin to Suel. He took a second forkful of food and said, "I'll be right back. I just thought of something." He hurried out before Suel could respond. He sat at his desk and dialed Emily's extension down in the Tech Lab.

She answered on the fourth ring. "Tech Lab."

"Hi, Emily. It's Dillon. Sorry to bother you. I had a thought. When you're going over those phones checking the calls made, could you also check the photo galleries on the phones? See if there are any common images or, God forbid, photos of the other victims."

"Interesting. Yeah, I'll do that. It may take some time. I hope to be on this by mid-afternoon, but that's just my hope, so don't hold me to that. Okay?"

"Yeah, thanks for your help."

"Okay, gotta go if you want this done," she said and hung up.

Dillon went back and dug into his pie. When they finished, they sipped their drinks for a couple of minutes, then headed back to their desks.

Dillon had been going over background information on the victims for the umpteenth time and was still coming up empty-handed. He kept thinking perhaps the victims had met in a bar, at a party, or a concert or something. It was close to 5:00 when his desk phone rang. Based on the short double-ring, the call was from inside the headquarters building.

He picked up the receiver and crossed his fingers. "Dillon."

"Oh good, you're still there," Emily said. "I've found a common number on the phones. You want to come down and take a look?"

"I'm on my way. Thanks, Emily. This is the first break we've had."

"Well, don't get your hopes up too much. Come down and take a look."

"See you in a minute."

He hung up and looked toward Suel. He was seated at his desk with his back toward Dillon, hunched over, facing the wall on his cell phone. He looked stressed, and Dillon wondered if he was talking to Kira and decided not to wait and find out. He hurried out of the office and took the elevator down to the ground floor. He made his way through the halls, almost but not quite running. He pushed the intercom button next to the Tech Lab door.

"Dillon?" Emily said a moment later.

"Yeah, Emily." The door buzzed, and Dillon stepped into the lab. Emily was at the back counter typing on the keyboard and looking up at the screen mounted on the wall.

"You must have knocked over a half-dozen people to get down here that fast," she said glancing over at Dillon. "Okay, so here's what I've found. This number, with the national dialing code of 86, appears on all three phones for incoming calls. Interestingly, on these dates," she highlighted a list of three different dates and times stretching back to early December. "The incoming calls were made to all three phones. No one ever called the number back, which suggests they answered and may have agreed to meet or do something. Now, I have not gone through the text messages or the photo galleries yet. That will be my next task, but I'm not going to be able to get to it until tomorrow morning."

"This is great. Thank you. Can you print that information for me?"

"Way ahead of you. I've already done that," she said and handed Dillon two pages stapled together. "Now, one more thing. Are you interested in where these calls came from?"

"You mean the geographic location? I guess I presumed it was a cell phone."

"Wrong again, Dillon." She ran her hands across the keyboard, and a Dublin Google map came up on the screen. She enlarged the map a number of times and then clicked on the red dot that appeared in the city center. "This is Pinky's pub in Smithfield."

"Pinky's in Smithfield? Never heard of it," Dillon said.

"That's because you only frequent nice places, Dillon. Pinky's has a bit of a reputation for, shall we say, the lower class. These three, with two-year records and no permanent employment, yeah, they'd probably fit right in."

"And you think they might have met up there?"

"No, I never said that. All I know is someone phoned them from Pinky's on at least three different occasions."

"What's the address on the place?"

"Let me warn you, the uniformed officers won't go there unless there's at least two of them, and even then—
"

"Address, please."

"Some people just seem to be intent on learning the hard way," she said and brought the address up on the screen.

Dillon wrote it down. He thanked Emily and went back up to Special Branch. Suel was nowhere to be found, he even checked the men's room, but Suel had apparently left. Hopefully, he was meeting up with Kira, and they could patch up whatever the problem was. He locked up his desk and headed out the door.

ELEVEN

Once home, Dillon let Lucifer out into the front garden. He took off his shirt and pulled on a Dublin jersey, hoping it would make him look like more of a local. He made a chicken sandwich, and after he'd eaten, he coaxed Lucifer back into the house with a dog biscuit.

He thought about the comments Emily made regarding Pinky's. Were they accurate, or was she joking? He debated packing a pistol and decided that wouldn't be a good idea. At 8:00, he pulled on a jacket and got back in his car. He input the address for Pinky's pub into his GPS and headed down to Smithfield, an area along the Liffey River in Dublin's city center.

The houses in the area were all buff-colored brick, attached units. Dillon guessed they were probably a hundred and fifty years old or older. His GPS directed him to turn onto Blackhall Place. The houses he passed were no more than twelve feet wide and right up against the sidewalk. Each had a front door with an arched window above it and one two-panel window with an arched top on the first floor. Two smaller windows were centered above on the second floor. A number of windows and doors featured peeling paint. The roofs were slate and covered with moss. Chimneys for coal-burning fire-places were on the roof of every unit.

At the end of the twenty-three attached units stood a two-story double unit with a sign over the door, Pinky's. Two men were leaning against the front of the structure, smoking. Dillon had half-expected the place to be painted pink. It wasn't. Instead, it had a rather small sign that was easy to miss, suggesting to him that Pinky's most likely served local residents who lived within walking distance.

He was lucky to find a parking place between two cars just around the corner, and he backed into it. Once he turned his car off, he double-checked the interior to make sure there was nothing identifying it as an An Garda Síochána vehicle. If there was, he'd be sure to come back to a broken window or slit tires. He climbed out of his car, locked the doors, and walked around the corner to Pinky's entrance. The two smokers were still there, and by the looks of their cigarettes, they had just lit up fresh ones.

They smiled and nodded at one another, and as Dillon stepped past them, he caught the distinct smell of marijuana. Inside Pinky's, the lights were dim. The moment he stepped in, he was aware the level of conversation had suddenly dropped. More than a couple of heads turned and studied Dillon, the stranger, for a long moment.

There was a bar running the length of the room just off to the left, with a series of mirrors behind the bar advertising Jameson, Paddy's, and Tullamore Dew whiskies. If there were twenty stools along the bar, easily half of them were empty. Off to the right was a series of wooden tables and chairs. All but two of the tables were empty. At one table, a heavy-looking, gray-haired woman sat leaning with her head on the table, apparently passed out. Her right hand was still wrapped around an empty glass. The other table had three people seated at it, two men and a blonde woman. The woman was attractive and appeared to be a working girl, as in a street walker. For some reason, she looked familiar. From what Dillon could see from his quick glance, she was wearing a very short, tight skirt and a low-cut top beneath her brown leather jacket. All three of them stared at Dillon.

He made his way toward the end of the bar and settled onto a stool in the middle of five empty stools. The barman looked to be in his sixties and needed a shave. He stepped in front of Dillon and said, "What'll it be?"

This wasn't the place to order a Guinness, so he said, "I'll take a Jameson, straight, no ice, and better make it a double."

The barman nodded, took a glass from beneath the bar, and then pulled a bottle of Jameson off the rack. Instead of doing a free pour, as Dillon expected, he filled a shot glass twice and poured the exact amount of whiskey into a glass. If that had been back in the States or most of the pubs in Ireland, using a shot glass instead of a free pour would make it the last time Dillon would come to the place.

"Eight euros," the barman said as he set the glass down in front of Dillon.

Dillon pulled the ten euro note Suel had given him for lunch from his pocket and tossed it on the bar. The barman waited for a moment, hoping Dillon would tell him to keep the change, and eventually left once it became clear that wasn't going to happen.

Dillon took a small sip of his drink and then occasionally glanced at reflections in the mirrors behind the bar. The barman returned with his change, and the conversational sound gradually seemed to rise to a pre-Dillon level. He looked up and down the bar for a telephone but couldn't see one. There was a door behind the bar at the very end, just two stools to the right of Dillon, and he wondered if perhaps that was an office with a phone.

He had been at the bar for the better part of an hour, and his glass still wasn't quite half-empty. He picked up a round coaster from a stack on the bar. The coaster was black and labeled 'Pinky's' in bright pink letters. He placed it on top of his glass, signaling he'd be back. He walked down a short hall past the ladies' room and into the men's room. There was one stall in the men's room and then on the far wall, what was referred to as a 'piss wall.' An eight foot length of porcelain ran halfway up the wall, and a stream of water ran down over the porcelain. A six-inch wide curb to stand on ran across just in front of a porcelain rim. Dillon put the wall to use and had just zipped up and turned around when a large man staggered in wearing a leather jacket with a fur collar and a green tie-dye t-shirt that said, 'Rub Me For Luck.' Dillon nodded, flashed a quick smile, and stepped off the curb to the right.

The man moved to his left, essentially blocking Dillon's path.

"Oh, sorry, excuse me," Dillon said and moved to his left. The man blocked his path again.

"Yous ain't from around here, is yas?"

"Just visiting friends," Dillon said.

"You American?" the guy asked once he heard Dillon's accent.

Dillon nodded and suddenly knew where this was going.

"Even better," the guy said, then leaned back, wound up, and swung a large right fist.

Dillon had more than enough time to avoid the attempt. As the meaty fist swept past him, he shot his right hand into the man's adam's apple, causing him to reflexively raise both hands up to his neck as he gasped. Dillon stepped back, half-jumped to gain additional force, and kicked him squarely between the legs. The man groaned, and his eyes seemed to cross as he began to collapse forward. Dillon stepped to the side, grabbed him by the collar of his leather jacket, slammed his face into the porcelain wall, then slowly lowered him into the water trough at the base of the 'piss wall.' His head was on the porcelain rim, and a small trail of blood from his nose began to head downstream toward the drain. Dillon reached into the man's back pocket, pulled out a wallet, and placed it in his jacket. He stepped back into the pub, lifted the coaster off his glass, and drained the remainder of the whiskey.

The barman gave him a questioning look as if to say, 'What are you doing back in the bar, and where's your man with the fur collar?'

"Thanks for the whiskey," Dillon said and headed for the door as two men climbed off their stools and hurried into the men's room.

Once outside, Dillon picked up speed as he hustled around the corner. He climbed into his car, backed up, pulled into the street, and drove off. Halfway down the street, he passed the blonde in the very short skirt and brown leather jacket. Her shoulders were hunched, and she had to be cold in that short skirt. She turned and smiled at the sound of his car, gave a subtle nod and a wave. Dillon accelerated and sped past.

TWELVE

Dillon headed to the office early the next morning. He thought he'd be the first one in but was more than a little surprised to see Suel at his desk. "What are you doing in here at this hour?"

Suel looked over and shrugged. "Couldn't sleep, so I figured I might as well get my ass in here and try to do something positive."

Dillon nodded as he hung his jacket over the back of his desk chair and said, "Kira trouble?"

Suel shook his head. "Not anymore. She phoned toward the end of yesterday and told me she didn't want to see me again. Apparently, she was over at my place sometime last night because, when I went out to my car this morning, there was a big cardboard box filled with my clothes, a paint tray, brushes, and a roller, along with a couple of other tools. I'd been doing some work around her place. Anyway, it's over and done with."

"You think if you gave her a couple of days, she might calm down, and you could talk over whatever is bothering her?"

Suel shook his head and walked over to Dillon's desk. "You know, I've been through this with other women. I guess we both have. I don't want to go through this with Kira again six months from now. I'm just going to cut my losses and get on with life. Part of which is trying to find a link between these three murder victims."

Dillon nodded and said, "Well, I'm still sorry to hear about it. I've been there, and it's not fun."

"I'll survive," Suel said.

"Yeah, I know you will, Paddy. Look, if you need anything or you just want to bitch, let me know. I'm here for you."

"Thanks, right now, I want to find a break somewhere in this case, but I'm coming up empty-handed."

"Glad you mentioned that. After you left last night, I got a call from Emily. She found a link on the three cell phones."

"Oh, thank God. I knew something had to happen, or we were looking at another cold case. What'd she find?"

"She's still looking at call logs, and she hasn't gone through the emails or photo galleries yet. But, she did find a common phone number that all three individuals received three calls from on specific dates. I've got the list here," Dillon said, unlocking the middle drawer on his desk. He pulled out the two sheets Emily had copied, listing the dates, the times the calls were made to each phone, and the length of the calls. He handed the list to Suel.

"What the…Any idea who this is? Who called these guys?"

"Not a name, as such, but that number is for a phone in a pub called Pinky's. You know the place?"

Suel started to shake his head but then stopped and said, "Wait a minute. Is this a little dive over in Smithfield? Pinky's, I think it's a meeting place for knackers and slappers. I might have been in there years back, not that I can remember, which may have been how I ended up in the place, over-served and out of touch."

"Yeah, that sounds like it. I was curious and decided to pop in last night."

"You went to Pinky's? For the love of…You must have stood out like a sore thumb."

"Apparently something like that," Dillon said and went on to tell Suel the story about the 'piss wall' and the guy who ended up getting a close-up look at the thing.

"You're just damn lucky he didn't step in there with two friends. We'd find you face down in the Liffey. He went in there to rob you?"

"Sure seemed that way. Fortunately, he was drunk and moving slowly." Dillon reached into his jacket pocket and pulled out the man's wallet. "I grabbed this from him."

"What the hell. You, you robbed him?"

"Not exactly. I was checking him for a weapon just to play it safe, and somehow, I ended up with that in my pocket."

Suel shook his head. "In-f'ing-credible."

"I was thinking you might give him a call. Offer to meet with him and return the wallet, and while you're doing that, you might get some answers to questions on the victims and Pinky's."

Suel seemed to think for a long moment and then nodded and said, "I like that idea."

The wallet belonged to a man named Paul Grady. There were a couple photographs, a credit card, a union card, and an insurance card. Suel called the Plumbers and Pipe Fitters Union, explaining he was An Garda Síochána and was hoping to get a phone number for Grady. The person he was talking to offered to call him back just to make sure he was actually with An Garda Síochána. Suel gave the man his extension number and hung up. The call came through two minutes later.

Suel laughed and chatted for the next five minutes and then hung up. "Got your man's phone number. Turns out Paul Grady is known as 'Porky' on the job sites. He's a pipe fitter. Apparently, he's had some interaction with the Garda, nothing too serious, and always seems to be alcohol-fueled."

"That would match up with last night. Would you mind giving him a call?"

Suel smiled and said, "I'm looking forward to it. You know, I'm thinking, what if I have him come down here? I'll be in an interview room, and you can watch through the glass."

"Yeah, I like that. You can explain to him how you're busy, and you can't bring it to him, and you need him to sign a document."

"Yeah, and then I'll ask him if he knows any of the shooting victims."

"Just don't mention they've been killed."

"Dillon, it's been all over the news. He's no doubt heard all about the shootings."

"You think a guy who hangs out at 'Pinky's' watches a lot of news?"

Suel thought for a moment and then nodded and said, "Good point."

Suel made the phone call to Grady while Dillon sat on the corner of Suel's desk, listening. "Hello, this is DI Paddy Suel with An Garda Síochána. I'm calling for Mr. Paul Grady. Yes, Mr. Grady, we had someone turn in a wallet last night that apparently belongs to you. Just a moment, and I'll check. I have it right here in front of me. Yes, sir, it appears to be a debit card from Ulster Bank. Cash? There's a five-euro note in there. The wallet is brown leather, by the way. Looks a bit worn. I'd guess you've had it for a while. Oh, I wish I could deliver it, sir. Actually, I'm at the headquarters building in Phoenix Park. I suppose I could pass this on to the Garda Station on O'Connell Street, might take a few days, possibly a week. If you don't need the wallet before then. I—Very good. This morning will work. Just ask for me, DI Paddy Suel, Special Branch. Thank you, sir. See you in a bit," Suel said and hung up.

"How did he sound?" Dillon asked.

"Hungover. Interesting that he isn't working at the moment. The trades are screaming for people. Good Lord, he could work the weekends if he wanted to."

"Who knows?" Dillon said.

Suel reserved Interview Room Two for 10:30. He got a call announcing Paul Grady was in the lobby on the ground floor at 10:50. Dillon hurried into the viewing room next to Interview Room Two while Suel took the elevator down to the ground floor and escorted Grady up to the interview room.

THIRTEEN

As they walked into the interview room, Dillon studied Grady through the glass. He looked pretty much as Dillon recalled, baggy jeans, a large belly hanging over his belt, the jacket with the fur collar, and what appeared to be the same green tie-dyed t-shirt that said 'Rub Me For Luck.' The splint covering his nose and the two black eyes were new. Dillon recalled Grady's bloody nose after being slammed into the piss wall. Apparently his nose had been broken.

"Really appreciate you taking the time to come down here today, Mr. Grady. Please have a seat."

"Am I gonna be arrested or something?" Grady asked as he sat down and quickly looked around the room.

"Arrested? No, not at all. Just wanted to return your wallet to you. If you can just sign these two documents," Suel said and slid two pieces of paper across the metal tabletop.

Grady signed the documents without reading them. As he signed, Suel set an evidence bag on the table containing the wallet. Grady quickly shoved the signed documents back to Suel. He reached into the evidence bag, pulled out his wallet, and checked for the five euro note.

"That bastard took my cash. I had two hundred-euro notes in here."

"Two hundred euro notes. Oh, dear. Let me see that," Suel said, holding his hand out.

Grady handed him the wallet, and Suel pretended to examine the five euro note. "You're right. They're not here. Interesting he wouldn't take the five-euro note. Just wait for a moment. I have to get the right forms, and you can fill them out." As he spoke, he placed the wallet back in the evidence bag and set it off to the side.

"Don't I get me wallet?" Grady said.

"Yes, I mean, you certainly will, eventually. It shouldn't take more than a couple of weeks to do an investigation, and then we'll return it to you."

"A couple of weeks? What am I supposed to do in the meantime?"

"I suppose you could go to your bank and get some cash."

"You gotta be kidding. No, I tell you what. Umm, forget about the two hundred euros. I ain't gonna file that report. Just let me get my wallet back."

"Two hundred euros? You sure you don't want us to investigate?" Suel asked.

"Yeah, very sure."

Suel pushed the evidence bag across the table once more. Grady took his wallet out, shoved it in his pocket, and pushed his chair back, ready to stand.

"Say, before you go, I've got a couple of questions. Hoping you might be able to help me out."

"I didn't do nothing wrong. I wasn't gonna rob that bastard," Grady said.

"Good, I just wondered if you knew a guy named Connor Dunne." Grady seemed to think and then shook his head. "You know Thomas Davy?" Grady shook his head again. "What about Neil Kinan?"

He paused, then shook his head one more time. "Nope, never heard of any of those lads."

"You ever hear of someone named Feargal Scully?"

"No, absolutely not," he quickly answered. "Never heard the like of him."

"Okay, well, nice to meet you, Mr. Grady. You take care of yourself. Bit of a fall with the nose?"

"Something like that. Three guys came after me. One of 'em landed a punch."

Suel shook his head. "We can never be too careful. Enjoy the rest of your day."

"So, I can go, now?"

"You sure can. There's an officer just out in the hall who'll escort you down to the lobby."

Grady hurried out of the interview room. Suel turned toward the wall of windows and shook his head. A moment later, he stepped into the viewing room. Dillon was still seated in a chair.

"What did you think?" Suel asked.

"At no surprise, he's a lying sack of shit. I don't know that he knew any of the victims you mentioned. But who is Feargal Skully?"

Suel grinned. "That's the name of the barman at Pinky's. Sixty-seven years old. He's been tending bar there since forever."

"Sounds like the barman last night. When I ordered a double whiskey, he gave me two measured shots."

"Yeah, that would be him. Yet another reason I don't go to the place. At least you have the pleasure of knowing you broke Grady's nose."

"And apparently, I made off with two hundred euros."

"I'm sure the only time he's seen a hundred-euro note would be on the telly. Your man's a pipe fitter. They're crying for workers, but he'd rather be on the dole. It's a shame, really."

"You know, Paddy, I'm still thinking. I'd like to see if that phone number goes to that room behind the bar. It could be an office. Feargal Skully doesn't own the place, does he?"

Suel shook his head. "No, it's actually owned by a business called Dublin Drink. They own six different pubs, all along the same lines as Pinky's. Small neighborhood places. Nothing fancy. Pinky's is probably the lowest of the low, but you'd never hear of the other places. Always a bit of a question as to how much money they're making. To my knowledge, they're all cash-only businesses. No credit cards. Questionable bit of customers."

Dillon thought back to the table with the two guys and the street walker, and then fat, drunken thug Paul Grady. "The way you describe it, those pubs sound like the perfect place to recruit criminals."

Suel seemed to think about that for a moment. "Yeah, could be. A lot of them would be like your man Grady this morning. Not exactly the brightest bulb on the tree."

"You think he knew Neil Kinan?"

Suel gave a shrug. "I suppose it's possible. Kinan was driving around the city in a stolen Mercedes. He'd certainly fit the standard description, served time, no solid job. The idiot apparently snuck a woman into his room at least once that we know of. Hey, what are you thinking?" Suel asked in response to Dillon's faraway look.

"Something you just said popped into my thick skull. I need to run down to the property room."

"You going to fill me in?"

"Let me check down there first," Dillon said as he hurried out of the office.

FOURTEEN

He took the elevator to the sub-level and headed down the hall to the property room. The property room counter was covered with five cardboard boxes. One of the property room officers was in the process of placing the boxes on a four-wheel cart. He looked up as Dillon entered and smiled.

"Hey, Marshal. How are things going?"

"I'll know in a couple of minutes, Kevin," Dillon said. "I'd like to pull an item we brought down the other day. It's a box of papers in the Neil Kinan file."

"Sure thing. I need you to fill out a request form," he said, taking a form from a stack at the end of the counter and handing it to Dillon. "Let me just wheel this cart back there, and I'll get whatever you need."

Dillon quickly filled out the form and then waited at the counter for five minutes until Kevin returned. "Sorry it took so long. We're in the process of moving some of the quarter-century files over to the warehouse. What can I get for you?" Dillon handed him the form. "Neil Kinan? This just came in a day or two ago, didn't it?"

"Yeah, one of the Finglas shooting victims. Kinan was the third one. There are four, now."

Kevin shook his head and said, "Back in a minute."

Dillon leaned against the counter, expecting another long wait. Kevin was back in less than two minutes, carrying the half-empty wine box from Neil Kinan's armoire with all the mail and envelopes. "You taking this upstairs to Special Branch?"

Dillon shook his head. "No, I just need one item out of there."

"Okay, grab a seat in a cubicle and have at it," Kevin said.

Thanks," Dillon said as he picked up the box and hurried over to one of the cubicles. As he set the box down on the counter, a security camera was activated. Dillon paged through the envelopes and papers until he found what he was looking for, the Christmas card with the photo of the naked blonde woman wearing a Santa hat and a pleasant smile. He looked at the Christmas card for a long moment. It was definitely the same woman that had been in Pinky's last night. The same woman who was walking down the street. The same woman who smiled and waved as he drove past.

He returned the box to the counter, filled out the form Kevin gave him, then placed the card in an evidence bag and went back up to Special Branch. Suel was seated at his desk reading a report on his computer screen.

Dillon dropped the card over his shoulder and onto the keyboard.

Suel glanced at the card in the evidence bag and said, "Oh, thank you. Someone who wants to date me?"

"I think she dates anyone with fifty euros in their pocket. She was in Pinky's last night. Sitting with two guys. When I left, she was walking down the street, and she smiled and gave me a wave."

"Well, that only proves she had no idea how awful you are. So, she sent this to Kinan?"

"Yeah, it's signed Gemma on the inside of the card. Remember the blonde hairs on his sleeping bag and the used rubber? I'm wondering if she may have been his partner, at least for a night."

Suel seemed to think for a moment. "So, all four of these victims are getting phone calls from Pinky's. Kinan gets a naked picture and possibly a night's entertainment from a woman you saw there last night. That's beginning to suggest Pinky's is more than just a casual stop."

"That's what I'm thinking."

Suel nodded at his computer screen. "Oh, I'm going through the background file on Thomas Davy, yesterday morning's Finglas victim at the bus stop."

"You finding anything?"

"That's the problem. No, I haven't. He worked for Dublin County Council. Had been employed in maintenance for eight years. Worked at the Bell Building over in Darndale, Dublin. No problems, he had two promotions, standard promotions, but still. Umm, he did a year of study at Dublin City University. Owns a house in Finglas."

"Is he married?"

Suel shook his head. "No mention of that."

"I wonder if they've done an autopsy yet."

"If you're wondering about the bullet, I called Ballistics while you were down in records looking at pictures of naked women, and they haven't received anything yet."

"Let me give Noel Leonard a call and see where they are on the Davy autopsy. He said they might be doing it yesterday afternoon." Dillon went over to his desk, set the evidence bag with the Christmas card on the desk, and phoned Dublin Morgue.

A woman's voice answered after two rings. "Good morning, Dublin Morgue."

"Hi Gráinne, Jack Dillon calling. How are you doing?"

"Oh, fine, thanks. You calling for Noel Leonard?"

"I am, as a matter of fact."

"Let me connect you," she said, and a moment later, the phone began to ring. Given the quick response from Gráinne, the receptionist, they must be busy, and he wondered if they were dealing with relatives of the latest Finglas victim, Thomas Davy.

Leonard answered on the fourth ring. "Noel Leonard."

"Hi, Noel. Jack Dillon calling. Just a quick question for you."

"Hi Jack. A quick question is about all the time I've got. What's up?"

"The Thomas Davy autopsy. Where do you stand? Have you sent the bullet to Ballistics yet? And, can I do anything to help?"

"That's three questions, and the answers are finished, no, and yes."

Dillon had to think for a moment. "So, the autopsy's complete, and the bullet is waiting to be transferred?"

"Correct. They thought someone would pick it up late today or tomorrow."

"I can be there in the next half hour if that would help."

"It would probably get the results to you twenty-four hours sooner. Our work here is basically finished. In fact, we have Rom Massey & Sons scheduled to pick up the Davy body at 1:00 this afternoon."

Massey and Son's was a large funeral home with a number of locations on the north side of Dublin. "If you can have someone get the paperwork lined up, I'll be there in thirty minutes."

"It will be waiting out front with Gráinne. Thanks, Dillon. Just one more thing off the growing pile on my desk," Leonard said and hung up.

Dillon stopped at Suel's desk on his way out of the office. "I'm headed to Dublin Morgue. I'm going to deliver the Davy bullet to Ballistics. I should be back in an hour. You find anything on Davy that connects him?"

"No, nothing. You might want to check with Emily and see if she's had a chance to look into his cell phone."

"I'll do that once I drop the bullet off in Ballistics."

"Safe journey," Suel said and returned to his computer screen.

Dillon's trip to the Dublin Morgue, about two miles from his house, took close to fifteen minutes. He parked on Griffith Avenue in front of the Postal Service delivery building and walked into the side entrance of the Dublin City Mortuary.

The reception area and Gráinne were just inside the door. Gráinne's desk sat behind a thick glass panel on the front wall. No one else was in the area as he entered, and Gráinne looked up, smiled, and waved as he headed toward her desk.

"Good morning, Dillon. Here to transport to Ballistics?"

"Yeah, another promotion for me," he said, and she laughed.

"Just need you to sign these and keep a copy for yourself," she said. She passed a number of forms and a pen through the opening in the glass. Dillon signed the forms. There were actually four, and he pushed three of them back through the opening.

Gráinne pulled the forms onto her desk and shoved an official-looking manila envelope out through the opening.

"Thanks, Gráinne. Have a good rest of the day."

"You too, Dillon. Good luck with everything you have going on in Finglas."

"We can use all the good luck you can find for us," he said and headed back to his office.

FIFTEEN

Dillon pulled into the secure parking lot at the headquarters building and headed for Ballistics. He pushed the intercom next to the door and was immediately buzzed in by Joseph Lane, not the person Dillon was hoping to deal with.

Lane was a by-the-book, wound-tight individual. Today, like every day, he was wearing a white lab coat over his starched white shirt and blue-striped tie. The gold name tag over his left breast read Detective Sergeant J. Lane. A name tag of his own creation.

"US Marshal Dillon, good morning, sir."

"Good morning, Detective Sergeant. Nice to see you. I have the round removed from the latest victim in the Finglas shootings, a man by the name of Thomas Davy," Dillon said and handed the manila envelope along with the Dublin City morgue form over to Lane.

Lane pursed his lips and said, "Why are you delivering this?"

"We're anxious to get any and all information on this case. My understanding is that the three earlier victims had all been shot with the same weapon, a nine-mil-limeter Glock. We'd like to learn if this gentleman was killed by the same weapon."

"I believe the morgue was planning to transport this evidence themselves."

"That's correct. They were, but like all of us, they are currently buried with work and understaffed. I made a special trip to pick up the evidence and deliver it to you in the hopes we might be able to learn if the same weapon was used in this murder."

"You do realize we're just as busy as everyone else, right?"

"I do, and I want to thank you in advance for any assistance you can provide. We've got a killer out there, and we're trying to learn who the killer is and get them off the street before another innocent is murdered. As you know, the research and investigation from your section is key to accomplishing that task."

Fortunately, that last comment seemed to bring a subtle hint of a smile to Lane's face. "I'll see what we can do."

"Thank you, wonderful to see you. Pardon me for interrupting your day," Dillon said as he slowly began to back up and make his way to the door.

Lane merely nodded, apparently dismissing Dillon as he quickly stepped out into the hall. He worked his way along the hallways and pushed the intercom at the Tech Lab.

"Tech Lab," Emily responded a half-minute later.

"Hi, Emily, Jack Dillon." The door buzzed, and Dillon entered the lab.

"Hi, Dillon. How's the day going? Please, don't tell me there's been another killing in Finglas," Emily called. Her back was to him as she continued typing, her focus on the large screen on the wall.

"As far as I know, nothing has happened in Finglas so far today. Everyone is keeping their fingers crossed. I'm just checking in. Anything else on the cell phones?"

"If you're asking about the phone from your man killed at the bus stop yesterday, no, nothing yet. I'll get to it shortly. I have found some common or at least similar shots in the photo galleries. Should have things lined up for you later this afternoon."

"Thank you. I'm out of your hair. Text me when you have something."

"Yeah, I will," she said, never looking back at him.

Dillon left and headed back up to Special Branch. Suel was still at his desk. Dillon told him about taking the bullet from the Davy murder to Ballistics and handing it over to Detective Sergeant Lane.

"Talk about a piece of work. Honest to God, that gobshite takes the cake."

"No argument from me, but I was kissing his ass in the hopes he'd get on that right away. They've already got three matches. How hard could it be to check this one out and determine it either matches or it doesn't?"

"Spoken like a man who doesn't have to do the work," Suel said and laughed. "Not to worry, I'm with you, Dillon. Say, I placed a call to the Technical Unit. You remember Jimmy Burke?"

"Burke? Is he the guy who was married last year and a former girlfriend showed up at the wedding?"

"It was two years ago, but yeah, that was Burke. He and the new wife ended up in separate rooms the first night of their honeymoon. Anyway, I gave him a call, and he put me in touch with the Photographic Section. They do the sketches."

"I think they're called Evo-Fit composites nowadays."

"Yeah, anyway, I sent him a copy of that sexy Christmas card photo from the batch of Neil Kinan's papers, and he's going to run it through their system and see if someone comes up."

"Did you give him the woman's name, Gemma?"

"No, on purpose. I didn't want them to automatically look for someone with that name. This way, they have to use the photo recognition program. So, we'll see. Hopefully, they can run something today. I told him it had to do with the Finglas murders. It's like, as soon as someone hears Finglas, they jump on the task."

"Yeah, I popped in on Emily, and she's going over the photo galleries in those phones and then is going to do the same with the Thomas Davy phone, so we might have something from that too. With all the phone calls from Pinky's, I'm crossing my fingers in the hopes she finds something."

"We need to find out who in the hell made those phone calls. Your favorite barman Feargal Scully might know," Suel said.

Dillon shook his head. "I'm pretty sure it won't be Feargal. Whoever made those calls was probably in charge, and that pretty much eliminates Feargal. He doesn't strike me as having the brains."

"I don't know," Suel said. "What if someone told him to make the calls and told him what to say? That's why the calls came from Pinky's. You know, just in case we ever got hold of the conversations, whoever was in charge could claim they were innocent."

"Hmm, not as far-fetched as I initially thought. I want to check on something with Tully Egan," Dillon said. "You have his cell phone number?"

Suel nodded and pulled out his cell. He swiped his finger across the screen and then tapped a couple of times. "Yeah, here it is. You ready for this?"

"Give it to me," Dillon said and then punched in the numbers on his phone as Suel read them. He repeated the number back to Suel.

"Surprisingly, you did that correctly," Suel said.

"No one's more surprised than me," Dillon replied.

He went back to his desk and phoned Egan. He thought he was going to be dropped into voicemail when Egan suddenly answered. "Hello?"

"Hi, Tully, Jack Dillon. Just touching base. You come up with anything on yesterday's victim, Thomas Davy?"

"We're at his home now. So far, nothing."

"You going to be there for a while?"

"Next few hours unless something happens. Keeping my fingers crossed."

"Would you mind if I stopped in?"

"The more, the merrier. You have something in mind?"

"Not really, but something's beginning to rattle around in my brain. Just can't figure out what yet."

Egan gave Dillon the address and disconnected. Dillon called the Dublin County Council and eventually got transferred to the HR department. "Human Resources," was how the woman answered the phone.

"Hello, my name is Jack Dillon. I'm with An Garda Síochána, Special Branch. I'd like to speak to someone who could confirm some information for me on a former employee."

"I'm afraid you would have to submit that request in writing, and we—"

"This is regarding our investigation into the murder of one Thomas Davy in Finglas yesterday morning. Mr. Davy was employed by Dublin County Council for eight years." Dillon read Davy's address off to the woman and finished up with, "Is there a supervisor I could talk with?"

There was a pause, and then she said, "One moment, and I'll transfer your call."

After two rings, a man answered. "Brendan Haggerty."

"Mr. Haggerty, thank you for taking my call. My name is Jack Dillon. I'm with An Garda Síochána, Special Branch. We are in the midst of investigating the murder yesterday of a County Council employee."

"Oh Lord, Thomas Davy. Terrible, absolutely terrible."

"I couldn't agree more. I'm sorry to call out of the blue like this, but I would like to check on Mr. Davy's employment. The information we have is that he has been employed by the Council for eight years. Is that correct?"

"One moment while I check on that. That's D-A-V-Y?"

"Yes sir, first name Thomas."

"One moment. Yes, here we are. That is correct, eight years. He was hired in June of 2014. Received two promotions over the next few years. He was working maintenance in the Bell—"

"Was he scheduled for work yesterday?"

"Yesterday, oh, I'm sure he was. He, oh, wait a minute. It appears he phoned in a family emergency of some sort, and he was going to be out of town."

"Can you tell me when he phoned in that request?"

"Yes, let me just bring that up. He called at…umm…6:25 a.m. yesterday morning, apparently."

"Thank you, sir."

"Hope I was of some help."

"Indeed, you were, thank you," Dillon said and hung up. He thought for a couple of minutes, went online, and checked the bus route from Finglas to the airport. The N4 stopped at the very stop where Davy was shot. The bus route made a thirty-seven-minute journey to Terminal One at Dublin Airport. Dillon thought for a long moment. *Davy wasn't going to work. He was leaving town. But then, where was his luggage? Where was he going?*

SIXTEEN

Suel was on the phone, so Dillon gave a wave and hurried out to his car. Thomas Davy's house was on Jamestown Road, not more than a six-minute walk to the bus stop where he was shot. Two squad cars and an unmarked car were parked in front of number 30 Jamestown Road, Davy's home.

The house was a cream-colored two-story attached stucco structure located at the end of four identical units. Dillon pulled into the drive next to Davy's place, backed out, and then pulled behind one of the squad cars parked at the curb. He draped his lanyard with the ID around his neck and climbed out of his car. A 2005 silver Toyota was parked in the drive, and a uniformed officer was standing at Davy's front door.

As Dillon approached, he held up his ID and said, "Marshal Dillon, Special Branch. I spoke to DI Egan about twenty-five minutes ago and told him I was on my way."

The officer nodded and said, "Yeah, he told me. Go on in. I think he's back in the kitchen."

"Thanks. Stay warm," Dillon said, although the temp was in the mid-forties Fahrenheit. Warm for Dublin in the middle of February. He glanced over at the Toyota and noticed two of the wheels were flat. "Did someone let the air out of those tires?"

"They were slit. It was supposed to be towed out yesterday, but the tow truck was being serviced. They'll be by later this morning. Not to worry, it's not going anywhere."

Dillon nodded, stepped into the house, and called, "DI Egan?"

"That you, Dillon? Back here in the kitchen."

The staircase leading to the second floor was on the right, and the entrance to the sitting room was on the left. Dillon could hear officers upstairs as he headed back to the kitchen. The door was open, and Egan was leaning against the kitchen counter when Dillon stepped in. At the moment, he was talking on his cell phone, and he gave Dillon a nod. Dillon gave a quick look around the kitchen.

It was pretty standard for a place that hadn't been updated in at least thirty years. There was a small table with two chairs and a pile of unopened envelopes in front of one of the chairs. The faded white cabinets looked plastic with a woodgrain pattern. The countertops were old, and scratched with scarred white Formica stained from sauces and wine glasses. Dillon bent over, bringing his eyes level with the Formica countertop, and noticed a lot of dust and crumbs. Nothing appeared to have been cleaned in the place for quite some time.

A tea kettle was on the counter next to the sink. A white mug with the name Batchelor's Coffee Company in black letters was next to the kettle. Dillon had been to the shop a couple of times, coffee, tea, and pastries. It was up on the north end of Finglas. He guessed the mug was probably stolen. He walked over and placed a hand on the half-full mug. It was cold, and based on the scum on top, had been there for at least a day, maybe two. A used tea bag was resting on the counter just behind the mug. A chocolate-covered biscuit with a bite out of it was on the counter next to the tea bag. The sink had two dirty plates, some silverware, and a bowl sitting in it.

Dillon had the sense that, based on the mess, there hadn't been a woman in the place. *Had Davy left in a hurry? With the slit tires on the car out front, could that be the reason he had been waiting at the bus stop?*

"Thanks, Brennan. You find anything, let me know," Egan said and set his cell phone on the counter. "How you keeping, Dillon?"

"All sorts of things banging around in my thick skull. I noticed the slit tires on the car out front. Apparently, someone didn't want him to go anywhere. I checked online, and the N4 bus makes a stop where Davy was shot. The bus heads out to Dublin airport."

Egan nodded. "His suitcase was in the boot of the car. They went through it yesterday, nothing other than some shorts, t-shirts, and a pair of sandals. Everything appeared to be packed in a hurry and just tossed in. Oh, and there was a diamond ring, unique, old, possibly belonging to a grandmother or someone. Something scared him, maybe the three shootings, maybe he saw someone. He had a ticket to Spain, Barcelona, as a matter of fact. He was booked on Ryan Air. We're guessing he was going to drive to the airport. I'm thinking he saw the slit tires after he put his suitcase in the boot. He freaked out and ran to the bus stop."

Dillon nodded. "That makes sense. I spoke to the HR department in Dublin County Council just before I came over. Davy phoned in an emergency at 6:25 yesterday morning and told them he couldn't go to work. That half mug of tea and just a bite from the biscuit, along with those dishes in the sink, I'd say something got to him, and he left in a hurry."

"Did the Tech Lab find anything from his cell phone?"

"I don't think they've been able to get to it yet. I hope to hear from them later today. Are you at all familiar with a pub called Pinky's in Smithfield?"

Egan seemed to think for a moment and shook his head. "I don't believe I've ever heard of the place."

"The other three guys, Terry Tebbot, Connor Dunne, and Neil Kinan, all received phone calls from the place on three particular days. The calls were made just a couple of minutes apart. None of them called the number back. I'm thinking they got some kind of instruction to meet somewhere. We should have information by the end of the day, but I'm willing to guess Davy also received the same messages, met up with the other three, and whatever they did was something that led to them being killed. It looks like Davy was the only one smart enough to catch on that something wasn't right, and he almost made it out of here. He was killed waiting for the bus to take him to the airport."

Egan just shook his head. "I can only hope and pray it's just the four of them and no one else will be killed before we find out who in the hell has been doing this."

There was some noise out in the hallway, and Egan glanced out the kitchen door. "Any luck?"

"Not really," a female voice said. "A couple of receipts in a dresser drawer. Looks like he had dinner with another person nine days ago. Hopefully, we can find something on the security tape, if they even have one and if they haven't erased it."

"You finished upstairs?"

"Just about. If he had dinner with a woman, I can only hope for her sake she didn't end up in his bed. Those sheets haven't been washed in at least six months, if ever. I'm going to burn these latex gloves."

"No sign of a woman? No clothes, makeup, anything?"

"You gotta be kidding. You'd be afraid to catch something just by using the bathroom. The place is dreadful," she said and shook her head.

"Oh, well, on that happy note, let me introduce you to Jack Dillon. He's with Special Branch, detailed to us along with DI Suel," Egan said and moved to the side so the red-headed woman could step into the kitchen.

She smiled and held out a hand, her brown eyes sparkled. "Oh, hi. Nice to meet you, DI Hannigan, Lucette Hannigan. You're the American, right?"

Dillon nodded and gave her a quick handshake. "Nice to meet you."

"Well, if you'll excuse me, I'm going to go back to the station, burn my clothes, and grab a scalding hot shower. Dennis has the receipts from the dinner upstairs in an evidence bag. Nice to meet you, Dillon. Anything else you need, Egan?"

"No, check out, go home, and get some sleep. You earned it."

"I just wish we could have found something, God, anything."

"Me too, Lucette, me too."

They both watched her walk down the hall and out the front door.

"She good?" Dillon asked.

"You mean as an investigating officer? Yeah, very good. Has a slightly different take on things and comes up with thoughts you and I wouldn't think of, like her comment on your man's sheets not being washed for six months. He's the odd duck in this foursome. You have to wonder if there's some sort of County Council connection."

"A connection? Like what?"

"If I knew that, I'd have the case solved," Egan said. "Come on. You can have a look upstairs. Another pair of eyes never hurts."

SEVENTEEN

Dillon followed Egan upstairs. What passed for the master bedroom was at the top of the stairs. When they stepped into the room, it was immediately obvious that Hannigan's description had been correct. The bifold doors to two closets were open. Clothes were on the floor of both closets and scattered throughout the room. A takeout pizza box was on the bedside table with half a pizza and scraps of crust. A pile of crumpled Kleenex rested in the pizza box, and Dillon didn't want to think about what the Kleenex had been used for. There were two pillows on the double bed. The pillowcases were marred with a number of sweat stains. There was a worn-looking chest of drawers pushed up against the wall opposite the foot of the bed. A TV rested on top of the chest of drawers. At the moment, a man was on his knees looking under the bed. He was using the flashlight on his cell phone to illuminate the area.

"Any luck, Dennis?" Egan asked.

"This Davy character was a first-class slob. All the clothes on the floor and in the closets aren't from me or Hannigan. If I didn't know better, I'd think the place was ransacked. Davy apparently liked to wallow in trash.

That pizza box next to the bed has to have been there for close to a week. To answer your question, no, we haven't come across anything other than some dinner receipts. We checked the other two bedrooms. One of them is piled with junk. Your man must have been some kind of hoarder." He clicked off the cell phone light, stood, and got a surprised look on his face when he noticed Dillon.

"Hi, Jack Dillon, Special Branch." Dillon held out his hand.

"Dennis O'Gara. God, you don't want to be shaking hands with the likes of me after going through this cesspool," he said and shook his head. "Your man was an absolute slob, Tully. Look at this place. The next two rooms are even worse. Nothing found here. No weapons, nothing like a stash of cash, or even drugs."

O'Gara pulled off his blue latex gloves and inserted them in a large empty paper coffee cup sitting on the chest of drawers. "Not to worry, that's my cup, Tully. Let me show you the other rooms."

They followed him out of the bedroom and into the next room. He pushed the door open with his elbow and stepped aside. A single bed with a bare mattress was pushed up against the radiator that was just beneath the window. The window overlooked the back garden. Cheap metal mini-blinds hung over the window. A number of the blinds were bent or missing. The left side of the blinds rested on the windowsill, while the right side was twelve or fourteen inches higher. There wasn't a dresser or a chair in the room, just the bed with the bare mattress. The bifold door on the built-in closet was open. Other than a half-dozen metal hangers, the closet was empty.

"You think someone might have been living with him? Maybe an older child, a student, or someone, and they finally couldn't stand it anymore and left?" Dillon said.

O'Gara shrugged.

"No mention of that in any records. I don't believe he rented the room out, at least not officially," Egan said. "We sent two lads around knocking on doors yesterday. No one really seemed to know your man. Said he pretty much kept to himself."

"Let me show you the next room," O'Gara said, and they followed him to the door opposite the bathroom, just a few feet away from the middle bedroom. This time, he pushed the door open using his foot and stepped back. Egan began to enter and stopped. There wasn't any space to enter. The room was filled with furniture, much of it looking antique. Tables, cabinets, and a couch uphol-stered with what appeared to be faded red velvet had four wooden chairs piled on top of it. A table with carved legs was stacked with piles of plates, bowls, and serving dishes. Two brass lamps stood in a far corner. Matching crystal wine glasses, covered in dust, were lined up on a side table. Dozens of boxes were stacked against the wall behind the furniture.

"Look at this. The place is a dump, and you've got all these classy antiques stacked up in here. Based on the dust, this stuff has been sitting here for years." O'Gara shook his head. "Now, you don't want to go into the bathroom. You're liable to get infected with some unidentifiable disease that will no doubt kill you."

Egan laughed but didn't make a move to enter the bathroom. "Have you checked the back garden? There's a shed out there."

O'Gara gave a loud exhale, suggesting he wasn't looking forward to it, "Unfortunately, that's going to be my next stop."

"Don't let us keep you. Dillon, have you seen enough?"

"I guess I have, Tully. I'll head back to the office. As soon as we get the results on your man's phone, I'll let you know. I'm keeping my fingers crossed that he received the same calls as the other three."

Dillon drove back to Special Branch with more questions than answers. Thomas Davy seemed even more out of touch with the other three victims than before. Who would slit the tires on his car? And, if they did that so he couldn't leave, did he run to the bus stop? Why would he take time to call the County Council to say he wouldn't be in for work if he was fleeing someone?

He parked in the secure lot at Garda headquarters and entered the building through the door in the parking lot. He debated stopping at the Tech Lab to see if Emily had anything new from the victims' cell phones and quickly decided that was not his best idea.

He took the elevator up to the third floor and entered Special Branch. Suel wasn't at his desk. Dillon stopped at his own desk to see if the red light on his phone was blinking, signaling a message. Unfortunately, it wasn't, but the lights were on, and the door was open to DCI McCabe's office, so Dillon walked over and knocked on the doorframe.

McCabe was at his desk. He looked up from the file he was reading and said, "Oh, Dillon, wonderful. Please, come in. You're just in time to save me from reviewing another budget file. Any news on the Finglas cases?"

Dillon told him what he knew, which wasn't all that much. He finished up with, "So I'm hoping the Tech Lab might be able to discover something, anything that would lead us to find whoever was apparently in charge. My suspicion is something was accomplished, a robbery, perhaps a murder, something that these individuals were recruited to do. Whatever it was, I believe they accomplished the task and were murdered so they wouldn't talk."

"But you can't prove that at this point, can you?"

"No sir, unfortunately, we can't. I just have a strong sense that is the case."

McCabe seemed to think and then smiled. "It would appear that, at the moment, all roads seem to lead to this place called Pinky's over in Smithfield."

"That's my thought as well, sir."

"Well, then, don't let me get in your way. Thank you for the update."

"Thank you, sir," Dillon said and hurried out of the office. He shook his head as a thought crossed his mind, thinking he should have done this next step in person. He sat in his desk chair for a moment, thinking, then picked up his phone and called Finglas Station.

"An Garda Síochána, Finglas," was how the phone was answered.

"Yes, This is US Marshal Jack Dillon, assigned to Special Branch. I would like to speak with DI Dennis O'Gara, please."

"DI O'Gara is out of the office at the moment, working a case and—"

"Yes, I know. I just left him and DI Egan at the home of the latest shooting victim, a man named Thomas Davy. Is there a way I might reach him? Can you give me his cell phone number, please?"

"I'm afraid I can't do that, sir. It's against policy. I can send you to his voicemail. He'll be notified on his cell phone that you've left a message. And, if able, I'm sure he would return your call."

That sounded like complete and utter bullshit to Dillon, but he also realized that was the best he could hope for. "Yes, please send me to his voicemail."

A moment later, the phone rang twice, and then O'Gara's message. "This is DI Dennis O'Gara. I'm unable to take your call at the moment. Please leave your name and number, and I'll get back to you just as soon as possible." Dillon was about to speak when O'Gara's voice continued and repeated the message in Irish.

He waited a second or two just to be sure the recording was finished. "Hi, Dennis, Jack Dillon here. Just wanted to say it was nice to meet you this morning. I have an idea regarding the four individuals murdered in Finglas. Please give me a call when you're able. All the best and thank you. Oh, and here's my cell phone number in the event I'm out of the office." Dillon left his cell phone number and hung up.

He placed a call to the Tech Department and asked for Officer Burke. His call was transferred and, a moment later, began to ring. Burke picked up on the third ring and answered in one word, "Burke."

"Hi, Jimmy. This is Jack Dillon. Don't know if you remember me, but I'm—"

"Oh, yes, I remember. You're the poor bastard that got stuck with Paddy Suel as a partner. How are you holding up?"

"Still here to tell the story."

"Can't ask for more than that. Would you happen to be calling on the facial recognition of the woman on the Christmas card?"

"As a matter of fact, I am."

"Well, I've got the file here, completed it this morning, and I was waiting for Suel's call. You're welcome to come down and pick it up. Sorry I can't deliver it, but we're up to our necks in cases and—"

"Not a problem, Jimmy. If I'm down there in the next five minutes, would that be okay?"

"That would be just fine. See you whenever you arrive. You know where we are?"

"Two doors down from the lab, I believe."

"You got it. Tech Department 1-A. See you shortly," Burke said and hung up.

EIGHTEEN

Dillon took the elevator down to the ground floor and made his way through the maze of halls. He walked past the Tech Lab and, two doors later, pressed the intercom next to the door labeled Tech Department 1-A. "Yes," a male voice answered. Even with just the one word, Dillon was pretty sure it wasn't Burke.

"Jack Dillon with Special Branch. I'm here to see James Burke. He's expecting me."

"Let me just check a moment," the voice said, and Dillon could hear someone shout something from the other side of the door.

A moment later, the door buzzed, and he pushed it open. He stepped into an office area with six cubicles. Each cubicle had a white card with the occupant's name in black letters. Burke's cubicle was the second on the right-hand side, and Dillon headed toward it just as Burke's head popped up above the wall.

"Oh, Dillon, great to see you again. Come on in. How are you getting on?"

"We're in the middle of these Finglas murders and not coming up with much. Were you able to identify the woman in the photo?"

Burke nodded. "You mean my favorite Christmas card? Yeah, she's been a somewhat regular individual with the department. A few shoplifting charges. She assaulted a tourist, an American tourist, actually, back in 2020. Failure to pay was the suspected reason, although she claimed he attacked her first. Are you aware that prostitution is no longer illegal here in Ireland?"

"Yes, if I understand the law, prostitution is no longer illegal, but paying for sex is, correct?"

"Yeah, that's pretty much it. I was able to identify the woman as Gemma McKee. I've printed off a list of past charges, all minor, by the way. She lives in Council housing over in Finglas and—"

"Council housing in Finglas? That wouldn't happen to be on Plunkett Avenue, would it?"

Burke shot a quick look at Dillon. "As a matter of fact, that's exactly where it's located. So, you're familiar with her?"

"No, not really, but one of the victims in the Finglas shootings was found there. Well, found in his car parked in front of the building. If I recall the structure, I think it's twenty units. A two-story structure. Interesting that's where she lives. You know how long she's been there?"

Burke shook his head. "I just know that she lives there, or at least that's the address that's on the court records. Unit number six, as a matter of fact."

"I know Finglas Station had officers going door to door in the building. Unfortunately, they never got much of a response from the residents."

"It's a different world in Council housing. The residents, at least the ones with any brains, are just playing it safe, and they're not going to say anything. The last thing they need is to be identified as a Gardai informant. That could bring all sorts of problems."

Dillon nodded. "Very true. May I take that file?"

"Absolutely, it's yours to keep. The world's best Christmas card is in there."

"Thank you, Jim. Nice to see you again. Do I need to sign anything?"

"No, it's yours to take. I've got a copy here that we'll file for future reference. Glad I could help." They shook hands, and Dillon went back up to Special Branch.

When he got back to his desk, the red light on his phone was blinking, signaling someone had left him a message. He punched in the code for voice messages and a moment later heard DI Dennis O'Gara's voice. "Yeah, Dillon, Dennis O'Gara, returning your call. Just finishing up at the Davy residence. I found absolutely nothing of interest here if that's what you called about. You can reach me at this number," he said, gave his cell phone number, and then disconnected.

Dillon listened to the recording again and wrote down the number. He input it into his cell phone and then called.

His call was answered on the third ring. "O'Gara."

"Hi, Dennis, Jack Dillon here. Thanks for returning my call and passing on your cell phone number."

"My pleasure, I think. What can I do for you?"

"Did you have a chance to get an update from DI Egan?"

"Depends on what you mean by an update."

"Did he mention Pinky's pub?"

"Pinky's? That shit hole over in Smithfield?"

"That would be an accurate description."

"He didn't mention it. What's up with that place?"

"Here's the deal, Dennis. The Tech Lab has found phone calls to the first three victims coming from a phone at Pinky's. We don't know who made the calls yet. The calls were short, no more than a minute or two, made all on the same day, one right after the other. No one responded to the calls. We think it may have been scheduling a meeting. The Tech Lab will be going through Thomas Davy's phone later today, and I'm expecting he will have received the same calls. I'd like to sit down with you, maybe over a pint or a tea, and see if we can come up with something. The other thing that happened is that Neil Kinan, the third shooting victim, received a Christmas card from a woman known to be at Pinky's. We had facial recognition done on her photo, and it turns out she lives in the council housing building where Neil Kinan was shot in his car."

"What's her name?"

"Gemma McKee. You know of her?"

"No, sorry, doesn't ring a bell."

"Well, I think there's some kind of connection. Don't know what, exactly. But Pinky's is definitely involved in some way. Both Suel and I would be recognized as Gardai if we went in there. I was in there a few nights back, and some idiot tried to assault me. I—"

"Did you lock him up?"

"No, actually, I knocked him out, apparently broke his nose, and laid him down in the piss wall trough."

O'Gara laughed at that. "Oh, much better, way better. Tell you what, you know where the Palace Bar is?"

"I do, if it's the bar close to Trinity. Is it right on the edge of the Temple Bar district?"

"That's the place. How 'bout we meet there, say 6:00? The way things are going something comes up, just give me a call, and we can do it some other time."

"Works for me. I look forward to it, Dennis. Thank you."

No sooner had he hung up the phone than Suel entered the office. Dillon waved him over.

"What'd I miss?" Suel asked as Dillon handed him the file on Gemma McKee.

"Jimmy Burke got a positive ID on Miss Christmas Card. Her name is Gemma McKee. She had some interaction with the court system, an assault, probably due to lack of payment." Suel gave him a look. "Nothing serious. Here's the interesting thing. Burke got an address. Turns out she's living in Council Housing, where Neil Kinan was murdered. Doesn't seem like much of a jump to tie her in somehow. I'm not suggesting she pulled the trigger or knowingly lured him there to set him up. It's just that things are beginning to look a bit more connected, maybe. Check the file and see if anything stands out to you. I also gave McCabe an update, and I just got off the line with Dennis O'Gara, out of Finglas Station. You know him?"

Suel nodded.

"He was one of the DIs going through Thomas Davy's place this morning. I'm going to meet him for a pint tonight at the Palace if you got time. I'd like to have him pay a visit to Pinky's."

"What do you think he'll find there, Dillon?"

"Not sure, but I'd like to have him grab a stool at the end of the bar by that office door behind the bar. I could call that number and see if he hears it ring. If nothing else, it would tell us where the phone is that called all these guys."

Suel seemed to think for a moment. "Yeah, that sounds like a good idea. Be interesting to see if someone steps in there to answer the phone."

"I wonder if the barman, Scully, would do it."

Suel shook his head. "Feargal Scully? I can't see him doing that unless he was given specific instructions to answer the phone. He strikes me as the sort who would never, ever go out of his way to do anything for anyone unless there was something in it for him."

"Can't say as I disagree. It would just be interesting to see what would happen," Dillon said.

"What time are you meeting up with O'Gara?"

"6:00 at the Palace. Figure I might get there a little early and grab a chair in the back. It would be great if you could join us."

Suel nodded. "I should be able to do that. Well, unless something unexpected should happen."

"Oh, please. Don't even go there. I'll drive if you want."

Suel shook his head. "Why don't we both drive? That way, we can leave when we want. We won't have to drive back here and drop the other off. Besides, there will probably be some gorgeous-looking woman who'll want to spend the night with me, and then you won't have to wait around and be in my way."

NINETEEN

Dillon was the first one in the Palace Bar. He ordered a pint of Guinness and settled into a chair in the back room. The Palace was one of the nicer bars in the city center. Located on the edge of the Temple Bar district, there were always a few tourists who stopped in for one drink, but it was usually populated by locals. The place was busy all day long, and at the moment, not quite 6:00, Dillon felt lucky to be able to grab a table with three chairs.

He watched as O'Gara wandered toward the back room, spotted Dillon, gave a wave, and stepped to the bar. He made his way through the crowd with his pint of Guinness and sat down across from Dillon. "How were you able to grab a table?"

"Nothing but sheer luck. Just as I came in, four people were leaving. I pushed some old lady out of the way and got here before she could get up off the floor." O'Gara looked at him for a moment. "Just kidding. The folks were leaving, and I just happened to be standing nearby. Paddy Suel's going to join us. Do you know him?"

O'Gara nodded. "Yeah, we've worked a couple of cases over the years. You two are partners, right?"

"Yeah, almost since the day I was attached to An Garda Síochána. He's a good guy, always has my back."

"You were involved in that shooting out at the airport a few years back, weren't—"

"Oh, look who finally made it," Dillon said, cutting O'Gara off as Suel approached the table. Dillon hoped the topic of the shooting out at Dublin airport wouldn't return to the conversation.

"Wait a minute, Dennis O'Gara? Dillon, I thought you said there was going to be a sexy-looking woman with us. This doesn't seem fair. How you doin', Dennis?" Suel asked and held out his hand.

"Good to see you again, Paddy. Dillon's been filling me in on all the work he has to do, keeping you on the straight and narrow. You better sit down before that sexy-looking woman gets here."

"Here's to the three of us. I hope we can come up with something that will make whoever is responsible want to turn themselves in." Suel raised his glass of Guinness in a toast.

"One can only hope," O'Gara said as they clinked glasses.

They sat and chatted for a good bit. Dillon reviewed the details of Gemma McKee and the fact that she lived in the Council Housing where Neil Kinan had been murdered.

"You think he was there seeing her?" O'Gara asked.

"We don't know for sure. At this stage, it seems to be more than just a coincidence. Maybe they had a relationship. Maybe it was business. Maybe she set him up. Hopefully, we'll be able to find out."

"Other than this McKee woman, do you have any idea what these four guys were up to? My sense is they were involved in something that either pissed off some very important person, or they did something that someone wanted to keep quiet. A robbery? Maybe a murder? No one at Finglas Station seems to have any idea."

"Well, we know almost everyone received a phone call from Pinky's. I was hoping to have confirmation on Thomas Davy this afternoon, but that didn't happen. Still, three out of four, that says to me the call wasn't some wrong number."

O'Gara drained his glass and said, "I think we should get another pint and then consider having me go into Pinky's for a drink. One of you can make the call while I'm seated at the bar minding my own business, listening for the phone to ring."

"You're sure the regulars won't know you?" Suel asked.

"As sure as I can be. It's been a couple of years since I've been in the place. That said, if someone happened to be at a trial where I was on the stand, they might recognize me. Or, if they were walking down the street when I was involved in making an arrest, I'd never know."

"I think the idea of another round is probably the best thing said thus far. I'll buy, and let's see what else we come up with," Suel said and signaled a barman over to the table.

The second round of pints had been delivered twenty minutes ago, and they'd not come up with any new ideas. Suel pulled out a copy he'd made of naked Gemma on the Christmas card and handed it to O'Gara. "Best to study this image intently, Dennis. She just may be in Pinky's tonight, and I think it would be best to recognize her. The infamous Gemma McKee."

O'Gara took the copy from Suel and studied it. "Certainly not hard on the eyes. If I see her, I'll just nod, give her my phone number, and then grab a seat at the bar. Once my drink is delivered, I'll send you both a text, and you can wait a minute and then place the call. What did you say the barman's name was?"

"Scully, Feargal Scully," Suel said as he took the image of naked Gemma McKee out of O'Gara's hands, folded it, and replaced it in his shirt pocket."

"I was hoping that would be mine to keep."

"Wrong again, Dennis. I'm keeping her close to my heart."

O'Gara drained his glass. "Okay, once the call comes through, I'll wait a bit and then leave. How 'bout afterward we meet up at The Glimmer Man Pub? You know the place? It's over on Stoneybatter."

Both Dillon and Suel nodded. Dillon knew of the place and where it was, but he'd never actually been in there.

O'Gara left a few minutes before Dillon and Suel. They followed with Suel pulling into a parking spot on Blackhall Place, halfway down the block from Pinky's. Dillon turned at the corner and drove a hundred feet or so beyond the back of Pinky's before he found a place to park. It was dark, misting rain, and cold. He turned off his lights and the engine and waited. It wasn't long before the text from O'Gara came across. 'Sipping my whiskey. Make the call.'

Dillon brought up the number from Pinky's that had been sent to the three murder victims and placed the call. He listened to the phone ringing and counted the rings. There were eight, and then the phone suddenly disconnected.

He sent a text to Suel. '8 rings then disconnected. Send again?'

'No,' was Suel's reply.

Maybe ten minutes later, another text came through from O'Gara. 'In my car on the way to The Glimmer Man.'

The Glimmer Man was just a little more than a five-minute drive away. It was an old pub located in a three-story brick building. Dillon parked across the street and waited for a couple of cars to pass before he hurried across Stoneybatter and into the pub through the door marked 'Lounge.' He stopped and looked around the place. Every square inch on the brick walls was covered with posters, matchboxes, and bric-a-brac. Bicycles, including a tandem, hung from the ceiling. The place actually looked comfortable in an odd way, and there was a table with padded benches on either side just in front of the fireplace. He ordered a pint of Guinness from the bar and settled down in front of the fireplace. Suel appeared a few minutes later with a pint.

They sat sipping their pints for fifteen minutes. Finally, Suel asked, "Where in the hell is O'Gara?" just as O'Gara wandered in the door.

"Oh, hi, lads. Sorry to keep you waiting. I was in need of some petrol, and there was a line at the station. Let me grab a pint, and I'll join yas." It was another five minutes before O'Gara was settled in front of the fire. "You know, I always find this wonderfully quaint. Now just look at the picture of Margaret Thatcher. Where else in Dublin would you—"

"For the love of God, would you tell us what you learned? What the hell happened in Pinky's?" Suel asked.

"What? Didn't you get my text?"

"I didn't see a text coming across," Dillon said and took out his cell phone. "No, nothing. See." He held up his cell phone to O'Gara, just to prove his point.

"What the hell? I'm sure I—Oh, here. Sorry about that. I guess I forgot to send it." O'Gara tapped his screen, and a moment later, both Dillon and Suel's phones signaled a text message coming through.

"Did you happen to see my blonde Christmas angel in there?"

"Sorry, Paddy, as soon as I gave her my phone number, she pulled on her coat, said she was going to get cleaned up, and she'd call me." They all laughed. "No, I didn't see her. The place was pretty full, but I got a stool at the end of the bar. Even with your lads talking away, I could hear the phone ringing in what must be an office. The barman, Feargal, you said?" Suel nodded. "He was pouring pints. He finished up and hurried to the door, but he had to take out a key, and by the time he unlocked the door, the phone had stopped ringing."

Dillon nodded. "I counted the rings. There were eight, and then the phone disconnected. No chance to leave a voicemail."

"Maybe that's why no one called back," Suel said.

"That's maybe why Feargal didn't check to see if whoever it was left a message."

They finished their pints, decided against getting another, and agreed to touch base in the morning. Dillon hurried home to let Lucifer out, and once he was back inside, they settled in front of the TV. They were upstairs in bed before 11:00.

TWENTY

illon had been up for the better part of an hour before Lucifer made his way downstairs the following morning. He let him out into the front garden and encouraged him back inside with a biscuit five minutes later. Once at work, he grabbed a coffee from the truck in Phoenix Park and headed into the headquarters building. There was a phone message from Emily down in the Tech Lab waiting for Dillon when he made it to his desk. He called her back immediately.

"Dillon?" was how she answered.

"I saw you called," Dillon said.

"Did you happen to listen to the message I left?"

"No, I just decided to check in. Do you have anything?"

"Why don't you come down here? I have a number of things. Unfortunately, no images of the actual murders, but I think we've got significant evidence that all four of the individuals were working together."

"So you were able to go through Thomas Davy's phone as well?"

"Yes, and he definitely linked up with the others. Come down when you can. I'll—"

"I'm on my way, Emily," Dillon said. He left a short note on Suel's desk. 'Down in Tech Lab, join us,' he wrote and hurried out of the office. Three minutes later, he was breathing somewhat heavily into the intercom after taking the stairs to the ground floor and rushing along the hallway.

"Dillon?" Emily answered the intercom.

"It's me," he replied, and the door buzzed.

Emily was at the back counter arranging what appeared to be a series of group photos on the large wall-mounted screen. "Take a look at these," she said without bothering to turn around.

He looked at the screen as he approached. There were five different individuals in a series of about twenty photos. None of the pictures had all five individuals. Dillon recognized the four murder victims, Terry Tebbot, Connor Dunne, Neil Kinan, and Thomas Davy. He studied the images for a couple of minutes. The fifth person, the guy with the neatly trimmed beard, looked somewhat familiar, but he couldn't place him, so he asked, "Do you know who that fifth person is? The one with the beard?"

Emily shook her head. "No, I was hoping you might have an idea. Is Suel in yet?"

"No, but I left him a note, so hopefully, he'll be down just as soon as he arrives."

"Couple of things with these pictures," Emily said. "Since everyone is dressed the same in each image, there's about a ninety-nine percent chance these were all taken on the same evening. I don't recognize the pub.

Oh, and the date on all the pictures is December thirty-first, New Year's Eve."

"New Year's Eve? I don't recognize the pub, but again, once we get Suel looking at them, he might pick up on the place."

"That painting on the wall behind the four of them of that unhappy-looking guy raising his glass looks familiar."

"You mean that bottom image? That's a copy of a street image in Summerhill, you know, a mural on the side of a building. That's Brendan Behan holding the empty glass with the typewriter in front of him. It was done a couple of years ago. I've seen the bronze statue of him along the Royal Canal," Dillon said.

"So, all you have to do is find the pub where this painting hangs, and that's where your lads met up."

"And you've no idea who your man with the beard is?"

Emily shook her head just as the intercom rang. She stepped over to an intercom mounted on the wall and said, "Tech Lab."

"Hi, Emily. It's Paddy Suel."

She pressed a button, and Dillon heard the door buzz. Suel stepped into the lab a second later and hurried toward them. "Oh, so I see you decided to start without me."

"Take a look at this, Paddy. All four of our victims having pints in some pub, and there's a fifth person. You know who this knacker is with the beard?"

Suel studied the images and said, "I'm not sure of your bearded man. But I recognize the pub, at least, I think I do. It's the Sunset House. There was a gangland shooting there a few years back. They changed the name to Brendan Behan something or other, then closed and went back to the Sunset House. Now, as far as I know, it's been closed for over a month."

Dillon shrugged. "Well, here's our proof that they were all together at least once. From the looks of it, everyone appears to be enjoying themselves. Can you print off a couple of the images with that bearded guy for me? I'll run them past Jim Burke. Hopefully, he can come up with who the hell that is through facial recognition."

Emily ran her fingers across the keyboard, and a moment later, Dillon heard the printer come on and begin printing off four separate images.

Dillon looked over at Suel. "While I run those images over to Burke, do you want to check on the Sunset House? Even if it's closed, find out who owns or owned the place. My money's on Dublin Drink. The same company that owns Pinky's."

"Shouldn't take but a couple of minutes." Suel continued to stare at the images and then asked, "What was the date of the most recent phone call everyone got from Pinky's? Late December?"

"December thirtieth. The day before New Year's Eve," Emily said. "Anything else you two need?"

"I don't think so. Suel?" Dillon asked.

Suel shook his head. "No, this is good. Thanks, Emily. Something's obviously cooking there." Suel nodded at the images on the wall screen. "I'm heading up to the office. Dillon, stop by once you're finished with Burke. With any luck, I'll have something on the owner of the Sunset House." With that, Suel turned and headed toward the door.

"Really appreciate your help, Emily. This is the first break we've had. If nothing else, it pretty much proves the shootings haven't been random."

Emily reached over to the printer, grabbed the four pages with images of the man with the beard, and handed them to Dillon. She had enlarged one of the images, just focusing on the face, although with the enlargement, the face was much more out of focus. "Hope those will work for facial recognition."

"There's only one way to find out. Thanks again," Dillon said and headed for the door.

The Tech Department was just two doors away, and Dillon pushed the intercom. The same voice as the other day answered, "Tech Department."

"Hi, Marshal Dillon in Special Branch to see Jim Burke."

"Is he expecting you?"

"No, just came across some items I need analyzed."

"Just a minute," the voice said, and then, just like before, Dillon heard the guy yelling. So much for high tech. A moment later, the door buzzed, and Dillon quickly entered and hurried toward Burke's cubicle.

Burke suddenly popped his head over the cubicle. "Well, if it isn't Marshal Dillon. To what do we owe the pleasure?"

"Thanks for seeing me, Jim. Sorry to barge in without an appointment. We've just come across a series of photos that place all four of the Finglas victims together on New Year's Eve. Along with them in a number of the images is someone we can't identify. I'm hoping you might have better luck." With that, Dillon handed the printed images to Burke.

Burke quickly rifled through the four pages and frowned. "Do you have these on your computer?"

Dillon shook his head. "Actually, Emily in the Tech Lab printed them off for me."

"So she has the images in the system?"

"Yeah, she pulled them off four different phones belonging to the murder victims."

"Leave these here with me. I'll give her a call and have her forward the images to me. She should know better. Not that we can't use these as a last resort, but the actual images will provide a much more accurate result and probably quicker."

"Okay…umm…we're interested in the identification of the guy with the beard. We have everyone else identified."

Burke quickly went through the four pages again and said, "Let me hang on to these. I'll give her a call right now. Anything else you need?"

"No, sir. If you can identify that individual, it would really help."

"I'll let you know when we have something," Burke said.

"Thanks, Jimmy. Much appreciated." Dillon held his hand out, they shook, and he hurried out the door. He debated giving Emily a heads-up but then figured if Burke was calling right now, he would only be in the way.

TWENTY-ONE

Once he left the Tech Department, Dillon took a deep breath and made his way to Ballistics. He pressed the intercom on the wall and waited. After nearly a minute, he pressed it again. A voice finally replied, "Yes."

Dillon felt some momentary relief. The voice clearly wasn't that of Sergeant Lane.

"Marshal Jack Dillon with Special Branch. I delivered a round to Detective Sergeant Lane on behalf of Dublin Morgue. It was the round from the fourth Finglas victim, Thomas Davy. I'm hoping you may have results."

The door buzzed, and Dillon stepped in. The man approaching in the white lab coat looked somewhat familiar, but Dillon couldn't come up with a name. He did make note of the fact that he wasn't wearing a gold nametag like the one Lane had worn.

"Hi, Dillon, don't know if you remember me, but I'm Finn McPartland. We met about two years ago. I was just getting started back then."

"Yeah, of course, Finn. How's it going?"

"Well, never a dull moment. Say, lucky you," McPartland said, then quickly glanced around and, in his Northern Irish accent, half-whispered, "Sergeant Lane is out at the moment, but I can bring up that information and print a copy off for you."

"Oh, Finn, thanks. That would really help."

"The victim's surname was Davy, wasn't it?"

"Yes, Thomas Davy."

"Yeah, Lane was reviewing the file with me. The same weapon was used in three previous shootings. You said this is part of the Finglas cases?"

"Yes, it is. Same weapon?"

McPartland nodded. "Yeah, identical. No question. Come on over here," he said, turning toward a counter with a keyboard. "I'll print that file off for you." He brought up the file, a total of eleven pages, including enlarged images of the round, along with a list of similarities to the rounds recovered from the three previous victims. Once the file was printed off, McPartland stapled the corner of the pages and handed the document to Dillon. There you go. Good luck in finding whoever is doing this."

"Can't thank you enough, Finn. I owe you a pint."

"Careful, I'm liable to take you up on that," he said.

Suel was at his desk in the process of grimacing after taking a sip of tea.

"Well, I see the tea is just what you expected." Dillon laughed.

"God, why do I bother? You were able to hand over those images to Burke?"

"I did. He took one look at them and is hopefully on the phone with Emily right now, having her send the computer images over to him. He said they'd work a lot better."

Suel seemed to think for a few seconds. "Jesus, that only makes sense. Unfortunately, he's dealing with us, two lads who grew up with phones you dialed."

Dillon chuckled. "You find out anything on who owns the Sunset House?"

"Yeah. It pains me to say this, but apparently, you were right. It's the Dublin Drink outfit. I'd say it's probably time we gave them a little closer look."

"I just got a confirmation from Ballistics. Thomas Davy was killed by someone using a nine-millimeter Glock. The exact same weapon that was used to kill the three previous victims. Let me make a call to DI Egan. I just want to update him on where we are on this. Let him know we've got pictures and a definite link between the four victims. Now we just have to figure out why."

Dillon settled in at his desk and phoned DI Tully Egan at Finglas Station. Egan answered on the third ring, "This is Egan."

"Hi, Tully. Jack Dillon, checking in."

"Oh, Dillon, please tell me you've got something, anything," Egan said.

"Actually, we do, or at least we're beginning to get something." He went on to tell Egan about the images of all four victims together at the Sunset House pub. He detailed the phone ringing at Pinky's the night before with DI O'Gara sitting at the bar and, last but not least, the confirmation from Ballistics that all four victims had been murdered by the same nine-millimeter Glock.

"Thank God. Finally, that's positive. You mentioned there was a fifth person in the photos."

"Yeah, the Tech Department was going to have the lab send them the images rather than trying to run facial recognition from printed images. Hopefully, they'll have something in the next day or two. I'm keeping my fingers crossed."

"All right, anything else?"

"Not at the moment. Did you ever get any other response from the residents in that Council Housing over on Plunkett Avenue? The site where Neil Kinan was murdered."

"No," Egan said, "and, to be honest, I don't expect to. Most, if not all, of the residents in those places are second or even third-generation residents. When it was originally conceived, Council Housing was meant to give people a hand and get them back on their feet. Now, it's multigenerational, and they've got it in their genetic makeup not to utter a word to us. I suspect we'd all be the same living like that. It's simply self-preservation. I'd be really surprised if anyone came forward, ever."

"Well, if we learn anything else, we'll let you know, Tully. If anything turns up on your end, please keep us informed. Oh, and pass on our thanks to Dennis O'Gara.

We wouldn't have confirmation regarding the phone at Pinky's without him working undercover last night."

"I'll be sure to pass it on," Eagan said and hung up.

"You learn anything?" Suel called from his desk.

"Yeah, unless Tully Egan is keeping things from us, and I don't think that's the case, all the information they have is coming from us."

"There's a part of me that's not surprised," Suel said.

"You interested in taking a little trip?" Dillon asked.

"Instead of sitting in front of my computer and reading the vague information on this Dublin Drink outfit? Hell, yes. I'll even drive. What are you thinking?"

"I'd like to go over to that Council Housing on Plunkett Avenue where Neil Kinan was murdered and see if your little Christmas Angel, Gemma McKee, is home."

"What are you thinking of asking her if she answers the door?"

"Maybe just have a little friendly visit. See what she could tell us about Neil Kinan. Then once she clams up, and she will, we pull a warrant and bring her in for questioning."

"You thinking she set Kinan up?"

Dillon shook his head. "That might be a bit harsh. But I think, at the very least, she might have some information that would be beneficial to our investigation. Since we finally seem to be having the beginnings of some luck today, it would be worth at least trying to find out what she knows."

"Let's go. Like I said, I'll drive. I'm thinking you knock on her door, and I'll stay in the car. If two of us go to her door, someone is going to spot us as Gardai right off the bat."

It was a fairly short drive, and Plunkett Avenue had almost no traffic. Suel pulled into the Council Housing parking lot, just six feet back from the ground floor units, and parked in the only available spot. He looked around at all the cars in the lot. "You find it interesting that on a workday in the middle of the week when everyone else is out busting their ass, apparently, just about everyone who lives in council housing hasn't even gotten out of bed."

"Maybe they all work the night shift," Dillon said.

"Probably not far from the truth, although not the sort of work, and I use the term loosely, that the rest of us would be involved in."

"Let me see if your Christmas Angel is out of bed yet. She's in unit six."

"How do you know that?"

"Burke told me. At least that was the address in the court records that came up when he did the facial recognition on her."

TWENTY-TWO

Dillon climbed out of the car, stepped onto the sidewalk, and gave a quick look around. There was no activity, and for a brief moment, he wondered if maybe Suel had been correct and everyone was still in bed. He walked along the sidewalk to unit six and knocked on the door. He was about to knock again when the door began to open, and a woman's voice said, "It's about time. You kept me waiting, and I was about to start without—Who the hell are you?" She held a half-empty wine glass with lipstick smudges. The black lace negligee sexy-looking Gemma McKee was wearing left nothing to the imagination. Then there was the large pendant with a blue stone surrounded by what looked like diamonds hanging from her neck. Dillon guessed it was glass, but if it was the real thing, he was probably looking at the most expensive piece of jewelry he'd ever seen.

"Hi, Gemma. We met a while back at Pinky's. You look lovely, by the way, if you don't mind me saying."

"We met? Was this a…umm…business meeting?"

"No, you were with a couple of guys. So it was brief, too brief," Dillon said.

She looked past him and glanced left and right. "Look, honey, I'd love to make your day better, but I'm expecting someone, and he's already late for his appointment. Maybe some other time?"

"Sure, how about later today? I'd like to talk to you about Neil Kinan."

She suddenly got a surprised look on her face, seemed to realize she was exposed in a couple of ways, and stepped behind the door, then peeked back around it. "Are you with the Gardi?"

"Just want to talk. You're not in any trouble, and I—"

"Please, just go away. Please. If they see you here, they'll kill me. Please."

Dillon pulled out a card and handed it to her.

"I don't want that. Really, I don't."

"Take it, Gemma, and I'll leave."

She snatched the card from his hand and tried to close the door. Dillon placed his foot in the way. "Call me when you can. I just want to talk."

"Please go, just go."

He moved his foot, and she slammed the door closed. He heard the lock click as he walked back to Suel's car.

"That didn't seem to go too well," Suel said as Dillon climbed back into the car.

"Wearing black lace and a smile. She's one pretty woman. Apparently, someone is about to show up for a business appointment. Maybe back out of here and park across the street. It would be interesting to see who shows up."

Suel put the car in reverse, backed out of the parking spot, and pulled across the street. They sat there for the better part of ten minutes. Suel was just about ready to leave when a gleaming Burgundy SUV raced into the parking lot and screeched to a stop in the spot they'd been in ten minutes earlier.

"Open the glove box and hand me the binoculars in there," Suel said.

Dillon opened the glove box and handed the binoculars to Suel just as the driver's door opened, and a man stepped out of the vehicle.

"Holy shit, look who it is," Dillon said as Suel brought the binoculars up.

"Yeah, I think it's our mystery man. Apparently, he shaved. God, I wish we had a camera. We're too far away for the cell phone to do anything."

The man was carrying a bottle, maybe wine. He knocked on the door, and it opened almost immediately. Gemma, still in her negligee, pulled him inside, glanced left and right, and closed the door. "Write down this license number," Suel said and read the number off to Dillon, who wrote it in the notebook in his pocket. "That's an Audi SQ8 he's driving. They don't come cheap. Over a hundred thousand euros."

They waited for a few more minutes, and then Dillon said, "He could be in there until tomorrow morning. I think we should head back. See where Burke is on your man's facial recognition. Find out if he owns that vehicle, and I think it's time to get a warrant on Gemma McKee, bring her in for questioning."

Suel started the car and drove back to the headquarters building. Once they were up in Special Branch, Dillon placed a call to Jim Burke down in the Tech Department. He ended up leaving a message. "Hi, Jim. Jack Dillon checking in. Just wanted to see if you had any luck running the facial recognition on that image. I think we have a vehicle license number on him, and I'm going to be running that. If I come up with a name, I'll call you back."

Next, he called the NVDF, the National Vehicle and Driver File. It was the database containing details of registered vehicles and their owners. After being transferred around to four different individuals, he finally got to someone who could actually help. Dillon gave the woman the license number and the description of the vehicle, a burgundy Audi SQ8.

"Here we are," she said a moment later. "That vehicle is actually registered to a business named Dublin Drink. Would you like their address?"

"Yes, please."

She gave Dillon the address. Dillon thanked her and hung up. It turned out that Dublin Drink was located on Summerhill, and from the building address, it couldn't be too far from the Sunset House pub, where the pictures of the five guys had been taken. Dillon brought up Google Maps and input the address. The image showed a busy four-lane street and a block of what looked like four two-story older residential units. Dillon clicked on the compass arrow until he got the image of the opposite side of the street. There it was, a three-story structure on the corner. The top two floors were painted white, and the ground floor, the actual Sunset House pub, was painted a dark green and located directly across the street from the Dublin Drink office.

He Googled Dublin Drink but just like before, there was very little information and no pictures. He wondered if the Dublin Drink Audi was still at Gemma McKee's place, but then what? He didn't have a warrant. Actually, he didn't even have the name of the guy McKee had been expecting. He could drive over to Dublin Drink, but it would be the same problem. He didn't have a warrant or even a name. He decided the better idea would be to fill out the paperwork requesting a warrant to question Gemma McKee. Based on the fact that Neil Kinan had been murdered not more than forty feet from her front door, and apparently, based on her naked Christmas Card, they had had some form of interaction. It only seemed to make sense.

It took the better part of an hour, but when he had finished and read through the warrant request three times, he felt it was ready to be presented to DCI McCabe. Dillon knocked on the doorframe of McCabe's office.

McCabe looked up from the file he was reading and waved Dillon in. "Dillon, good afternoon. Please tell me there's movement in a positive direction on the Finglas murders."

"Things appear to be starting to move in our direction, sir." Dillon went on to give McCabe an update on the progress and then handed him the warrant request. "Once we learned Gemma McKee had some sort of previous relationship with the third Finglas victim, Neil Kinan, we decided to pay her a visit. DI Suel remained in the car so as not to attract attention to both of us knocking on her door. She answered the door wearing a black lace negligee, clearly expecting someone else. In fact, she said, 'It's about time,' and then noticed it was me and asked, 'Who the hell are you?'

"And she was wearing a black lace negligee?"

"Yes, sir. Very revealing."

"Lucky you."

"I think so," Dillon chuckled. "I left, we waited across the street, and a man pulled up in an Audi SQ8. Just for fun, I looked it up online. They go for about a hundred and ten grand. Anyway, he pulls up. We recognize him immediately from the images the Tech Lab recovered from the shooting victims' phones. Still no name on him. The car he was driving is registered to Dublin Drink, a company that owns a number of pubs in town. Obviously, Gemma McKee is involved with him in some way. Even if it's just a business relationship, she most likely has information that would be pertinent to our investigation."

"Do you think she's in any danger?"

"I do, sir, for two reasons. First, Neil Kinan was murdered in his car, not forty feet from her front door. It would seem a pretty strong possibility that he was either coming to or leaving her unit. Second, the individual she was expecting turned out to be the fifth person in the group of five, four of whom have been murdered in Finglas."

"Rather succinct, Dillon. I like that. I don't see any problem with this request. I'll attach a note, and hopefully, tomorrow morning, maybe even before the end of day today, we should have it. Thank you once again for following procedure and not barging into her unit or arresting the individual calling on her and compromising the investigation."

"Thank you, sir," Dillon said, picking up on the fact he was being politely dismissed. As he walked back to his desk, Suel gave him a questioning look. Dillon gave Suel a thumbs-up.

TWENTY-THREE

Back at his desk Dillon called Jim Burke in the Tech Department. Burke answered on the second ring. "Hi, Dillon. Great minds think alike. I was just about to call you."

"Were you able to identify the bearded guy?"

"Yes, I phoned Emily in the Tech Lab, and I think she sent the images to me before I was able to hang up the phone. I'll send you the file as soon as we're off the line, but your man has been identified as an individual named Jasper Sullivan."

"Jasper Sullivan? Why does that name ring a bell?"

"Might be a couple of reasons. His father, of the same name, was an undertaker on the south side of Dublin. He passed away at a young age, ten years ago. Cancer, I believe. The other is that Jasper, the son, was a midfielder on the Dublin Hurling team, I think, for three years, and he owns a number of pubs."

"Not sure either one of those would be the reason the name rings a bell. But this is a definite identification?"

"Yes, it is. I'm sending the file to you in just a moment," Burke said.

"Back up for a minute. You said he owns a number of pubs?"

"Yes, well, actually, he's president of a company that owns—"

"That company wouldn't be Dublin Drink, would it?"

"That's exactly the company. Sullivan is founder and president. So, I would guess money isn't much of an object with him."

"Interesting. Thank you, Jim. Very much appreciated," Dillon said and hung up. A moment later, his computer signaled an incoming message. Dillon clicked on the message, and the facial shot of Jasper Sullivan suddenly appeared. Dillon scrolled down, and along with Sullivan's name and date of birth, April 3, 1986, was his phone number and address.

Dillon brought up Dublin Google Maps again and input the Sullivan address on Kincora Drive in the Dublin area known as Clontarf, one of the nicer areas on the north side of Dublin. He clicked on the red point indicated on the map, and it brought up an image of Sullivan's home. A large, two-story attached structure with a curved entrance over the front door set back by a few feet. Dillon guessed the place would go for somewhere between eight hundred thousand and maybe a million euros. Not bad, but then again, Dublin Drink did own six pubs, and yes, they might all be in the nature of Pinky's, meaning neighborhood pubs. But still very profitable neighborhood pubs, with the exception of the Sunset

House. Based on where he lived, Jasper Sullivan seemed to be doing rather well for himself, which brought Dillon back to the question, what was he doing with Gemma McKee?

Dillon waved Suel over to his desk. "Just off the phone with Burke. He's got a definite ID on our man with the beard. His name is Jasper Sullivan. Turns out he's the president of Dublin Drink, the company that owns six pubs, including Pinky's and the Sunset House. Burke suggested that means money isn't much of an object for Sullivan, but I don't know."

"If he's president of the company, does he own it?"

"As a matter of fact, he does. Founder, owner, and president. So, I didn't mention this, but when Gemma answered the door in that black negligee, she had this great big pendant around her neck. A blue stone with what looked like diamonds around it. I thought it was probably a fake. But what if it was jewelry that Jasper Sullivan gave her? That could be a reason she lured Neil Kinan over to her place and—"

"And you're suddenly spouting a hell of a lot of conjecture, Dillon. Just for starters, if this Jasper Sullivan is as wealthy as you suggest, he doesn't have to give someone like Gemma McKee a fancy necklace to wear around her neck. As pretty as she is, there are lots of beautiful women and a lot classier women than a slapper the likes of Gemma McKee. Do you know, is Sullivan married?"

Dillon shook his head. "I don't know."

"Well, before we go jumping off a cliff with speculation, maybe we should stick to the facts as we know them. If someone like Gemma McKee had a real piece of jewelry like that, I'd think she'd either sell it or pawn it about twenty-four hours after she got it. It's the way they operate, the way they think. Hell, she'd probably trade the thing for drugs."

"Yeah, I guess you're right. I was just thinking—"

"Let's stick to the facts, Dillon. That said, one of the facts is that this Sullivan was the person she had apparently been waiting for. That's something. So, what was Sullivan doing with these three former criminal low-lifes? Once we figure that out, the next question is, what is Thomas Davy, the only one of the four with a full-time job, doing with them? He works for Dublin County Council, for God's sake. None of this is making any sense."

"What were the charges that got the three guys sentenced to prison?"

"Burglaries," Suel said. "I went through the cases. They're all unique, but a couple of things stand out. It would be almost impossible for them to have worked together on the burglaries. All three burglaries involved breaking into businesses with a vault, or in Terry Tebbot's case, a large safe. Tebbot is in prison when Connor Dunne is arrested. Dunne is in prison when Kinan is arrested. There is nothing that points to them being together, except for the series of New Year's Eve photos."

"Well, and the fact that they were murdered one after the other over the course of ninety-six hours by someone using the same nine-millimeter Glock. Look, I'm with you, Paddy. It doesn't make any sense, but in a way, it kind of does. We just don't know why yet."

"Don't forget the phone calls from Pinky's, Dillon."

Suel went back to his desk, and Dillon continued searching online for anything and everything on Jasper Sullivan. There wasn't much. For a successful businessperson in the drink business, he apparently kept a pretty low profile.

Toward the end of the afternoon, his cell phone rang. "Dillon," he answered without looking at the screen.

"Well, apparently, it's my turn to call since I haven't heard from you for a while."

"Oh, Shannon. God, I'm so sorry. I didn't think I'd be very good company, just involved in a case and—"

"Neil's murder?"

"Actually, all four murders in Finglas. I'm sorry, but I really can't say anything about them. How is your mother doing?"

"Oh, she's doing well under the circumstances. She leans heavily on the church. It's what her generation was raised to do, and to tell you the truth, the parish priest has been very kind and gracious. He's been a big help."

"Any problem with someone stopping at her house?"

"No, thank God. Other than that one night, absolutely nothing. I know it's short notice, but I was wondering if you had any plans for dinner this evening?"

"Dinner. Umm…well, no, I don't have any plans. Did you want to meet somewhere?"

"Actually, I was wondering if you'd like to come over to my place. I made a lasagna and—"

"Oh, God. I love lasagna. I'll bring the wine. You tell me what time, and I'll be there."

"Whatever time works best for you."

"Okay, how does 7:00 sound? That way, neither one of us will have to rush home from work."

"That will be just fine."

"Great. Now, Shannon, just two things."

"Oh?"

"Yeah, first of all, thank you for the call, and second, I'm going to need your address."

"What? Oh God, spacey me," she said and gave Dillon her address. He wrote it down and then repeated it back to her just to make sure he'd written it down correctly.

"I'll see you at 7:00, Dillon. Now get back to work," she said and disconnected.

Suel called over from his desk just before 5:00. "You interested in a pint tonight?"

"I'd love to, but I've got something else I have to do. Can I take a rain check?"

"Not a problem. You're not meeting up with Gemma, are you?"

"Yeah, there you go. I thought I could fool you, but you caught me. She's going to meet me at Pinky's wearing that black lace negligee."

"I knew it," Suel said and laughed. He locked up his desk and called out, "Behave tonight, and I'll see you in the morning. I'll want a full report."

"I'm taking a rain check on your offer to buy my pint, Paddy."

Dillon went through the motions on his computer for the next twenty minutes but never found anything of interest regarding Jasper Sullivan. He shut things down, locked up his desk, and headed home. Lucifer met him at the door and then assumed the position in front of the car and did his business. Dillon took his mail into the kitchen. He checked the first floor for any Lucifer mess but thankfully didn't find anything. He grabbed the leash and they headed out for a walk. Once they arrived back home, he filled Lucifer's water dish, treated him to a biscuit, and hurried upstairs to change. He grabbed the only bottle of wine in his refrigerator, tossed another biscuit to Lucifer, and headed out the door. He carefully bypassed the most recent deposit on his driveway, climbed into the car and drove up the lane.

TWENTY-FOUR

Shannon lived in an area on the north side of Dublin known as Marino. Not all that far from Artane, where she grew up and where her mother still lived. Dillon drove down Griffith Avenue. He followed his GPS directions and turned right onto Turlogh Parade, and then took a left onto Brian Avenue. Her home was halfway down the street. It turned out to be the corner unit of four attached units, with the standard layout of two-story structures. A two-story addition had been added to Shannon's unit, basically increasing the size by another fifty percent.

Dillon drove halfway over the curb and parked partially on the footpath. He grabbed the bottle of wine and headed for the front door. He was just about to ring the doorbell when Shannon opened the door. She was dressed in tight-fitting blue jeans and a white blouse with a shiny gold chain around her neck. A lovely perfume scent drifted over Dillon as he stepped into the house. "I thought that might be you parking in front. Any problem finding the place?"

"No, I put it into my GPS, and that delivered me right to your door. Oh, a bottle of wine. If you have another going, don't worry. Just keep this one in the refrigerator and have it for some other time."

"Thanks, that's sweet of you," she said and gave him a peck on the cheek. "Just toss your jacket on the bench and come on into the kitchen," she said. She waited while Dillon quickly removed his jacket and tossed it on the wooden bench. "Hope you don't mind. We're going to be dining very informally this evening. I've got a bottle of wine open. Can I pour you a glass?"

"Yes, please. Anything I can do to help?"

"Yes, you can sit down in that chair," she said, pointing to a chair at the table as they entered the kitchen. The table was lightly stained oak, and the chairs were upholstered in brown leather. The table was set for two with white china plates and silverware resting on white linen napkins. Three white candles were lit on the table. A china tray with a wedge of cheese and crackers was on the table. "So, how was your day? Did you, oh wait, sorry. I didn't mean to ask. How about this? What did you do in your free time?"

Dillon was about to say he really didn't have much free time but quickly caught himself and said, "I took my dog for a long walk. I live just two or three minutes from Albert Park if you know where that is." Shannon nodded. "I've found over time that my life is a lot better, and there seems to be a lot less damage if we go for a walk and Lucifer lets off some steam."

"Lucifer? You named your dog Lucifer?"

"He was named when I got him. I thought about changing the name, but I learned rather quickly that it really fit."

"Oh, funny. Listen, go ahead and help yourself to some crackers and cheese. That's a French Camembert I happen to be fond of. I'm just going to toss this salad."

"Don't mind if I do." Dillon spread the cheese across a cracker and tossed the whole thing in his mouth. "Mmm-mmm, very good. Make you one?"

"Yes, please. Are you partial to any particular salad dressing? I've got French, Balsamic, Caesar, or Italian."

"I'll have whatever you're having," he said as he spread cheese across the cracker and handed it to her. She placed the entire cracker in her mouth, smiled at Dillon, set the salad bowl on the table and began to toss the greens lightly.

"So, I noticed you have a fairly substantial addition on the house. Did you do that?"

"No. It was here when I bought the place. That was seven years ago. I have to say, I can't imagine life without it. Absolutely wonderful. I'll take you on a quick tour after dinner. Oh, God, I almost forgot," she said and raised her wine glass. "Here's to an enjoyable evening."

They clinked glasses, and she took two healthy swallows, then dished up the salad and handed a plate to Dillon. He watched her for a brief moment, and when she set her salad plate on the dinner plate, he did the same.

It was an enjoyable meal, delicious lasagna, and just to prove the point, Dillon had two pieces. There was homemade garlic bread and, for dessert, a two-layer tiramisu. Dillon thought about having a second piece but stopped himself from asking lest he appear the ultimate pig.

Shannon emptied the wine bottle into Dillon's glass and said, "Care for a two-minute tour of the place?"

"I'd love it," Dillon said. "Let me just clear the table for you, and we—"

"No, leave everything right where it is. Come on, let me show you around," she said and headed for the door at the opposite end of the kitchen. Dillon grabbed his wine glass and followed her into a lovely den with a gas fireplace that was burning. She pointed a couple of things out, and then they climbed a set of stairs in the back of the den that led up to the second floor. Except for the fact that there were four bedrooms instead of the standard three, it was pretty much the same as the hundreds of Dublin homes Dillon had been in. Everything was neat, clean, and orderly, and Dillon suddenly had a momentary image of Thomas Davy's home with dirty clothes scattered all over and the bedroom with pieces of antique furniture stacked on top of one another.

Shannon bypassed the master bedroom, led them downstairs, and settled onto the couch in front of the gas fireplace in the den. She poured two more glasses of wine and was about to dim the lights.

Dillon had a fairly strong sense of where this was headed and cursed himself for following the rules. He set his wine glass on the coffee table and said, "Shannon, I can't thank you enough for the lovely dinner. I'm afraid I have to head out. I have an early morning meeting and still have to prepare. Thank you so much."

"You're, you're leaving? Now? I thought we might have an enjoyable—"

"Shannon. Please, don't misunderstand. I would love it. But if someone is charged with Neil's murder and it somehow came out that we were intimate, it could lead to them being found innocent, receiving a lesser charge, or a bunch of other things."

"I, I just wanted to thank you and get to know you better. I didn't think—"

"I'd love to get to know you better, too. But right now, my focus is and has to be on finding whoever did this and putting them in prison. Okay?"

"That's really nice of you, Dillon." She took a deep breath. "Okay, I guess I'll be waiting. If that's what you want."

"Believe me, not what I want," Dillon smiled. "But it's what has to be. Thank you. I'll let myself out," he said.

He walked out to the front entry, straining his ears for her footsteps. He never heard them. He grabbed his jacket from the bench and turned around as he pulled it on. Shannon wasn't there. He frowned, mumbled to himself that he was one stupid bastard, and stepped out of the house. He checked to make sure her door was locked, hurried to his car, and drove home, calling himself a number of vile names along the way.

TWENTY-FIVE

Suel stepped out of the break room as Dillon settled in behind his desk. "So, was your last night successful?"

Dillon set the cup of coffee from the vendor's truck next to his computer screen and turned the computer on. "Had a nice dinner and then possibly one of my dumber moves. I turned down a beautiful woman who I'm pretty sure was looking for a late-night partner."

"You didn't go back to see Gemma McKee, did you?"

"What? No, of course not. No, this was someone else, who, well, let's just say, a night with me may not have been in her best interest."

Suel laughed. "Dillon, you've possibly just described every woman in Dublin and beyond. Aw, good on ya, Dillon. Not fun, but you're both the better for it."

"Yeah, that's what I keep telling myself, but it's not really sinking in."

"Well, look at it this way. She probably woke up this morning a happy woman." Suel walked over to his desk, shaking his head and chuckling.

The door to Special Branch opened, and a younger-looking man walked in carrying a manila envelope. Dillon recognized him as a delivery person and presumed he was going to drop something off at DCI McCabe's office, even though McCabe wasn't in at the moment. That meant he'd want to leave the envelope with Dillon.

Sure enough, he stopped at Dillon's desk. "Marshal Dillon?"

"Yeah, something for DCI McCabe? I'll sign for it."

"Well, I want your signature, but actually, it's for you. A warrant, I think," he said and held out the envelope. Dillon signed the form attached to the envelope and then pulled it off and handed it to the guy. "Thanks, have a good day and stay safe," the man said and headed out of the office.

Dillon watched him leave, then crossed his fingers and opened the envelope. There it was, the warrant for Gemma McKee. "Suel," Dillon called and waved the warrant back and forth as Suel looked over.

"Please tell me that's your invitation to get up close with Gemma McKee."

"It is indeed. All I need now is a chauffeur."

"I'm on it. Let me just call down to the garage and line something up. If we transport her back here, I want some protection between the front and back seat." Suel picked up his phone, punched in three numbers, and nodded at Dillon.

Fortunately, it was an unmarked car they were traveling in. Not that it couldn't be identified as a Garda vehicle with no whitewall on the tires, a screen between the front and back seat, the spotlight attached just outside the driver's door, and the flashing light equipment mounted on the rear deck. Still, it was better than arriving in a squad car, and in a way, should Gemma McKee happen to look out the window and see them approach, she probably wouldn't pick up on the fact it was a Garda vehicle. If she did recognize it, there was a subtle sense of authority that the dark-colored vehicle evoked.

It was almost 10:30 in the morning, but the Council Housing parking lot was still full. From what Dillon could tell based on the two times he had been here, all the vehicles belonged to the residents. That wasn't a guess but rather the identification of the required parking sticker on the front windshield of all the vehicles. Suel parked on the street just past the Council Housing building and remained in the vehicle.

Dillon climbed out of the car. He had folded the warrant in half and placed it in the inside pocket of his jacket. His pistol was attached to the back of his belt, just next to the pair of handcuffs should he need them. He stepped into the parking lot, headed for the sidewalk up against the building, and made his way to unit six, Gemma McKee's place. Along the way, he looked at the parked vehicles, making note of the parking sticker on each vehicle's windshield. He slowed as he approached unit six, looking left and right. The sidewalk and parking lot were devoid of anyone.

He stepped to the door, was about to knock, and then noticed the boot print next to the doorknob and the broken doorframe. He knocked on the door forcefully, not pounding but not exactly gently either. The door swung partway open, exposing two broken pieces of white wooden trim on the floor. Dillon glanced back at their vehicle and waved, indicating Suel should join him.

Suel quickly stepped out of the car and hurried over as Dillon pulled his pistol from the holster and moved to the side.

Suel hurried onto the sidewalk toward Dillon. "What the hell is—"

"Apparently, someone kicked in the door. I'm going in. Watch my six," Dillon said and stepped inside with his pistol extended. "Gemma? Gemma McKee? It's Jack Dillon, An Garda Síochána. Gemma?" Dillon called from the front room. He quickly pointed his pistol at the worn brown leather couch, then turned back toward the hall that led to the kitchen. Suel was just behind him with his pistol pointed down the hall.

"Gemma?" Dillon called out again, then heard and felt something crack beneath the sole of his foot. He looked down at pieces of shattered glass and a few flowers on the tiled floor. Blood was on the floor and splattered across the wall. He stepped past the entrance to the cooking area. A sink, a four-burner stove, six Formica cabinets, three up and three down, and a small refrigerator made up the area. There was nowhere to hide.

He moved four steps down the hall toward the closed door. "Gemma? Gemma? You in there? It's Dillon with An Garda Síochána. Gemma?" He stepped back to the side, took hold of the doorknob, and pushed the door open, revealing a small bathroom with a toilet, a sink, and a shower/tub. Remnants of dried blood were splattered in the sink bowl.

Dillon moved forward toward the bedroom. The door was open, and he noticed another boot print next to the doorknob. He peeked into the room. A sliding window on the back wall was open, and a worn lace curtain fluttered in the gentle breeze. Dillon kept his pistol pointed on the far side of the bed as he approached, eventually peeking over. He shouted, "Clear," to Suel, standing at the door with his pistol pointed at a wooden wardrobe.

Dillon stepped over to the wardrobe, glanced at Suel, nodded, and then pulled the door open. Suel's eyes widened, and then he puffed his cheeks and blew out a breath. "Empty, thank God."

"You notice the blood on some of that glass by the kitchen?" Dillon asked.

"Yeah, and in the bathroom sink. You think that was her or someone else?"

Dillon shook his head. "No idea. This open window? I don't know. Maybe she made it out of here. You know, someone kicks the door in. She cracks him on the head with a glass vase, the guy is bleeding, and she runs back in here, opens the window, and hops out."

"I suppose it's possible. I think we'd better call Finglas Station and get a crew out here to go over the place. Maybe get a blood sample and see if it's hers. She's got a record, so her blood type should be on there."

"I'll give Tully Egan a call," Dillon said as he pulled out his phone.

Suel nodded. "We should get our asses out of here. Don't touch anything. They'll be looking for prints."

Dillon followed Suel back down the hallway, side-stepping most of the broken glass as they headed outside. Once he was outside, he pulled a latex glove from his jacket pocket, slipped it on, and closed the front door.

He phoned Tully Egan at Finglas Station and gave him the news.

"No one shot?' Egan asked.

"No, at least it doesn't look like it, fortunately. Broken glass on the floor with some blood and blood splattered on the wall by the kitchen. The bathroom sink has blood in it. Looks like someone cleaned themselves up. It doesn't look like a shooting. A rear window was open in the bedroom. I'm wondering if she hit someone over the head with a flower vase, ran into the bedroom, and made it out the window. If she did, and she's still in town, she's probably hiding somewhere. Can you have someone check to see if she owns a car?"

"Yeah. Let me get a team together and head over there to go through the place. Can you stay there until someone arrives? I don't want some knacker wandering in there and going through the place looking for something to steal."

"We're here until you show."

"All right. Appreciate the call, and thank God there wasn't another body waiting for us," Egan said and disconnected.

"They'll be here as soon as they can," Dillon told Suel. "You want to pull the car into the lot, and we'll wait there. Once the crime scene team gets here, we can start knocking on doors and have people tell us they don't know anything."

TWENTY-SIX

A squad car arrived ten minutes later. The officer spoke with Dillon and Suel, and then they settled into their separate vehicles and waited for an investigative team to arrive. It was close to an hour before the team pulled into the parking lot. None of the residents had come out to their car during that time.

Dillon and Suel gave the team their brief story and then started knocking on doors. It didn't take long. There were nine other units on the ground level. Three people answered their knock on the door. All three had no idea anything had happened. No one heard any noise. In fact, they all stated that they didn't know Gemma McKee. The second floor was slightly better from the standpoint that five people answered the door, but once again, no one was aware of the incident, and four of the five swore they had never heard of Gemma. The one person who did recognize the name, a woman, said, "That's what the slapper deserves," and closed the door on them.

"Well, there you go. I'm so glad my taxes go to help pay for this lot," Suel said and shook his head.

As they came down the stairway attached to the side of the building, DI Tully Egan climbed out of his car. "Any luck?" he asked.

"What do you think? Half of them wouldn't even answer the door. Of course, it's early, not quite noon, so they're probably still in bed," Suel groaned.

"No surprise. Listen, lads, appreciate you helping out on this. It could have been days before we found out about it, if even then."

"Any idea where she might have gone?" Dillon asked

Egan shook his head. "Not really. She's hardly on our radar. She's pulling tricks, probably with the same dozen or so men every month or week. Keeps a low profile, you know. There is one thing that comes to mind. I can't recall the name, but someone posted bail or paid the fine or something for her. This would have been a year or so ago. A Finglas woman, not her mother, but an older woman, maybe in her fifties. Damn it. I can't recall her name. Tell you what. Let me make a call, and I'll have the desk sergeant pull the file. The woman's listed as posting bail. Linda, Lana, Laurie, something like that. Might be worth a call to her see if she knows where McKee might be."

Dillon nodded. They spoke for a couple more minutes. Egan promised to keep them posted should anything come to light. Dillon and Suel climbed back in the car and drove to Finglas Station.

They parked just in front of the station in a no-parking zone. Suel put the flashers on the vehicle, and they hurried inside.

"Dillon? Suel?" The desk sergeant asked.

"No one else would want to be us," Suel said, which brought a smile to the sergeant's face.

"God's honest truth," he laughed and handed Dillon a file. Dillon opened the file. Gemma McKee's most recent arrest had been sixteen months earlier. The charge had been failure to pay a hotel bill of six hundred and eighty euros for a one-night stay at the Westbury Hotel. The case was later dismissed once the bill had been paid. A woman by the name of Louisa MacBride had paid the hotel and the fine. Her address was listed as being on Casement Park, just a few blocks over from Gemma McKee's Council Housing on Plunkett Avenue.

"I know the area," Suel said. "Five minutes away. Let's go." They handed the file back to the desk sergeant, thanked him, and hurried out the door. "If it's the area I'm thinking, and I'm almost positive it is, there's actually a parking area in front of a row of houses. All attached. Nice enough area. I'm wondering if this woman is a social worker or a madam."

Dillon looked over at Suel. "Nice thought, but I can't see a social worker stepping up to pay over seven hundred euros."

"Well, she clearly paid the bill. Maybe Gemma McKee is paying her back with interest."

Suel pulled onto Casement Park. The houses were all attached, two-story, white stucco structures. The long line of units had a slight curve to it, and out in front was a parking area with a series of lined, perpendicular parking spaces.

Dillon had never seen this setup before. "Is this unique? A convenient parking lot, essentially for the residents?"

"Yeah, nice, isn't it?" Suel pulled into an empty spot and turned the car off in front of Louisa MacBride's unit. "It made sense, and then the light went on in someone's thick skull, and they realized that, for every four parking areas like this, they were losing out on more housing units. They halted the design immediately. Probably fired whoever came up with the idea in the first place. Let's pay this MacBride woman a visit and see if she knows anything."

TWENTY-SEVEN

They climbed out of the car and walked to the front door. It had just started to mist, and Suel knocked on the door and then raised the collar on his jacket.

The door opened a moment later. A ginger-haired woman in her fifties, looked at the two of them, shook her head, glared, and said, "What do you want?"

"Good day, ma'am, Miss MacBride?"

"Were you listening? I asked what yous want."

"We're looking for Gemma McKee. We've reason to believe she might be here, and we'd like to talk with her."

"You're the feckin' Gardai, I can tell. How'd you get my name?"

"Practice makes perfect," Dillon said. "I can assure you, we're not here to arrest her. We just want to speak with her regarding the unfortunate incident yesterday and make sure that she's okay."

She seemed to think about that for a long moment, shook her head in disgust, and said, "I knew this was bound to happen. Gemma?" She waited a moment before she turned toward the kitchen and shouted, "Gemma, damn it. Get your bleedin' arse in here, now. Do you hear me? Now."

Dillon thought he heard what sounded like a chair being pushed back. A moment later, a blonde-haired woman peeked around the corner. It was definitely Gemma, the same woman who'd answered her door in a neglige. Right now, her right eye was black and nearly swollen shut. The right side of her lower lip was swollen and split. She sniffled and ran a hand beneath her nose.

"Come here, darlin'. They want to see that you're all right." Gemma tentatively moved next to and a little behind MacBride.

"I wonder if there might be somewhere we could possibly sit down," Dillon asked. "We'd like to find out what happened, and we want to be sure you're okay."

MacBride turned to Gemma and said, "Let's go into the sitting room, darlin'. I'm not going to leave you. I'll be right there," she said as she shot a look at Dillon and Suel, almost daring them to tell her no.

Dillon nodded. "I think that would be a good idea, Gemma. Louisa will be right next to you." They followed the two women into the sitting room. The room was clean, and everything seemed to be in perfect order. Two controls for the TV were lined up next to one another on a coffee table in front of the couch. A box of Kleenex rested at the other end of the table. The women settled onto the couch behind the coffee table, facing the TV. Suel took a seat in the wingback chair just in front of the window that looked out into the back garden and closest to Gemma. Dillon sat in a smaller, less comfortable chair close to Louisa and gave Suel the evil eye for a split second. Suel smiled back.

Louisa took hold of Gemma's hand. Gemma just stared at the coffee table.

"We stopped at your unit this morning, Gemma. We were checking on all the residents in the building after the murder the other day," Dillon lied. "We wanted to make sure everyone was okay. We noticed your door had been kicked in, and when you didn't answer our calls, we were afraid you might be injured or, well, even worse, so we went through your unit."

Gemma nodded but didn't say anything. Dillon noticed her lower lip and chin seemed to be trembling. "We saw the broken glass, the blood on the wall in the hall and in the bathroom sink. Can you tell us what happened? It looks like someone attacked you."

She gave a slight nod.

"Can you tell me what happened, Gemma?"

She looked up at Dillon as a tear ran down her left cheek. "He called and made an appointment. Said he'd be there in an hour," she whispered.

"Do you know who he was?"

She shook her head. "No, he'd been over twice before. Told me his name was Adrian the first time and Colin the second time. He never told me a last name. As soon as he was finished, he would leave, just leave me there on the bed. He'd throw a fifty euro note at me and walk out. Never even said thanks or anything, just left. But I needed the money, so I didn't really care, I guess.

"He had an appointment yesterday and then came back in the afternoon. He just left his car in the middle of the parking lot. I watched him get out of the car. Something didn't seem right. He looked all around like he was checking things out, and then he walked between two parked cars, and I saw the gun. He knocked on the door, and I just said, 'I can't see you. Go away.' It was quiet for a moment, and then, all of a sudden, my front door flew open, and he came at me. I tried to hit him, but he just laughed and pushed me. So I kicked him and ran into the kitchen. I was gonna get a knife, but he was right behind me. He spun me around and hit me a couple of times. I grabbed a vase with some flowers from the counter and hit him in the head as hard as I could. The vase broke, and he fell down. I ran into the bedroom, slammed the door, then slid the window open, and got out. I just ran and hid in one of the other buildings. After a while, I called Louisa, and she, she came and got me," Gemma said and then burst into tears, sobbing.

Louisa wrapped her arms around Gemma and pulled her close. As she did so, she gave both Dillon and Suel a look as if to say, 'See what you've done. Are you happy now?'

Dillon waited for the better part of two minutes before Gemma calmed down enough that he could say something.

"You just know him as Adrian or Colin?"

Gemma nodded and reached into the Kleenex box. She blew her nose, took two more pieces of Kleenex, and dabbed at her eyes. "Yeah, he never told me a last name, and I've no way to know if one of those is even his real name. The two times I saw him, he brought me a bottle of champagne."

"We'd like you to come down with us and look at some pictures. Maybe you could identify him."

She got a worried look on her face, and she started to bite her lower lip but then flinched and stopped, having forgotten for the moment that it was swollen and split.

"Maybe I could bring her over. Are yous in Finglas Station?" Louisa asked.

"No, actually, we're in the headquarters building in Phoenix Park. That would be much better than Finglas Station. More private, a secure parking lot. You'd be safe there, Gemma. We can have the two of you in a private room, get you a tea and some biscuits if you like."

"I don't know. I don't want to do this. I just want it all to go away."

"I understand that, Gemma. Really, I do. But here's what we know because we deal with people like this man all the time. You were lucky to get away. The only reason you are here today is because you had the courage to fight back and were smart enough to flee from your unit. Unfortunately, this person, Adrian, Colin, or whatever his name is, he's not going to give up. He's looking for you right now." Gemma gave a frightened look to

Louisa. "He won't stop until he finds you, and when he does, he's not only going to hurt you, but he's going to hurt Louisa, too. We want to protect both of you and keep you safe. The best way for us to do that is to have you identify this man, and then we'll deal with him."

"They're right, Gemma. He won't stop until he finds you. Until he finds us," Louisa said and wrapped her arms around her.

Gemma began sobbing again as Louisa held her tight. "I'm sorry, Louisa. I'm so sorry I got you into this. I didn't know. I had no idea. Neil said it was a reward for doing a job for them. He said he was on his way to making it big time, and he gave me that necklace. Stupid me, I left it in my unit. I wasn't thinking. He killed him. I know he did. I know it was him, and he was going to kill me, too."

Dillon and Suel looked at one another. "What job did Neil do for him, Gemma?" Suel asked.

"I don't know. He just said he was going to make it big, and we would be a couple and…and…oh God. I'm so stupid. I'm so stupid," she sobbed.

"Louisa," Dillon said. "Let's get the two of you to headquarters. We can find a safe place for you to stay until we get this guy off the street. We'll let Gemma pack some clothes. You should do the same thing. Sooner or later, he's going to put two and two together, and he'll find both of you. You know he will. We don't want that to happen."

Louisa kept her arms wrapped around sobbing Gemma, but she nodded and said, "Okay. Unfortunately, I think you may be right."

While the two women went upstairs to pack a suitcase for Louisa, Dillon and Suel remained in the sitting room. Suel was on the phone explaining things to DI Tully Egan, and Dillon had the pleasure of informing DCI McCabe of their plan.

"Dillon, do you believe what she's telling you? You believe she didn't intentionally lure this Kinan individual to her home with the promise of sexual favors, all the while setting him up to be murdered?"

"I believe she was in something more than a business relationship with Neil Kinan. I believe they were both set up, and that is exactly why whoever is behind this either sent someone or arrived himself with the intent of killing her. It's only sheer luck that she isn't the fifth victim in this case, sir. Now, we're going to bring them both in, hopefully, to identify a suspect. They are going to need round-the-clock protection until we get whoever is involved off the street. With all due respect, sir, if we pressure them, threaten them, they will shut down, and we're liable to have two more victims on our hands, which will bring our total to six."

Dillon could hear McCabe take a deep breath. "Very well, Dillon. I pray you're right," he said and hung up.

The women were back downstairs, each carrying a suitcase, just as McCabe hung up.

"Both packed?" Suel asked.

"No, these are just my things," Louisa said. "We'll have to stop at Gemma's so she can pack."

"Oh sure, we can do that. Happy to help," Suel said and rolled his eyes at Dillon.

TWENTY-EIGHT

This time there was an open parking slot just two doors down from Gemma's unit. Two squad cars were parked out on the street, and Dillon recognized DI Tully Egan's car at the far end of the parking lot.

Both Dillon and Suel realized it was a waste of time to attempt to separate the two women, who were now acting like conjoined twins and holding each other's hand as they approached unit six. The door was closed, and Dillon went to push it open, but it didn't move. He turned the doorknob, and the door opened. Apparently, someone had reattached the two broken pieces on the door frame.

DI Egan stepped out of the kitchen, sipping a tea, and gave a wave. He held a cup from the shop next to the Finglas Station.

Dillon waved back and said, "Just here to pick up some clothing and incidentals."

"Go ahead and pack. In fact, I'm glad you're here. Do you have a key to your front door, ma'am?"

"Should be hanging on a hook in the kitchen, just behind the tea kettle," Gemma replied.

"Oh," Egan said, stepped back, and saw the key on the hook "Well, I'll be damned. There it is."

Gemma and Louisa, still holding hands, passed Dillon and headed back to the bedroom. Dillon gave Suel a nod to follow. As they walked past, Dillon noted that the shards from the glass vase had been removed, although the blood on the floor and on the wall appeared to be untouched.

"You find anything?" Dillon asked Egan.

"Maybe, we were able to get pieces of glass with some blood samples. The worst scenario is we'll have a blood type. Best outcome would be DNA identifying whoever it was. You said she hit him over the head with the vase?"

"That's what she told us. From here, we're going to an interview room to have her look at photos and see if she can ID the man. We'll tape the whole thing and ask some more in-depth questions. Do you want to be present for the interview?"

"I'd love to, but we're up to our necks. You know she can't come back here, and if she stays at the friend's place, that's probably not safe either."

Dillon took a deep breath. "Yeah, we've told that to both of them. We'll figure something out. I'm just hoping she'll be able to identify someone from the mug book."

"Good luck with that. They're probably scared out of their wits, and rightfully so. They'll just want all of this to go away. We're going to want to interview the

McKee woman at some point. Based on this situation, she's bound to have information on the Kinan murder."

"She alluded to a relationship, or maybe the beginning of a relationship, with Kinan. I'd still like to have them look at the mug shots. See if maybe they can come across someone. If they do, he would seem to be a potential suspect in the Kinan murder, if not all four of the murders."

Egan nodded and said, "If we get a DNA match on that blood, you'll be the first person I call."

"Hopefully, someone will be identified," Dillon said. He phoned Special Branch and reserved Interview Room Three. Just as he disconnected, Gemma stepped out of the bedroom with a backpack strapped to her back, a makeup bag in her right hand, and wheeling a suitcase with large flowers all over it. Dillon breathed a sigh of relief happy she hadn't packed as much as Louisa, but then Louisa stepped out, wheeling a second suitcase, and Suel followed, carrying a large overnight bag. "Is that everything?"

"Just a few things, but it should cover me for a couple of days," Gemma said.

Dillon waited for the rest of the joke but then realized she hadn't been kidding. "Okay, let's get those into the car, and we'll head down to Phoenix Park," he said, purposely not saying the words 'Headquarters' or 'Special Branch.' They loaded the luggage into the boot, and then Suel held the rear door open for the women. As they slid into the back seat, Dillon looked around for someone watching but, fortunately, didn't see anyone.

He climbed into the passenger seat, turned to the women, and said, "Buckle up."

The drive to the headquarters building was uneventful. The guard at the entrance gave a look at the women in the backseat. They were holding hands and sitting close together. He smiled, nodded, raised the gate arm, and Suel drove into the secure parking lot.

As Suel pulled to a stop, Dillon said, "We'll leave your luggage in the boot of the car. It will be safe, and there's a guard at the entrance twenty-four hours, seven days a week."

"Are you going to lock us up?" Louisa said, and they seemed to move closer together.

"No, no, nothing like that. We're going to have you look at photos. See if you can identify the man who attacked Gemma. I just thought it would be easier than carrying your luggage up to the third floor. We can bring it up if you want."

They seemed to think about that for a moment, and then Louisa nodded and said, "I think it will be all right here. Is it okay with you, honey?" she asked as she turned toward Gemma.

Gemma nodded but didn't say anything.

They entered through the secure door in the parking lot and took the elevator up to the third floor. Both Dillon and Suel breathed a sigh of relief that no one got on the elevator with them.

They walked down the hallway past Special Branch and headed into Interview Room Three. "Grab a seat, ladies," Dillon said as he pulled off his jacket and draped it on the back of a chair. Suel did the same thing as the women stepped over to the far side of the table. Gemma still carried her backpack. She pulled it off, leaned it against the wall, and settled onto a chair.

Louisa looked around and then sat down next to Gemma.

"Okay, now this may take a while. Can we get you a tea or a soda, maybe something to eat?"

"I'm starving," Gemma said.

"Shepherd's pie sound okay?" Dillon asked, and Gemma nodded. "Louisa?"

Louisa nodded and said, "And a tea, no cream or sugar."

"Same for me," Gemma said and seemed to relax just a bit.

"If you would do the honors, please, Paddy," Dillon said.

Suel gave a quick nod and headed out of the room.

Dillon opened the laptop on the table in front of him and input a security code. "I'm going to be taping this for your own protection. I don't want it to look like we've forced you to pick an individual image, or you get tired, and we make you continue to work going through a pile of pictures, okay?"

Both women nodded, and Dillon began recording. He introduced them by name. Asked if they were there of their own free will and briefly explained the assault on Gemma.

"If you want to open up the computer in front of you, the images should appear on the screen in just a moment. Hopefully, you'll be able to identify the individual who attacked you yesterday, Gemma. Just take your time. What did you say the two names are that he called himself?"

"Adrian and Colin," she replied, almost in a whisper.

Dillon ran his fingers across the keyboard, and an image suddenly appeared. "Okay, we'll start with individuals using those names. Now you should have an image on the screen in front of you."

Gemma nodded.

"See those arrows in the lower right-hand corner of the keyboard? If it's not the person on the screen, click that arrow on the right, and it will bring up the next image. Take your time. There's no rush. If you think there might be someone, but you're not sure, let me know, and we'll mark it as such. No pressure, and no one knows you are doing this, so do not worry about that. Okay?"

Gemma nodded and moved on to the next image, which was a good thing because the first image was that of DCI McCabe. There were actually two images of each individual. The person facing into the camera, as well as a side view. Louisa leaned closer to Gemma as she began to press the arrow key, bringing up one image after another.

TWENTY-NINE

Gemma had been going through mug shot images for the past twenty minutes and hadn't found anyone, although she did identify two individuals to Louisa as former 'clients.' The door to interview room three opened, and Suel stepped in with a shopping bag and a cardboard tray with four cups. "Dinner is served," he said, and there was an audible sigh of relief from Dillon and both ladies.

Suel handed teas to the women, set one in front of the empty chair where he planned to sit, and then gave a cup to Dillon, saying, "Decaf coffee so you can sleep tight tonight."

"I don't think sleep is going to be a problem tonight."

Suel pulled out four takeout food trays, setting one in front of each individual, then handed everyone a plastic fork and sat down. "Anyone look familiar?" he asked Gemma.

She shook her head and said, "Not really. There were two men I was familiar with, but I haven't seen either one for at least a year or more. How many of these pictures do you have?"

"Quite a lot," Dillon said. "You've barely scratched the surface, and I eliminated men over fifty, bald guys, anyone not Caucasian, anyone taller than six feet two inches. Not to worry, just take your time."

"You never asked me what kind of car he drives."

"You know what kind of car he drives?" Dillon asked as he sat up and grabbed a pen.

"Well, not the kind, exactly, but it's black, and it has four doors."

"Good to know that," Dillon said as he wrote down 'black 4-door.' It was going to be a long night.

Dillon and Suel had finished their shepherd's pies, and the women were little more than halfway through. They kept up a casual conversation with Gemma, asking if she'd been out with the man and, if so, where they had gone. Up until the other day, she'd only been with him twice, both times in her place. Both times he brought her a bottle of champagne, and he was out of there in less than fifteen minutes. Slam, bam, thank you, ma'am.

For a half-second, Dillon thought, *fifty euros for fifteen minutes worked out to be two hundred euros per hour*, then quickly decided that the best idea might be to keep that thought to himself. Once the women had finished their shepherd's pies, Suel pulled out a tray and opened the top. Four chocolate brownies with chocolate frosting sat on the tray. Surprisingly, Louisa was the first one to reach for a brownie. Gemma quickly followed. Suel picked up the tray and held it in front of Dillon.

"I really shouldn't," Dillon said.

"You're right, you shouldn't, but you're going to all the same. We all know that, so take one and get it over with. Besides, you need the sweetening."

Dillon took a brownie. Suel set the tray down in front of him, took a brownie, and bit into half of it. "Mmm-mmm, just what I needed."

"Never enough sweetening for you," Dillon said, and everyone laughed.

Suel collected the trays, pie tins, plastic forks, and napkins and dumped them into the bag. "Anyone need to use the loo?" he asked, and Gemma raised her hand. "Come on. It's just down the hall."

"I'll go with you," Louisa said.

Suel looked like he was about to say something, but Dillon caught his attention and shook his head. "Might be a good idea if we all made the trip," Dillon said.

Suel picked up the bag and led the way to the restrooms. Once the women stepped into the ladies' room, Dillon turned to Suel and said, "You hit the can, and I'll wait here until you get back."

"How do you think it's going?"

"I think they're being honest with us, and she's trying to find the mug shot of the guy, but it's a steep curve. Hell, for all we know, the guy may not even have a record."

"What are you going to do with them tonight, Dillon? Do you have anything lined up? Where are they going to sleep?"

"I haven't even had time to think about that. To tell you the truth, I've got two spare rooms. Now that you mention it, I'm thinking maybe my place."

"Who's on duty tonight?" Suel asked.

"The Night Officer? I think it's Bennett."

"Let me talk to him. We get on well. Best to have it okayed officially, or it will no doubt come back to burn your ass."

Dillon nodded, said, "Thanks," and waited outside the ladies' room. He could hear some quiet conversation on the other side of the door but couldn't make out what was being said. After close to ten minutes, they stepped out of the ladies' room, and Dillon led them back to Interview Room Three, where they continued going through images. Unfortunately, with the same result, in other words, nothing. Suel returned, sat down, and when the women were focused on their computer, he gave Dillon a thumbs-up with his hand just beneath the table.

After another hour, Gemma gave a loud sigh and said, "I'm really sorry, but if I look at many more pictures, I'm not going to be able to see straight. No one looks like him, and we've been doing this for hours."

"I think it's time we knocked off," Dillon said.

"Are you going to send us home because I couldn't find anyone?"

"No, Gemma. We have a place lined up for you in Glasnevin. You each get a private room with a bathroom just across the hall. I'll be there for security overnight."

"And there'll be an officer outside, so you'll be safe," Suel added.

"I just want to sleep," Gemma said.

"Let me just tidy up here, and we'll be on our way."

Ten minutes later, after transferring the luggage, they were pulling out of the security lot in Dillon's car and heading toward Glasnevin and Dillon's house. He took a left onto Ballymun and drove up to St. Pappins Road, just across from DCU, Dublin City University. Dillon turned onto St. Pappins Road, drove past the shops, and took a left down Dean Swift Road. A half-minute later he pulled into his drive and parked.

"Is this some undercover place you have?" Louisa asked from the back seat.

"It serves a number of purposes," Dillon said, dodging her question. "Best to mind your step as you get out. There's a dog here that uses the front garden if that translates."

They climbed out of the car, and Dillon opened the boot. He pulled two suitcases out, and the women loaded up the rest. They followed Dillon up to the front door, side-stepping Lucifer's various deposits.

Dillon unlocked the door, and there was Lucifer, prepared to jump out, only he stopped and looked at the three of them.

"Oh, he's darling. Does he live here? Is he a guard dog?" Gemma asked.

"He's called a number of things," Dillon said without going into detail. He stepped aside so the women could enter. They set their luggage down, gave Lucifer a pat on the head, and he hurried out the door.

Dillon did a quick peek into the sitting room and the kitchen. Thankfully, Lucifer hadn't left a mess.

"If you follow me upstairs, I'll show you the rooms," Dillon said and grabbed two of the suitcases, and headed up the stairs. He opened the door to the middle room, then took three steps and opened the door to the bedroom at the end. The rooms were pretty much the same size, and he said, "You two can decide who sleeps where. The bathroom is right there. I'll get some towels out for you. The bed linens are clean, and the radiators in both rooms are on."

Louisa brushed past Dillon and said, "I'll take the room closest to the bathroom." Gemma stepped into the middle room and dropped her backpack and bag on the floor.

"Not sure which one of you belongs to these suitcases, so I'll let you deal with it. If you'll excuse me, I'll let Lucifer back in the house."

Lucifer and Dillon were down on the first floor in the sitting room, watching TV. Other than someone using the bathroom upstairs, Dillon didn't hear anything. He let Lucifer out after the evening news and headed up to bed just before 11:00. Both bedroom doors were closed. He left the bathroom door open and the nightlight on and went to bed. He woke to the sound of a door closing right around 2:30. He opened his bedroom door a crack and peeked out. The bathroom door was closed, but he could see the light streaming out from the bottom of the door and waited. After five minutes, the door opened, and just as naked Gemma began to step out, she turned off the light. The night light flashed on in the bathroom, and he watched as she tentatively opened the door to the room Louisa was in.

He wanted to say something but didn't and waited for her to step out once she realized her mistake. Louisa's bedroom door never reopened. He heard a soft moan a moment later, waited another five minutes, and climbed back in bed, wondering if there was perhaps more to the relationship than he realized. He drifted off to sleep and woke before his alarm went off.

Dillon shaved, took a quick shower, dressed, and tiptoed downstairs. He made a pot of coffee and set the table for three. He figured scrambled eggs and toast would make a decent breakfast and set out the eggs and the loaf of bread. Lucifer was downstairs thirty minutes later. Dillon glanced out the front window and saw an officer sitting in a squad car. He took a cup of tea out to him and followed up ten minutes later with two fried eggs and bacon rashers.

THIRTY

At 8:30 he sent a text message to Suel, 'Waiting for my guests to wake up.' He sent another message a little after 9:00. 'Still waiting.'

Just after 9:30, he heard two voices upstairs in the hall. The bathroom door closed and then he heard the shower come on. "Good morning, ladies," was how Dillon greeted them forty minutes later as they stepped into the kitchen. "How did you sleep?" he asked and smiled.

They both gave a faint smile, and Louisa said, "It was very nice. I take it this is actually your home rather than some undercover place the Gardai have?" she said, looking around.

"Why? Does it have that look that a guy lives here?"

"Well, no offense, but it could do with some attention," Gemma said. "The door in my room doesn't close completely."

"Oh yeah, been meaning to fix that," Dillon said. "Why don't you grab a seat? Would you like coffee or tea?"

"Tea," they said in unison,

He turned the kettle on, placed tea bags in two mugs, and set milk and sugar on the table. He poured the boiling water into the mugs, ran outside, collected the empty breakfast plate and mug from the officer, and hurried back inside to start breakfast.

"Let me just get that door fixed," Dillon said, grabbing a toolbox next to the back door. He hurried upstairs, tightened the hinge screws, and tested the door. It worked. He set the toolbox in his bedroom and went back downstairs. Once they finished breakfast, he sent a text to Suel saying they were headed into Special Branch and that they would pick up where they left off in Interview Room Three. Twenty minutes later, they settled in at the table and resumed the process of Gemma looking at mug shots. By 1:15, she'd gone through every image that had met the set descriptions as to age, hair, height, and whatever else they could think of. Still, no mug shot of her assailant had come up. Dillon had even added random images of the four murder victims. Other than Neil Kinan, which wasn't a surprise, she didn't recognize anyone.

Dillon was at a loss as to what to do, so Suel hurried over to Phoenix Park and returned with a bag of tacos and, for dessert, since Valentine's Day was coming up, chocolate hearts.

"These are really good," Dillon said as he unwrapped his first soft shell taco. "They're as good as the ones I get back in the States."

"The guy who runs the food truck is named Luis. Dillon and I probably get lunch or dinner from him at least once a week. I guess he owns a number of trucks and has them all around the city. I've seen one over by Trinity College. I think he's got another one up in Skerries. He parks it just outside of the County Council offices in Skerries. There's always a line up there because the food is so good. He's competitive because he's buying in quantity for five or six trucks, and he . . ."

"You okay, Dillon?" Suel suddenly asked.

Dillon had a look on his face that seemed to put him a million miles away.

"Dillon, you okay?" Suel asked again and set his taco down on the table.

Both women stared at Dillon.

"What you just said about Luis owning five or six trucks. Hang on just a minute," Dillon said and Googled the company Dublin Drink. Once the site came up, he clicked on the image of Jasper Sullivan, the same image Jimmy Burke had sent him. The image was a casual photo, Sullivan, with a full beard, was seated at a desk devoid of everything except a neat, open file centered on the desk in front of him. With dark hair, the full beard, and blue eyes, he appeared to be in fairly decent physical condition. He looked like the kind of fun guy you'd want to ask over for dinner or go out and have pints with. Dillon turned the computer around so it was facing Gemma and said, "Does this guy look familiar?"

Gemma stared at the screen for a long moment and then looked up at Dillon and slowly nodded. "I'm pretty sure that's him. It's just that the man that paid me and brought me champagne didn't have a beard."

"Okay, bear with me a minute here," Dillon said. He turned the computer back toward him, copied the link to the Dublin Drink site, and sent an email to Emily in the Tech Lab. 'Check this site out. Is there a way to determine when the image of the bearded company president was posted? Thanks, Dillon.'

He stepped over to the phone on the wall, punched in the three-number extension, and waited. Emily answered just before he thought he was going to be dropped into voicemail. "Tech Lab," she said, not sounding too pleased with the call coming through.

"Hi, Emily. Dillon calling. Just sent you an email. Can you check it out? We're in an interview room looking at mug shots. Just want to know if you can determine when a photo was posted."

"If it's a mug shot, the date should be right below the image. Isn't it there?"

"This isn't a mug shot image. It's from a company's site." Dillon thought he may have heard the 'F' word whispered.

"You're in there with a suspect?" Emily asked.

"An assault victim, trying to help us out. We've been going through mug shots for hours. I checked, and this guy in the image doesn't have a record."

"And you emailed me?"

"Yeah, just a minute ago."

"Let me check, and I'll get back to you. Which interview room are you in?"

"Interview room three, Special Branch."

"All right, I'll check it out," she said and disconnected.

Dillon hung up and returned to his chair.

"What'd they say?" Louisa asked.

"She's going to check it out. If anyone can find out when that image was posted, she will. How long have you known this guy?" he asked Gemma.

She shrugged and shook her head. "If it's him, the guy I'm thinking of, I probably met him just in the last three, maybe four, weeks. I think he's the one who gave my name to Kinan. At least that's what Kinan said, except he never said his name. If he's the same guy, he was Adrian once, and the next time, he told me his name was Colin. I usually don't know their names. It's not important to me," she said without looking at either Dillon or Suel. "Kinan just said a guy he knew gave him my number, and then he said that the guy told him he brought me a bottle of champagne. Only one man ever did that, but he never stayed long enough to have a glass. He just did his business and left."

"He ever say anything about what he did for a living? Mention his business, or tell you where he lived?" Suel asked.

She shook her head. "You ever been with a woman you paid? You guys just want to get the job done and then get your ass out the door. You're with me for one reason and one reason only, and I'm okay with that. I'm just providing a service, and you're gonna pay me for doing that," she said as she nodded and raised her eyebrows.

The phone on the wall suddenly rang, and Dillon jumped off his chair. "Emily?"

"That image of your pal, Jasper Sullivan, was posted back in 2019. Don't tell me you're thinking of buying a pub."

"No, just having some difficulty recognizing him with the beard, but if that picture is four or five years old, that makes sense."

"Anything else you need?"

"No, thanks. I'll let you get back to whatever you were doing."

"Much appreciated," she said and disconnected.

"You said that picture is four or five years old?" Gemma asked.

"Apparently, it was posted back in 2019."

"Can I look at it again?"

Dillon sat down, brought the image back up on the computer, and turned it around toward Gemma.

She studied it for a long minute and slowly began to nod. "Yeah, that's him. Definitely him. The blue eyes, I remember, I think he has a Celtic tattoo on his right shoulder." Dillon made a note regarding the tattoo. "You're sure this is the man who assaulted you the other day?"

"Yes, now I am. The blue eyes. He doesn't have the beard anymore, and like I said, he's got that tattoo. If you make him take his shirt off, you'll see it."

Dillon turned the computer around and then said, "Let the record state that Gemma McKee has identified the individual who assaulted her as one Jasper Sullivan. Founder, owner, and president of the company known as Dublin Drink. He is now a suspect in the murder of Neil Kinan. Kinan was found murdered in an automobile parked in front of Gemma McKee's residence on Plunkett Avenue, in Finglas, County Dublin."

"Ladies, if you'll excuse us for a few minutes. We're going to get things organized. Shouldn't take long. Dillon, if you'd join me outside, please," Suel said and headed for the door.

"Back in a bit," Dillon said and followed Suel out of the interview room.

"What do you think, Paddy?"

Suel shook his head. "All well and good, but the questionable identification by a Dublin prostitute isn't going to get us an arrest warrant, let alone a charge of murder that would stand up in a court of law."

"But you saw her. She's sure Sullivan is our man. We could be looking at him for all four murders, Paddy."

"I agree, but not on the questionable identification by a prostitute who saw him for no more than fifteen minutes."

"What about the tattoo?"

"Come on, Dillon. You know as well as I do that we can't bring him in here on unfounded charges to see if he has a tattoo. And even if we did? Then what? For starters, we need to be in touch with Egan in Finglas. See if they have a blood type or, God forbid, a DNA result."

Dillon shook his head. "You know as well as I do, we're looking at weeks, if not months. In the meantime, what are we supposed to do with these two?"

"Well, we can't send them home. We can't put them up in a hotel. My sense is the safest place is probably a house in a quiet neighborhood, you know, like your place on Dean Swift Road."

Dillon mouthed the 'F' word and shook his head.

"You got a better idea?" Suel asked.

"Yeah, I know. I know. Okay. Can you touch base with your pal, Bennett? Is he still the night officer?"

"Yeah, he is. I'll give him a call right now. Shouldn't be more than a couple of minutes, and I'll let you know if there's going to be someone out in front of your place tonight."

"Okay, Paddy. Thanks," Dillon said and headed back into the interview room.

THIRTY-ONE

The drive back to Dillon's house was quiet. Neither Dillon nor his two passengers spoke. He found it interesting that they were both sitting in the back seat, holding hands. Not that he cared. Whether it was just because they were stressed out or they were in a relationship, temporary or otherwise, it didn't matter. He turned onto Ballymun Road and thought for a brief moment that he might stop at The Grape Vine and pick up a bottle or two of wine. He quickly realized what a stupid idea that was and accelerated up the hill to Pappin's Road. As he turned onto Dean Swift Road, he slowed and watched in the rearview mirror for a vehicle. Fortunately, nothing appeared. He drove down the hill, pulled into his drive, turned off the car, and they all stepped out.

As Dillon headed for the door, Louisa said, "You could use a bit of a clean-up out here, if you don't mind me saying. Looking around, your neighbors must think you have a half-dozen dogs inside instead of just that one."

Gemma chuckled as the two of them side-stepped three or four of Lucifer's deposits.

Dillon's first thought was to hand her a plastic bag and the poop scoop. Instead, he said, "You know, you're right. I'll get on that in just a moment. Let's get you two settled inside. After the day we've had, how 'bout you settle in on the couch in the sitting room and turn on the telly. I'll get a fire going, and we can all just take it easy. It's been a crazy couple of days."

He unlocked the door and opened it. Lucifer bounded off the front stoop, turned to face Dillon and the ladies, and assumed the position. *Perfect timing*, Dillon thought as he stepped inside. The women followed and, keeping their coats on, headed into the sitting room. Dillon walked into the kitchen and quickly returned the debris Lucifer had scattered throughout the room back into the wastebasket. He unlocked the back door, reached outside for his poop scoop, and relocked the door. He set the scoop and a plastic bag next to the front door, then stepped into the sitting room.

The women were seated on the couch with Louisa's coat open and spread over the two of them. Gemma was in the process of dialing a phone number. "Gemma, no calls, please. We want to keep you safe. Let me get the fire going, and it will warm up both of you. In the meantime, here," he said and handed Louisa the leopard skin fleece blanket lying on the chair.

"Oh, wonderful," she said as she unfolded the fleece and placed it over them. That seemed to cause Gemma to smile and snuggle a little closer to Louisa.

Dillon placed a starter log on the iron fireplace grate and lit both ends of the package. "Now, just let that burn. Once it gets going, I'll place some logs on it. Back in a minute," he said.

He went back into the front hall, grabbed the scoop and trash bag, and stepped outside. He started on the driver's side of the car and, in short order, realized that Louisa had been right. There were way more deposits from Lucifer than he had thought. He worked his way around the car, across the drive, and then onto the front lawn. Yeah, the more he thought about it, the more he realized it hadn't been just a week, but maybe more like three weeks since he'd picked up after the dog.

Once he finished, he glanced up and down the street. It was dark, and no one appeared to be outside. He stepped out of the front garden, closing the gate behind him so Lucifer couldn't follow, and hurried across the street. He took another quick look around, then placed the trash bag in the neighbor's bin and hurried back across the street. He coaxed Lucifer inside, repeating, "Biscuit," a couple of times, and locked the door behind them.

He grabbed a biscuit from the cookie jar in the kitchen and tossed it to Lucifer, then headed into the sitting room. The starter log was burning nicely, and Dillon placed three logs around it. One in the front, one in back, and one at an angle across the top.

"Oh, thank you, Dillon. That's very nice," Gemma said.

"Yes, and thank you for your effort outside. I'm sure things are much better. We won't mention a word to your neighbor across the street," Louisa said, and they both laughed.

They sat in front of a romance movie Dillon would never have watched and, in fact, apparently didn't because Gemma shook him on the shoulder and said, "Good night, Dillon. Thank you for not snoring too loud." More laughter from the two of them as they headed upstairs to bed. Dillon sat in his chair for a minute or two, listening to the noise from the bathroom, and then he heard the bedroom door close. He waited for more bathroom noise and another bedroom door closing but never heard it.

He headed into the kitchen, set the table for breakfast, filled the water kettle, and arranged the mugs for tea just in case his guests were up before him. He double-checked the locks and glanced out the window just as a car came down the street and began to slow as it approached. Dillon quickly turned off the front hall light and watched in the dark as the car pulled to a stop in front of his drive. Fortunately, it turned out to be a Garda vehicle. He hurried outside, gave a wave at the officer, and approached.

The officer lowered his window and said, "Good evening, sir, Marshal Jack Dillon?"

Dillon nodded and said, "Yes, no one else would want to be me." The officer laughed, and Dillon asked, "Can I get you a tea or make you a sandwich."

He seemed to think about that and said, "A tea would be nice, black if it's not too much trouble, sir."

"Coming right up," Dillon said and hurried back into the house. He turned the kettle on and grabbed a handful of chocolate-covered biscuits from the cupboard. Once the tea was ready, he took it out to the officer along with the biscuits. "I'll be up and make you breakfast in the morning. Scrambled eggs and rashers all right?"

"That would be perfect, sir, but don't go to any trouble."

"No trouble," Dillon said. "Thank you for being here."

"My pleasure, sir. We've got a baby on the way, and I'm getting paid double time."

Dillon went back into the house. The fire had burned into not much more than a pile of hot coals. He woke Lucifer, turned off the lights in the sitting room, and they headed upstairs. He brushed his teeth, applied some cream to his face, and stepped out of the bathroom. The door to Louisa's room was closed.

Lucifer was stretched out on the carpet in front of the bedroom door. He gave Dillon a look but didn't move. The door to Gemma's bedroom was partially open. Dillon peeked into the room and saw the empty bed, confirming his suspicions. He climbed into his bed and was asleep in less than a minute.

THIRTY-TWO

When Dillon woke, it was still dark out. He tiptoed down the hall, past Lucifer, who was fast asleep in the hallway. He shaved, grabbed a very quick shower, and was dressed and downstairs in about fifteen minutes. He glanced outside. The squad car hadn't moved, and he set about scrambling eggs and frying up bacon rashers. He placed two pieces of brown bread in the toaster, then buttered them and arranged the eggs and rashers on the plate. He grabbed a knife and fork, a steaming hot tea, and stepped outside.

As he approached the driver's door, the officer lowered the window. "Oh, God bless. This is better than I'd get at home."

"I doubt that very much, but thanks all the same," Dillon answered. "Anything else you need?"

"I should be fine, sir."

"Believe it or not, I've got a bathroom inside if you need it."

The officer laughed. "Traveling with the plastic jug my wife issued me," he said and nodded at the half-gallon plastic milk jug sitting on the floor of the passenger seat.

"Probably a good idea. Still, if you need, you know, porcelain, just give a knock."

"Thank you. I'll keep it in mind. I'll be leaving in about a half hour. If it's okay, I'll just set the plate and silverware on your front stoop."

"Not a problem, just as long as you feel free to use the loo, or if you need something, don't hesitate to knock. Stay safe," Dillon said and hurried back into the house.

He heard noise upstairs an hour later. He added water to the kettle and cracked eight eggs into a mixing bowl. He added feta cheese, some red pepper, mushrooms, and sliced black olives. He cut six slices of brown bread and left them on the cutting board. Maybe thirty minutes later, it sounded like the ladies were about to head downstairs, so he turned the kettle on. He placed the bread in the toaster, dumped the egg mix into a frying pan, and placed six bacon rashers in a larger frying pan.

They entered the kitchen just as Dillon was pouring the boiling water into the tea mugs. "Have a seat, ladies. Breakfast will be ready in a minute," he said and pushed the tea mugs across the counter to them.

Louisa walked over to the refrigerator and took out the small pitcher of milk. Dillon watched as she put not two but three drops of milk into her tea.

"You sure that's enough?" he joked.

"Yes, it's perfect. It's what I do every morning," she replied, not picking up on the fact that he had been joking.

The toast came up, and he quickly placed the pieces on a plate and set it on the table. He dished the eggs up on the three plates, added two bacon rashers to each plate, and set the plates on the table. He turned off the stove, poured himself a coffee, and sat down. "All right, ladies, enjoy your breakfast. So, how did everyone sleep last night."

"It was just what I needed," Gemma said, and they both smiled.

After breakfast, the ladies loaded the dishwasher while Dillon wrote out a grocery list off the top of his head. If they were going to stay for any length of time, he needed to stock up on food.

"You writing a grocery list?" Gemma asked as she wiped down the kitchen counter behind Dillon.

"Yeah, just looking at getting the basics. Three people, three meals, three times a day, it starts to add up."

"Can you add blackberry jam, please?" Gemma suggested. "That would really be good."

"As long as you're doing that, some lettuce, tomatoes, maybe sunflower seeds, oh, and put down a balsamic vinaigrette salad dressing. That would be perfect," Louisa said.

"Might be nice to have some crisps, you know, something to nibble on if we're watching the telly at night," Gemma added.

"I've got an idea," Dillon said. "Let's all hop in the car and go to the grocery store. I'm sure once we start walking down the aisles, more ideas will pop up. Let's start with you two cooking dinner for us tonight. Okay? Come on. Grab your coats and let's go before it gets too busy."

Once again, both women climbed into the backseat, and Dillon, acting as the chauffeur, drove them over to the Lidl store on Upper Drumcondra Road. After he parked, he opened the boot of the car and pulled out four shopping bags. He placed a euro coin in the slot to free a shopping cart, and they entered the store. His plan was to work off his shopping list, but that quickly went out the window once the women began to peruse the items on the shelves. Gemma set a jar of blackberry jam in the shopping cart, then added a jar of orange marmalade and a jar of strawberry jam. Dillon had chicken breasts on his list, to which Louisa added smoked salmon, ground beef, and black pudding. Vegetables, three kinds of salad dressings, oranges, apples, grapes, plus a liter of cranberry juice, apple juice, a twelve-pack of bottled water, and two different herbal teas.

It went on and on, and then they arrived at the wine section. Two bottles of Sauvignon Blanc, two bottles of Cabernet, Merlot, Pinot Noir, and a bottle of dessert wine Dillon had never even heard of.

"Okay," Dillon said. "It's time for all of us to head to the checkout, or I'm going to end up destitute, and we'll be sleeping in my car." Reluctantly, they headed toward the front of the store and the checkout lane.

Dillon had inserted his credit card into the card reader. Louisa and Gemma were standing at the end of the checkout counter, placing various food items back into the shopping cart once they'd been rung up.

"Gemma, dear, maybe start filling one of those shopping bags," Louisa said.

Gemma grabbed one of the shopping bags and opened it up just as a man stepped next to her and asked, "Hey, darlin', don't I know you?"

Gemma looked up and immediately shook her head. "No, I think you must have me mistaken for someone else."

"No, now I'm sure it was you. You live on Plunkett Road, don't you? Council housing? I drove my boss there. He, umm, had an appointment to see you. Brought you a bottle of champagne. I always wanted to give you a call, but he never gave me the number." He quickly glanced around, lowered his voice, and said, "My name's Barry. I'd love to get together with you sometime. I'd make it worth your while. I manage the Lamplighter pub. You should stop in some time, drinks on me, and I'd make it very enjoyable if you get what I'm saying."

"Thanks, but, like I said before, you must be mistaking me for someone else."

"God, I'm sure of it. Remember, you answered the door in black lace. Your unit's on the ground level, ain't it? I never forget a pretty face."

"It wasn't me with your boss," Gemma said, maybe a little too loudly.

"You got the wrong girl. She's been asking you nice like, so get out of here," Louisa snarled.

"Okay, okay. Sorry to bother yous. Maybe give me a call if you're interested. Like I said, I'd make it worth your while." He tossed a business card into the shopping bag.

"Would you like a receipt, Mr. Dillon?" the cashier asked

"No, thanks. Everything okay here, ladies?" Dillon asked, staring at the guy as he pulled his credit card from the card reader.

"Relax, man. I'm leaving, just leaving," the guy said.

"Probably a good idea," Dillon replied, then watched as he walked out of the store and into the parking lot.

"Sorry about that," Gemma said as she opened another shopping bag and began to fill it.

Once the bags were packed, Dillon pushed the shopping cart out of the store and over to the car. He opened the boot, arranged the shopping bags, then slammed the lid closed and pushed the shopping cart over to the line of available carts. He hooked the cart up to the other carts, recovered his one euro coin, and hurried back to the car. He glanced around. Fortunately, the Barry character seemed to have disappeared. Dillon took a long way home, checking the rearview mirror more than a couple of times.

THIRTY-THREE

illon placed a pan with three chicken breasts in the oven. Gemma was working on a salad. Louisa was coating slices of potatoes in olive oil and garlic and placing them on a cookie sheet.

Once everything was in the oven and the salad was made, Dillon poured three glasses of Sauvignon Blanc. They settled around the dining table, munching on brie and crackers while chatting until dinner was ready. When the oven timer went off, Dillon removed the chicken and potatoes from the oven. Gemma dished up the salad on three plates. Louisa topped up the wine glasses and set the three bottles of salad dressing on the table.

Dillon couldn't remember the last time he'd had two people over for dinner, and he'd certainly never had two women. The meal was lovely, followed by a caramel and sea salt ice cream that Dillon had insisted on getting at Lidl. When they were finished, the ladies, along with Lucifer, headed into the sitting room while Dillon cleaned up the kitchen and got things ready for the morning.

A few hours later, Gemma once more shook Dillon on the shoulder to wake him and told him they were heading upstairs to bed. Lucifer followed.

Dillon turned off the TV, spread the coals around in the fireplace, and glanced out the front window. There wasn't a squad car out front. He debated calling DI Bennett the Night Officer but decided against it. Whoever was pulling duty here tonight probably got delayed somehow, and they'd be along. Dillon didn't want to appear to be a complainer.

He waited downstairs for another fifteen minutes, and once the noise in the bathroom subsided and the doors closed for the last time, he turned the lights off in the sitting room, turned on the house alarm in the front hall, and went upstairs. Lucifer was stretched out in the hallway in front of the door to Louisa's room. Dillon headed ito the bathroom, and glanced into Gemma's empty room on the way.

Lucifer watched as he approached but didn't bother to move. Dillon sidestepped him and went into the bathroom. He turned off the upstairs hall light and, just like the past two nights, left his bedroom door open an inch or two. He was asleep in a couple of minutes.

He blinked awake, waited a moment, and decided he'd been dreaming. He glanced at his digital clock. It was just after 3:30. He turned on his side and was about to close his eyes when he heard the sound again. A low, steady growl, Lucifer. He was about to call him, tell him to settle down, then came fully awake. Something wasn't right. He climbed out of bed, pulled on a pair of jeans, and peeked out the bedroom door. Louisa's bedroom door was closed. Lucifer was up, standing just outside Dillon's room, staring down the staircase. He let off another low growl. Dillon listened but couldn't hear anything.

Other than the night light in the bathroom, the house was dark. Then Dillon heard it, a click, subtle, but a click all the same. A mouse? He glanced out the bedroom window. The street was empty. There was no squad car in sight. He grabbed his phone and dialed 999.

"Emergency Services," a woman answered.

"US Marshal Jack Dillon, Special Branch. Someone's breaking into my home." He gave his address and then heard what sounded like the front doorknob. Lucifer growled again, this time louder. Dillon tossed the cell phone on the bed, pulled his pistol off the table, and shoved it in the back of his jeans. He noticed the toolbox next to the bedroom table and opened it. He had just reached for the hammer when the house alarm suddenly went off. The sound was ear-splitting.

Lucifer gave a whimper, ran into Dillon's bedroom, and scurried underneath the bed. Dillon crouched down as a figure suddenly appeared on the lower landing and charged up the stairs. He waited a half-second until the figure reached the top of the stairs before he attacked. Swinging the hammer with all his might, catching the man squarely on the chin, and actually lifting him up off his feet.

The man seemed to hover in the air for a moment before landing on his back halfway down the staircase and bouncing down the rest of the way, eventually stopping at the landing. In the process of his retreat, a pistol fired twice.

Dillon charged down the stairs, picked the pistol up off the third step from the bottom, and pointed it at the unconscious man on the landing. He was bleeding from his mouth, and then Dillon noticed blood dripping down from the man's leg and onto the stairway carpet. Apparently, he'd shot himself in the foot.

Dillon held the pistol out in front of him as he stepped to the alarm keypad. He input the code to turn the alarm off, then gave a quick glance outside, slammed the front door closed, and double-locked it. The man on the staircase was slowly beginning to move his head back and forth. Dillon stepped over him, hurried upstairs, and grabbed his handcuffs off the table. He picked up his phone, shoved it in a front pocket, and went back downstairs.

The man's eyes were still closed, but he was groaning. Dillon grabbed him by the jacket collar, pulled him none too gently off the landing, and handcuffed his hands around the bottom of the newel post.

"Ga, my foo, my foo," the man groaned, then coughed as blood continued to drip out of his mouth.

"Who are you?" Dillon growled and pressed the pistol against the man's head.

"My foo, my fuing foo."

"Dillon?" one of the women called from upstairs.

"Everything's okay. Stay in the bedroom and lock the door."

"The alarm went off, and we—"

"Stay in the bedroom and lock the damn door," he shouted. He held the gun at the ready and quickly checked the kitchen. It was empty, and the back door was still locked. He stepped back into the hall.

"You ha to hel me. I…I nee a octor. You fuin' sho me."

"You shot yourself, you piece of shit. I'm gonna let you bleed to death," Dillon said, then headed toward the sitting room with the pistol out in front of him. He stopped at the door, reached into the room, and turned on the light. The room appeared to be empty. He pushed the door all the way open until it bounced off the wall, just to be sure no one was hiding behind it. He glanced into the room and approached the far end of the couch. No one was there, and he could hear a siren in the distance.

He stepped back into the front hall and approached the man handcuffed to the newel post. There was a puddle of blood about the size of a small plate surrounding the man's foot. For the first time, he actually studied the man's face and thought he looked familiar.

"Come on, ma. Ca you see I nee a fuin' ocor? I'm bleein, for Gos sake."

"You broke into my house, you're bleeding on my refinished floor, and I'm supposed to help your worthless ass? Let's start with you telling me your name."

"I nee a ocor. I bleein."

"I'm going to ask nice just one more time. What's your name?"

"I tol you, I nee—" Blood dripped from both sides of his mouth.

"That does it," Dillon shouted and stomped on the bleeding foot hard.

The man screamed in pain, and Dillon stomped on his foot again, this time grinding his foot back and forth on top of the man's bleeding foot.

"Ahh, ahh, ple sop, sop, it's eclan. My ame is eclan O'rien," the man screamed.

"And what the hell are you doing here? How did you find out about—"

"Declan?" Gemma called from upstairs. She suddenly appeared, leaning over the banister in the upstairs hallway. "Declan? What the feck are you doing here?" she screamed, then disappeared for a half-second and was suddenly racing down the steps. "You worthless, miserable bastard. I told you on the phone I couldn't see you. So, you broke into this house? You came here to kill—" She had apparently slipped on a t-shirt before leaving the room. Based on the look on her face and the screaming, Dillon didn't say anything.

"I was gonna che on ya. See if ou were all righ an—"

"You lying, worthless feck," she screamed and kicked him hard on the side of the head. His head bounced off the side of the newel post with a large thud just as two wailing sirens and flashing lights pulled in front of the house. He appeared to be out cold. So much for questioning him. "God, I hope he's dead," Gemma shouted.

"I think you just knocked him out," Dillon said. "Might be a good idea to run upstairs and get some clothes on. The Garda will be in here in a few seconds."

"I want to strangle the bastard."

"That makes two of us. You know him?"

She nodded and said, "Declan O'Brien. An occasional customer."

"Thanks, better hurry upstairs, Gemma, please."

Dillon quickly rolled the man over and checked his pockets for a wallet or ID. Not surprisingly, the pockets were empty except for a set of car keys. Dillon set the pistol on the bench and opened the front door. Four officers were just stepping into the front garden. "Everything is okay. Thank you for coming. I'm Marshal Jack Dillon, Special Branch. I'm the one who called Emergency Services. I've got the burglar inside."

THIRTY-FOUR

The man was being loaded into the Emergency Ambulance that had backed into the drive next to Dillon's car. One of the officers had returned Dillon's handcuffs to him and then cuffed the man to the gurney with his own set of cuffs. Not that he would be able to run anywhere, given the bullet hole in his recently broken foot.

Dillon was in the kitchen handing mugs of tea to two of the responding officers seated at his kitchen table. He was now dressed, as were Gemma and Louisa, although the women were out in the sitting room with two other officers.

"So you said you knew the man?" one of the officers asked.

"No, I said I thought maybe I recognized him. I'd seen him a few nights ago in a pub named Pinky's."

"Pinky's? That place in Smithfield?" the other officer asked.

"I was working undercover in an ongoing investigation," Dillon quickly added, so they didn't think he was a regular there. "He was at a table with another guy and Gemma McKee, the blonde in the sitting room."

"So you think he was coming here to talk with her?"

"To talk? No, that was the last thing on his mind. He was coming here to kill the two women in the sitting room. Gemma has information on the Finglas murders. She's been in Special Branch for the last two days, going through mug shots, looking for the man we suspect could be the shooter."

"They're up to four random shootings in Finglas, aren't they?" the officer with the ginger hair asked.

Dillon nodded. "We're working on something that might link the victims together, hopefully."

"So, your door wasn't damaged. How'd your man get in here?"

Dillon went over the events again, starting with Lucifer growling at the top of the stairs.

"Where's your dog now?"

"He's probably still hiding underneath my bed. As soon as the alarm went off, he scurried under the bed, and I haven't seen him since. The alarm was piercing, and it hurt my ears. I can't imagine how bad it was for him."

"Any thoughts on where your man may have parked his car?" the dark-haired officer with the mustache asked and held up the set of car keys Dillon had taken from the man's pocket.

"Not specifically, but if I had to guess, I would take a look just around the corner or up around Dean Swift Green. I don't think he would have parked too far away just in case he had to make a run for it."

The ginger-haired officer chuckled. "He's not going to be running anywhere for a while with that hole in his foot."

"Yeah, that pistol fired twice as he bounced down the stairs."

"You think he was aiming at you?"

Dillon shook his head. "Much as I'd like to say he was, just to make sure he receives an extended sentence, I'm pretty sure he was unconscious. The pistol firing was just a reaction to him bouncing down the stairs."

"Still, he broke into your house with a loaded gun and was running up to the second floor in search of the two women. How did he even know they were here?"

"That's one of the many questions I have for him. Any idea where they'll take him? I'm thinking probably St. James's Hospital."

Both officers nodded. "That would seem to be as good a place as any. Give a call to Glasnevin Station later this morning. They should have it on the books by then. Once he's good enough to transport, he'll be locked up in The Joy. Attempted murder on two women, not to mention an officer, Special Branch no less. He'll be going away for a fairly long time."

Dillon had a comment on the tip of his tongue but decided it would be better to keep it to himself. He heard footsteps out in the hallway, and a moment later, an officer stepped into the kitchen. "We've got statements from Miss McKee and Miss McBride, and we're pretty much finished."

"Unless you have anything else to add, Marshal, I think we're finished for the time being. No doubt you'll hear from someone wanting to interview you further," the ginger-haired officer said.

"Yeah, no doubt," Dillon said. "I want to thank all of you for the quick response. I've had someone out front the last two nights. I don't know what happened tonight."

"Well, after tonight's incident, I'd say it's a pretty safe bet you'll have someone out there."

"That would be nice," Dillon said. "Let me see you out, and then I'm going to try to get some sleep."

"Good luck with that," one of them said, and everyone laughed. The officer in the sitting room joined them. Dillon, Gemma, and Louisa said a few more thank yous and waved as the squad cars drove off and disappeared around the corner.

As Dillon closed and locked the door, Gemma said, "What a night. You think there might be a chance for a glass of wine? Just to see if I can get back to sleep."

"I think that sounds like a good idea. What about you, Louisa?"

"I'll surely take the wine, but I don't know how much good it will actually do."

"Well, it can't hurt. Come on into the kitchen," Dillon said. He cleared the table of tea mugs and set three wine glasses on the counter, filled them, and handed one to Gemma and one to Louisa. He raised his glass and said, "Here's to good luck and the fact that we're even here to do this."

"Amen, to that, and thanks to little Lucifer. Where is he, by the way?" Louisa said and looked around.

"I'm sure he's still under my bed. The alarm really frightened him." Dillon took a long swallow of the red wine. "Gemma, you phoned that O'Brien guy?"

She shook her head and said, "No, honest, I didn't. He called me, and I told him I couldn't see him and hung up. Really, I did. It was just a few seconds."

He made a mental note to find out where, exactly, O'Brien had been taken. He wanted to question him at the earliest possible moment.

They finished their glasses of wine, and the women headed upstairs, making no secret they would be sharing the same bed. Dillon was planning to stretch out on the couch in the sitting room, but when he looked out the window, there was a squad car parked in front of his drive. Better late than never.

He rinsed out the wine glasses, left them in the sink, and climbed the stairs. It took some encouragement, but he eventually got Lucifer out from underneath the bed, and they gradually drifted off to sleep. Dillon woke two hours later, just after 8:00. He took a long, hot shower, dressed, and tiptoed downstairs. He started a pot of coffee and looked out the front window. The squad car was still out front, and Dillon hurried out to see if the officer would like a tea.

"That would be wonderful, sir. Thank you. Don't know what the deal was last night. Our information said you would only need two nights. Someone screwed up somewhere."

"Just glad to see you here. I'll get that tea for you, and are eggs and rashers okay for breakfast?"

"I'd like nothing better. Oh, by the way. I'm here until I'm relieved. You'll have security twenty-four-seven until we're told otherwise."

"Believe me, I appreciate that," Dillon said and hurried back into the house.

THIRTY-FIVE

Dillon had just stepped back inside after delivering a mug of tea to the officer parked out front when his cell phone rang. Paddy Suel.

"Good morning, Paddy."

"What in the bleeding hell happened? Are you okay? I just got a call."

"Yeah, I'm fine. We're all fine. I don't know what happened, exactly, but apparently, the Night Officer, Bennett, had us down as needing someone out front for just two nights."

"Is anyone there now?"

"Yeah, there's a squad car out front. The officer told me we'll be getting security twenty-four hours a day, seven days a week, until further notice. The prick that broke in was one of the two guys I saw with Gemma the night I was down at Pinky's on my own."

"You think she called him or something?"

"No, she was screaming at the guy. He shot himself in the foot, and I had him cuffed to the newel post. No idea how he knew they were here. His name is Declan O'Brien, by the way. But here's the problem. If he knew, I'm thinking it's a pretty safe bet he can't be the only one. I think we need to find somewhere else to move the women, not your place, by the way.”

“I’ll get on that immediately,” Suel said.

“While you’re doing that, see if you can find out what hospital they took O’Brien to. I’m thinking probably James’s. I want to talk to him, find out how he knew they were here.”

“I’ll check and get back to you. Don’t come in this morning. Stay where you are. As soon as I hang up, I’m going in to see McCabe. He’ll go ballistic. There was a shot fired?”

“Two shots, actually. O’Brien shot himself in the foot. I hit him pretty hard on the chin and sent him down the stairs. I’m guessing he’ll be cuffed to a bed for maybe forty-eight hours before they lock him up. But I want to talk to him.”

“They may not allow that, Dillon.”

“That’s why we need to find out where in the hell he is so I can get in to see him before they can stop me.”

“I’ll see what I can do, but don’t hold your breath,” Suel said and disconnected.

Dillon cooked up eggs and rashers for the officer parked out front and took them out to him. “Thank you, sir. Very kind. I see on the reports they took your man to St James’s early this morning. Shot in the foot, a concussion, a broken jaw, and a host of other problems. He’ll be there for at least two or three days, and then they’ll lock him up in The Joy. Serves him right, the bastard.”

“I think you just made my day,” Dillon said.

"They're piling on the charges now, breaking and entering, three counts of attempted murder, assault of an officer, parole violation, and possession of a firearm. He'll be looking at twenty-plus years. Not to mention the fact that he'll never be able to run properly."

Dillon shook his head. "I only wish he'd shot himself in his thick skull."

"That would save us all a lot of time and money," the officer said. "Thanks for the breakfast. Much appreciated, and you didn't have to do that."

"I'm just glad you're here," Dillon said and hurried back into the house. He heard some noise upstairs in the bathroom, so he refilled the kettle and set it to boil. Louisa was the first one down. She had showered but still appeared to be sleep deprived.

"Did you get any sleep?" Dillon asked.

"Bits and pieces off and on. I think just about the time I was going to fall into a deeper sleep, I'd wake up and stare into the dark, listening for any noise for twenty minutes until I drifted off and repeated the process. Gemma just squirmed back and forth and kept talking gibberish."

"Is she up now?"

Louisa nodded. "She should be down any minute."

The kettle suddenly clicked off. Dillon filled two tea mugs. He set one in front of Louisa and the other in front of Gemma's spot. He called upstairs to her and then poured himself a coffee. Just as Dillon sat down, Gemma stepped into the kitchen. She looked exhausted.

Once she took a sip of her tea, Dillon said, "I'm going to see about moving us someplace else. There's no telling who or how many people may know you're staying here, and I don't want to wait around to find out."

"Where will we go?" Louisa asked.

"I don't know yet. But after breakfast, I think it would be a good idea if you packed up your belongings. Better be prepared to move on a moment's notice."

Both women nodded.

"Is there any way you can think of that Declan O'Brien found out you were here?" Dillon asked.

Gemma started to shake her head 'no' but then stopped. "You know, remember the man at Lidl yesterday, Barry?"

"Yeah, but he didn't follow us home. I took a long route and was checking for him in the rearview mirror."

"Yeah, but remember the cashier? When she asked if you wanted your receipt, she called you Mr. Dillon. Barry runs one of Sullivan's pubs. He'd probably have the type of computer system or maybe even a contact that could find out where you lived."

Dillon closed his eyes and silently swore. He was on his computer a half-hour later going through arrest records on Declan O'Brien when his cell phone rang. Suel calling.

"Yeah, Paddy, what's up?"

"I'm just turning onto Pappin's Road. I'll be at your place in a minute."

"Okay, there's an officer parked out front. Show him your ID and ask him if he wants a tea. I'll turn the kettle on for both of you. See you in a minute."

Dillon turned on the kettle and then went out to the front hall and opened the door. Suel had just turned onto Dean Swift Road and was heading down the hill. He watched as Suel pulled up over the curb and parked on the sidewalk.

Suel draped his ID around his neck and headed over to the squad car. He chatted for a moment, laughed, and headed toward Dillon, standing at the front door. "How are you doing, Mr. Excitement?"

"We're all fine. Come on in," Dillon said and held the door open.

Suel stepped in, and once Dillon closed the door, Suel wrapped his arms around him and gave him a bear hug. "Damn it. You scared the hell out of me, Dillon."

"Thanks, I'm okay, Paddy. We're all okay, it could have been a lot worse. Except for Lucifer waking me up, that bastard would have been upstairs and shot me before I could have gotten out of bed."

"The women?"

"They're both upstairs. Let me get you a tea. Did you ask your man outside?"

"Yeah, he'd like one. Black."

"Come on into the kitchen. I just boiled the water, but I know what a pain in the ass you are, so let me put it back on. What have you got for me?"

"O'Brien is in James's. They've got him in a private room cuffed to a bed. There's an officer outside the room, and McCabe will be going over with a team to interview him. Along with shooting himself in the foot, apparently, the foot is broken. His jaw is broken, and they're going to wire that this morning." Suel glanced at the clock on the wall. "They may have already done that by now. He's got a fairly severe concussion, a number of vertebrae problems, along with some fractures. Oh, and when you hit him on the chin, apparently, he bit off a section of his tongue," Suel said and grinned.

"That explains his speech impediment. I still think he got off easy," Dillon said and turned the kettle back on. He set two mugs on the counter and dropped a tea bag in each. "Any idea when McCabe will be over at St James?"

"Probably not until sometime this afternoon. Right now, he's in the process of tearing Bennett, the night duty officer, a new one. From there, he's working his way up the ranks. I gotta say, I wouldn't want to be on the receiving end. You know how he can get when one of his team was attacked," Suel stopped for a moment, blinked back tears, and cleared his throat. "Jesus Christ, I'm just glad you're okay, Dillon."

"Thanks, Paddy. Yeah, me too, it's your turn to buy drinks, and I didn't want to miss that."

Suel laughed and said, "I'll buy you all the drinks you want and damn happy to do so."

The kettle clicked off, and Dillon filled the two mugs. Neither one said anything for a half-minute, then Dillon said, "Let me take this tea out to your man. I'll be right back."

He hurried out with the steaming tea and gave it to the officer seated in the squad car. "If you need anything, just let me know. Feel free to use the loo inside."

"Thank you, sir. Sorry to hear about last night. Don't know what the hell happened."

"Yeah, thanks for being here. Much appreciated. Let me know if you need anything," Dillon said and went back inside."

"You thinking of going over to James's?" Suel asked as Dillon stepped into the kitchen.

"What do you think?"

"I think if you want to go, you'd better do it now before your man O'Brien brings on a solicitor that tells him to keep quiet. From what I understand, he works for Jasper Sullivan or did up until last night. No idea what he did for him. Maybe a barman, or hell, maybe he swept floors."

"You want to come with?"

Suel shook his head. "Best if you go on your own. You won't attract as much attention, and you in there alone might be just enough to impress on your man he'd better talk. I'll wait here until you get back. Just mind yourself and don't spend too long. Here's his room number, and I'm not going to tell you who the officer on duty is but mention my name. He's expecting you."

"Thanks, Paddy. I'll be back as soon as I can."

THIRTY-SIX

It was a fifteen-minute drive to St. James Hospital. Dillon took the Father Mathew Bridge across the Liffey, drove past the Brazen Head pub, up the hill, and then took a right, driving through the Liberties section of Dublin. He turned onto the grounds of St. James Hospital. He could have parked right in front of the hospital building and put the An Garda Síochána paper on his dashboard, but he didn't want to attract attention, so he pulled into the parking ramp instead and parked on the second level.

Wearing the lanyard with his ID around his neck, Dillon entered the hospital through the main door on the ground floor and took the elevator up to the third floor. Declan O'Brien's room was in the Intensive Care section. Dillon wound his way along a number of halls before he arrived.

Just like Suel said, there was a uniformed officer seated in front of a room at the end of the hall. Dillon headed toward him. "Hi, DI Paddy Suel sent me. I've some preliminary questions to ask the patient before the interview team arrives this afternoon."

The officer focused on the magazine in front of him, not looking up, and said, "Don't take too long. They got hospital folks going in and out of the room. One just left a moment ago."

"I'll make it quick," Dillon said and stepped into the room. O'Brien was lying in bed with his eyes closed and three pillows propping his shoulders and head up. A vital monitor checking his blood pressure was mounted on the wall behind the bed. Just now, it read 125/75 in green. His body temperature was reading at 36.5 Celsius, and just below that, his oxygen saturation was at 97. An IV pole with two bags was next to the bed, with tubes running down to the intravenous device inserted in his left arm. His left foot, where he'd shot himself, was wrapped in gauze and cloth bandages and raised ever so slightly on a blue foam pillow. Both his cheeks were swollen, and Dillon figured they'd already wired his jaw.

Dillon cleared his throat a couple of times, and O'Brien slowly blinked his eyes open. As he focused on Dillon, his eyes grew wide, and he reached over for the cord with the nurse call button. Dillon grabbed it first and said, "You don't want to call a nurse. They're busy taking care of patients that matter. You don't matter. You're just in the way. You want to live to see another day you're gonna answer my questions."

O'Brien groaned, and the monitor screen on the wall displayed an increasing blood pressure, now at 135/81 and rising. He opened his mouth to speak, but Dillon couldn't understand whatever he was attempting to say.

"I'm going to ask you some questions. You can nod yes or shake your head no. You answer my questions, and I'll leave. You understand?"

O'Brien just stared at Dillon with a worried look on his swollen face.

"I'm going to ask again, and you'd better answer. Nod your head for 'yes' or shake your head for 'no' Do. You. Understand?"

O'Brien gave a slight nod.

"Did a man named Connor tell you where I lived?"

O'Brien shook his head slightly.

"Good, that was good, Declan. Did Jasper Sullivan tell you where I lived?" Dillon waited a bit and then said, "Declan, I'm going to ask you again. If you don't answer me, I'm going to make things very difficult for you. Don't make me do that, Declan. I'll bring Gemma back here and she'll get an answer. I just want to get this over with. Did Jasper Sullivan tell you where I lived?"

Dillon was about to ask again when O'Brien gave a slow, almost imperceptible nod.

"That's all I needed to know, Declan," Dillon said and tossed the nurse call button onto O'Brien's chest. He walked to the door and then turned toward O'Brien. "The perverts in The Joy are going to love you."

"Faa ooo," O'Brien said.

"Oh yeah, they're really going to love you." He stepped out of the room and said, "Thanks, man," then hurried down the hall. He climbed in his car up on the second level and pulled out of the ramp. He paid six euros for his quick visit and was just wondering if it had been worth it when two squad cars and an unmarked car pulled in front of the hospital building. He watched as the officers got out of the squad cars and then held the doors of the unmarked car. DCI McCabe and another uniformed man stepped out of the back seat. Dillon figured it was McCabe's boss in the uniform. The group headed into the hospital, and Dillon pulled out of the parking ramp and headed home, thankful he'd barely missed their arrival.

He was back home fifteen minutes later. Suel's car was still parked, partially covering the sidewalk. The same officer was still in the squad car out front. Dillon approached the squad car and said, "You need anything?"

"No, but thank you. I'm just fine. I've got someone relieving me in about a half-hour."

"Thank you for putting the time in and keeping everyone safe," Dillon said. He stepped into the house just as Suel was coming down the stairs wiping his hands on his jeans.

"You know, that's why I have towels hanging in the bathroom," Dillon said.

"Yeah, but I figured, with you in charge of the laundry detail, they probably never get washed. How'd it go?"

"Good. Your man at the door let me in. They've got O'Brien hooked up to monitors and an IV. He's all bandaged up and, based on his inability to say anything I could understand, I'd say he took a hell of a bite out of his tongue."

"Did you learn anything? If you couldn't understand the muppet, how could he—"

"I told him to nod or shake his head. He tried to call a nurse, but I snatched the call button from him. Anyway, he nodded when I asked if Jasper Sullivan had sent him. That was enough for me. Then, when I was pulling out of the parking ramp, I saw DCI McCabe pull up with two squad cars and his boss."

"Larkin?"

"Yeah, that's your man. I couldn't think of his name. I missed them, or they missed me by only a couple of minutes."

"Good thing because we'd both be out of a job," Suel said.

"You have time to stay for lunch?" Dillon asked.

Suel shook his head. "No, I want to stop over at Finglas Station and chat with Tully Egan for a bit. Bring him up to date. Any word on moving you and the ladies?"

"I haven't heard anything. Have you?"

Suel shook his head. "I'm wondering if we should do it ourselves. Just quietly get all of you the hell out of here."

"Let me think about it. Obviously, the big question is, where would we move to?"

THIRTY-SEVEN

The ladies were in the sitting room on the couch. Lucifer was stretched out on the floor in front of them. They were all watching TV. Two people were interviewing so-called stars that Dillon had never heard of. Just now, they were talking about minimizing their use of water, and so they were showering together once every three days and flushing the toilets in their South Dublin mansion only once a day.

"Sorry to interrupt, but have you had anything for lunch?"

"Oh, no, but thanks for mentioning it. How about if I make us a salad?" Louisa said as she climbed off the couch.

"A salad? I was thinking I'd maybe make us each a grilled cheese sandwich, and we haven't opened that bag of cinnamon bread. That would make some delicious toast."

"I think a salad would be better for us," Gemma said.

"Well, yeah, okay, if you want to make it. I'll do my part and turn the kettle on. It's okay if you have tea, isn't it?"

"Very funny," Louisa said. She gave him a soft punch on the shoulder and headed into the kitchen. Gemma followed, and while Louisa put together the salad, Gemma poured taco chips into a bowl and set a jar of salsa on the table.

Dillon turned on the kettle and made two teas, then filled a glass with water and sat down. They talked about nothing specific for a while, and then Dillon brought up the subject of finding a new location.

"Well, you mentioned this before you left this morning, so both of us are already packed. You just say when, and we'll load up the car," Gemma said.

Louisa nodded. "I think it's a good idea. That knacker last night can't be the only one who knows we're here. Even with someone outside, what if they just stop in front of the house and use a machine gun to shoot out all the windows? I'm for moving and the sooner, the better. No offense, Dillon, you've been wonderful, but after last night, well . . ."

Dillon nodded and said, "Let me make a couple of phone calls after lunch. I have an idea."

They chatted on for the next twenty minutes, and then when they had sort of run out of subjects, Dillon said, "Why don't you two make yourself comfortable in the sitting room, and I'll make some calls."

Dillon placed a call to Suel. "Everything okay?" was how Suel answered.

"Hi, Paddy. Yeah, everything's fine. I was just talking to my guests. We all think we'd better move. There's no telling who else knows they're staying here. O'Brien said that Jasper Sullivan sent him. I'm sure by now Sullivan knows that didn't work too well, but I can't believe he's given up, and I—"

"Just for your information, a team was out to Sullivan's less than an hour ago. He wasn't there, and no one knows where he is. He drives a black Mercedes, and that was still at his home and has been impounded, but hell, he could be driving a beer truck around the city now, and we wouldn't know. We have someone posted at his office, but there's been no sign of him. Why don't you load up the car and meet me in the parking lot at the Croke Park Hotel? You know where that is?"

"The Croker? Yeah, who doesn't know where—"

"Were you listening, Dillon? Not the bleeding stadium, the hotel. It's—"

"I know where it is, Paddy. It's on Jones Road. Right across from the stadium. You think we should stay there?"

"I think you should stay there, at least for tonight. We have to find out where this plonker Jasper Sullivan is. We can get security lined up at the hotel. A couple of off-duty lads will make sure you're all safe and sound. If it's okay, I'll book the rooms. The call coming through from An Garda Síochána might just give it the sense of importance to score a little better room at a discount rate."

"You'll book it in my name?"

"No, let me see if I can book it as An Garda Síochána. I don't want to use your name. I'll meet you over there."

"Yeah, okay, Paddy. Thanks, we'll see you there. Oh, and two adjoining rooms, please."

"Yeah, let me see what I can do. Oh, one more thing, Dillon. Just in case, check your car for a tracking device."

"Good idea. I'll do it now. See you shortly," Dillon said and disconnected. He stepped into the sitting room. "Ladies, bring your luggage down and leave it in the hall. I'm going to pack a suitcase, and we'll head out of here shortly. Just going to check something on the car first," he said and stepped outside.

He got a wave from the officer in the squad car and waved back, then set about checking his car. He examined the wheel wells, the bumpers, the front grill, the lights, and underneath the car frame, and fortunately, came up empty-handed. He hurried inside, ran up to his room, and quickly packed a suitcase. He heard the women making a couple of trips up and down the staircase. He stepped out of his bedroom, and there was Lucifer, staring up at him.

"Oh shit. You? Okay, come on. You're going too."

Lucifer seemed to understand and hurried down the stairs ahead of Dillon.

Dillon told the officer in the squad car that they were leaving but didn't mention where they were going. He opened the lid on the boot, and they loaded the luggage into the car. The ladies, along with Lucifer, settled into the back seat, and Dillon resumed his role as chauffeur. He took a roundabout way to the Croke Park Hotel, once again constantly checking in the rearview mirror to see if they were being followed. They weren't.

He pulled in front of the hotel, and before he could even step out of the car, Suel had pulled in behind him. Dillon climbed out and said, "Great to see you, Paddy. You're just in time to help us carry the bags in. Were you able to reserve two adjoining rooms?"

"Yes, under the name of An Garda Síochána, so get your ID around your neck." He glanced in the backseat, nodded at the women, and said, "Lucifer. You brought fecking Lucifer?"

"Relax, I'll tell them he's a guard dog or something. Part of our investigation."

"Maybe use a different word than investigation. I don't want them thinking we're looking into them."

Dillon nodded and said, "Good point." He pushed the car fob and the lid on the boot rose just as the women climbed out of the back seat. Dillon took hold of Lucifer's leash, grabbed his bag, and headed into the hotel. He draped the lanyard around his neck as he approached the front desk.

"Good day, sir," the man behind the counter said. He was wearing a dark blazer with the Croke Park Hotel logo emblazoned on the front pocket. His nametag read Finnegan.

"How do you do, Finn? I believe we have a reservation under An Garda Síochána for two adjoining rooms."

"Oh, yes, sir. Just a moment, please. Our manager would like to have a word."

"Thank you," Dillon called, all the while thinking, *damn it,* as Finn headed toward an office door.

The manager stepped out of the office a moment later, all smiles. He extended his hand as he approached. They shook hands, and the manager said, "I just wanted to introduce myself. Thank you for choosing the Croke Park Hotel. Should you need anything, my name is Thomas Micklin. Please feel free to contact me at any time."

"Thank you, Thomas. We'll be keeping a rather low profile."

"I understand. Umm, perhaps you would prefer meals delivered to your room? If so, I'll be happy to arrange that for you at no additional charge."

"Yes, that would be wonderful."

"Excellent, well, don't let me hold you up. Oh, and your name, sir?"

"I'm Marshal Jack Dillon. I'm with An Garda Síochána, Special Branch."

"Very good, sir. Very good," Micklin said as he shook Dillon's hand once more and then headed back to his office.

THIRTY-EIGHT

Their rooms were up on the fourth floor. At the moment, Dillon and Suel were on their computers in Dillon's room. The door to the adjoining room was open. Gemma and Louisa, along with Lucifer, were in their room watching another episode of Derry Girls.

"They're not finding Jasper Sullivan anywhere," Suel said. "They've sent a notice to all the airlines at Dublin airport. They've checked his home twice, his office, almost all of his pubs, including the Sunset House and—"

"You said almost all the pubs. Which pubs haven't they checked?"

"Just the one, Pinky's, but they don't open until 4:00."

Dillon checked the time on his laptop screen. It was just after 3:00. "If they don't open until four, wouldn't that seem like a logical place for him to be? He could use the phone there and not give away his location. He could park down the street or in a parking ramp nearby."

Suel seemed to think. "You want to head over there?"

"One of us needs to keep an eye on those two," Dillon said and nodded toward the adjoining room with the women.

"You want to flip a coin for who stays here and who goes?"

"Why don't I just go, and you stay here," Dillon said. "See what else you can find out on Sullivan. Maybe he's got a place on a lake, a home in the mountains, or something. I'll drive over to Pinky's and look around."

"Yeah, just do me a favor and give me a call once you get over there and a call when you're leaving and heading back here."

Dillon nodded, turned off his laptop, and rolled off the bed. "Let me just check on our guests before I go. I'm not going to tell them I'm leaving."

"Good idea."

Dillon wandered into the adjoining room. Louisa and Gemma were both stretched out on the double bed closest to the TV. They were each resting against two pillows propped up against the headboard. Lucifer was stretched out between them, sound asleep. Dillon noticed Gemma's phone on the table between the beds. "Need anything, ladies?" Dillon asked.

"No, we're just fine," Gemma said.

"Okay, just checking. Gemma, if I see you on that phone, I'm going to take it from you," Dillon said.

"I promise I'm not making calls."

"Okay, I don't want you answering calls, either." He noticed the three empty little wine bottles next to the TV.

Since there were only four of the little bottles in the refrigerator, there was no point in making an issue out of it. He headed back into his room, slipped on a jacket, and gave Suel a wave.

"Remember to phone me once you get there," Suel said.

Dillon nodded, gave another wave, and quietly closed the door behind him. He drove over to Pinky's in record time and parked around the corner. He sent Suel a text saying he'd arrived. He climbed out of his car and walked around to the front of the building. The door was locked. He knocked on the door a couple of times, but no one answered. He walked back around the building and tried the back door. It was locked too.

He checked the time on his cell phone. It was 3:40. Pinky's presumably opened in twenty minutes. He glanced around and then walked across the street and down about twenty feet. He leaned against the wall of a garden, and from where he stood, he could keep an eye on the front door to the pub and the rear of the pub. If Jasper Sullivan, or anyone for that matter, left the pub from the back of the building, Dillon would see them.

Five minutes later, an older man, badly in need of a shave, walked up and stopped at the front door of the pub. Feargal Skully, the barman. Even from across the street, he looked ten years older than the sixty-seven years Suel had said he was. He pulled out a set of keys, unlocked the door, and stepped inside.

Dillon kept his eyes peeled. If Sullivan was in there, now would seem to be a good time to leave before customers began to arrive. Dillon waited, and Jasper Sullivan never appeared.

Four people from four different directions arrived and waited out front until the door was unlocked. One of them looked like the older woman who had been passed out face down on the table the night Dillon had been in there. He waited another fifteen minutes after the door had been opened, but he never saw anyone leave.

After fifteen minutes, he was about to cross the street and enter when a squad car pulled to a stop, and both officers stepped in through the front door. Dillon kept his eyes on the back of the building. If there was ever a time something would force Jasper Sullivan out of the place, the arrival of two officers might be it. Still, nothing happened. Ten minutes later, the officers stepped outside, climbed in their squad car, and drove down the street. The driver glanced at Dillon as they drove past but didn't acknowledge him. For his part, Dillon didn't recognize the officer.

He crossed the street and climbed into his car. He sent Suel a text message, 'Nothing. Headed back to the hotel. See you shortly.'

Dillon pulled his car into the parking lot, looked around for a long moment, saw nothing out of place, and entered the hotel. He took the elevator up to the fourth floor, walked down the hall, checked to make sure no one was following, and then entered his room.

"Nothing?" Suel asked, still stretched out on a bed with his laptop.

"An absolute bust. I waited for fifteen minutes after the place opened, but nothing happened. I was about to go in when a squad car pulled up, and two officers entered Pinky's. They were there for a bit and left."

Suel shook his head. "You think they were looking for Sullivan?"

"I don't think they went in there for a drink, if that's what you mean. You find anything?"

"Maybe, remember the pictures of all these victims together, drinking at the Sunset House with Sullivan?"

"Yeah, they were taken on New Year's Eve."

"Check this out," Suel said and turned his laptop toward Dillon. The headline on the article read 'New Year's Day Heist.' "Go ahead and read it," Suel said.

Dillon read the article. A large jewelry robbery happened back on New Year's Day. The estimated value of the jewelry was two point five million euros. "Was this the robbery where the jewelry was going to be displayed in the Bell Gallery?"

Suel nodded. "Yeah, they've worked very hard to keep it quiet. The show was actually going to be at the Bell Art Gallery and was scheduled to run for thirty days, classic jewelry designed and made by Irish jewelers. A lot of pieces over a hundred years old."

"But how does this fit with the victims?" Dillon asked.

"A couple of thoughts. We've got New Year's Eve images of all the victims together at the Sunset House. With the exception of Thomas Davy, they'd all been arrested in the past for safe cracking. Here's the deal with Davy. The robbery occurred on New Year's Day at the Bell Art Gallery. Davy worked maintenance at the Bell Building. Let me rephrase that. He wasn't just a guy who swept floors. He was the manager, and he scheduled and managed the maintenance crew. He had access to the building, including the Bell Art Gallery, where the robbery occurred. The diamond ring that was found in Davy's suitcase has been transferred to the Gallery to see if they could identify it."

"A diamond ring. And if it's been sent to the Bell Art Gallery, would it be a fair comment that it was unique enough to stand out?"

"Yes, the interesting thing is that it was in his suitcase in a business envelope, and at first, it was thought to be some family heirloom. Apparently, someone in stolen property saw it, immediately recognized the ring, and delivered it to the Bell Gallery."

"What did they say?"

Suel shook his head. "Nothing that I can find."

"Can you check and see who the officer was that sent the ring to the Bell Gallery? Give me a minute. I want to check on something," Dillon said and headed into the adjoining room.

THIRTY-NINE

Both women were immersed in another episode of Derry Girls and were stretched out on the bed. Lucifer had moved, or been moved, to the other bed.

"Gemma, can I talk to you for a moment?" Dillon said.

"Oh, can it wait? There are only twelve more minutes in this episode, and—"

Louisa grabbed the remote and clicked the button. The screen froze just as one of the Derry Girls was about to scream. "We've got all day and night to watch this. Let him ask you a damn question, honey."

"Okay, sorry," she said, faking a groan.

"Thanks. The umm…the first time I saw you, I knocked on your door, and you answered it rather scantily clad. Do you remember?"

"Well, I was expecting someone else. In fact, it was going to be that Sullivan plonker, only I didn't know that was his name then. He'd told me Adrian the first time and Colin the second time."

"Yeah, that's what you said. But when you answered the door, you were wearing a necklace."

"Oh, yeah. Neil gave it to me the night he told me he loved me. No one had ever said that to me before, well, you know, unless I was riding them."

"Yeah, of course. Did you happen to pack that necklace?"

"Yeah…umm…why do you want to know?"

"I'd like to look at it. We're thinking it just might be the reason someone is trying to kill the both of you."

She shook her head. "That doesn't make any sense. Umm, except for you, no one has ever even seen me wear it. Well, Neil did, of course. But I've never told anyone about it."

"But you had it on when Sullivan came to see you, didn't you?"

"Well, yeah, I guess I did. But that was only for a second or two, and then he was on top of me on the floor. He couldn't even wait to take me into the bedroom. We just did it on the sitting room floor. I took the necklace off, you know, in case he was going to get a little crazy. I didn't want to slow him down. It usually means I get paid a bit extra. Once he was done, he simply pulled up his pants, paid me, and left."

"Can you get it for me so I can take a look?"

"Yeah, I suppose," she said, sliding off the bed and walking over to the four suitcases. She set the one with the large flowers all over it on the floor, unzipped it, then lifted the top and unzipped the net pocket on the inside of the top of the suitcase. She reached in and pulled out a plastic bag with the Arnott's department store logo, opened it, and carefully removed the necklace. "Is this what you're thinking of?"

"Yeah, thanks. I'm going to take it into the other room to show DI Suel. I'll let you get back to the Derry Girls."

"Okay," she said and climbed back on the bed next to Louisa.

"You never told me you had that," Louisa said.

"Yes, I did. I told you Neil gave me a necklace."

"Yeah, but you never said—"

"Oh, big deal, come on, put the TV back on. I want to see what happens."

Dillon heard one of the Derry Girls screaming as he stepped into his room and settled in on the edge of the bed across from Suel. "Here, check this out. Neil Kinan apparently gave this to Gemma. With the blue stone and the diamonds around it, I just presumed it was fake. But after what you said, I'm having doubts. You think you could get ahold of the DI who sent that ring to the Bell Gallery and maybe have him take a look at it?"

"Let me see if I can get ahold of him right now. DI Jimmy Flannery, I know him to say hi, but I've never worked with him."

"I don't think I know him at all. Go ahead and give him a call."

Suel called the switchboard, got transferred a couple of times, and then said, "DI Flannery? Yeah, this is DI Paddy Suel in Special Branch. I have a question for you. I see that you sent a ring over to the Bell Gallery." Suel nodded and said, "Yes, that was the robbery on New Year's Day, wasn't it? Have you heard from anyone at Bell? Oh, really," Suel turned and gave a nod to Dillon. "Well, here's the thing. We're working a case, Marshal Dillon and me. We've come across a piece of jewelry. We're wondering if you would be able to take a look at it. Yeah, I get that. Yeah, I could meet you tonight. You know where the Autobahn pub is on Glasnevin Avenue? Yes, that would be great. I'll see you in an hour. I'll buy a round," Suel said and disconnected.

"Okay, I heard you're going to meet him in an hour at the Autobahn?"

Suel nodded.

"God, I hope this works. It could suddenly connect all the dots and help in getting Jasper Sullivan locked up. See if he can give you a name at the Bell Gallery. I'm thinking I'll load the women up, and we can head over there tomorrow. We might also want to call Egan and suggest he do another search of the victim's homes. I'm guessing all four of them may have pocketed something. It might just be the reason they were killed."

Suel nodded. "I'll head over to the Autobahn in a bit. You want to call McCabe and give him an update, and I'll call Egan and do the same."

Dillon pulled out his phone. Once his call was transferred, McCabe answered on the second ring. "Good afternoon, sir. Marshal Dillon calling."

"Dillon, where in God's name are you? I've been worried sick."

"Still in Dublin, sir. You're aware of the incident early this morning."

"I most certainly am. Believe me, everyone knows I'm aware, and they're all keeping their distance from me. You're safe?"

"Yes, sir, I've both women with me. We're in Dublin, but I'd prefer not to mention where. No offense to you, sir, but—"

"No offense taken. I'm just glad you're all right."

"Yes, sir. DI Suel is in touch with Finglas Station at the moment. We think we've found a common thread between the four victims and Jasper Sullivan, the individual we suspect has committed the four Finglas murders."

"You've found a common thread?"

"Yes, sir, at least we think so. It's the jewelry heist at the Bell Gallery on New Year's Day. We've been able to link all four victims together the evening before the heist. One of them, an individual by the name of Thomas Davy, was the maintenance manager at the Bell Building in Darndale, where the Gallery is located. He would have had access to the Gallery, possibly alarm codes, and may have known where the jewels were stored. A ring in Davy's possession was identified by an officer, DI Jimmy Flannery. It's been confirmed as part of the stolen jewelry. He's going to be looking at another piece of jewelry later this evening that we've come in contact with. Suddenly, things may be coming together. Thus far, the events appear to be pointing to an individual named Jasper Sullivan as the mastermind."

"Sullivan? I'm not familiar with a Jasper Sullivan."

"Neither were we, sir. We've checked, and there's no previous record, but he's linked to the victims. We have photographs of them together on New Year's Eve, the night before the Bell Gallery heist. That's what we know thus far."

"Excellent, finally, something is beginning to work. All right, keep me informed and stay safe."

"Thank you, sir, I intend to," Dillon said and disconnected.

FORTY

Dillon had paced back and forth in his room for the past hour. Gemma and Louisa were watching another season of Derry Girls while eating dinner in the next room. Suel had left with the necklace with the blue stone surrounded by diamonds over two hours ago. Dillon was currently in the process of doing yet another set of twenty pushups in an effort to calm himself and not phone Suel.

The door to the room suddenly opened. Suel stepped in and looked down at Dillon on the floor. "What the hell are you doing?"

"Pushups, trying to relieve stress," Dillon said and counted off five more before he stopped and rose off the floor.

"Is it working?"

"I'll tell you in a minute. What did Flannery think?"

"You would have liked him, very enjoyable. He's been working the New Year's Day heist at the Bell Gallery ever since it happened. They're down to him and just another officer at this point. They chased up one dead end after another and continued to come up empty-handed until the diamond ring from Davy's suitcase appeared. It's been officially identified as one of the items stolen. Apparently, it was some special kind of cut diamond. He described it to me, but it went right over my head, and I—"

"What did he say about the damn necklace?"

Suel grinned. "He was ninety-nine percent sure it was stolen from the Bell Gallery. He had an image of the necklace on his laptop. The necklace appeared to match the image. Apparently, it has an estimated value of over a hundred thousand euros. It was made back in 1891 by an English jeweler for Prince Albert. He gave it to his fiancé, Princess Victoria Mary of Teck, as a Christmas gift that same year, and then he died in a pandemic a couple of weeks later."

"So, where's the necklace?"

Suel pulled a folded sheet of paper from his pocket. "He signed this. It lists Gemma McKee as the individual who returned the item to the Bell Gallery. He called someone at Bell, and they were going to meet him at the Gallery tonight. They should shortly be in the process of confirming the fact that it is one of the items stolen on New Year's Day. In the event it's not, he'll return it to Gemma."

"I suppose I'm the one who has the honor of telling Gemma her necklace has been confiscated."

"Might be better if you took another route. What if you told her the Gallery was so interested in it that they wanted to have their staff examine it?"

"I think I might not mention it at all and just hope she forgets she gave it to me. She's been more involved watching Derry Girls than asking me where the necklace is."

"You thinking at all about dinner?" Suel asked.

"The girls already ate, and I've been worrying about the necklace. What if we just grabbed a couple of burgers from Fagan's over on Drumcondra?"

"That sounds perfect. You go ahead and phone it in, and I'll drive over there in just a minute."

Dillon pulled out his phone and called. Two minutes later, he said, "They'll be ready in twenty minutes. Hey, I'm thinking, let's presume the necklace is part of the loot. It's not far-fetched that all four members of this group pocketed something, thinking it would never be missed. That could be another common link, along with the New Year's Eve pictures. So, what about Sullivan? Where the hell is he hiding? Apparently, he's not at his home in Clontarf, or at least hasn't been the few times it's been searched. Same thing with his office and the various pubs."

"Yeah, you were outside of Pinky's before they opened, and two officers went in there and searched the place, including that little office behind the bar. No sign of him."

"What about the Sunset House?" Dillon asked. "It's been closed. Someone checked it out, but maybe he shows up late at night or something."

"The other thing is, where in the hell are the jewels? This isn't something you'd hide in the closet. There were a lot of pieces of jewelry. Has anyone checked for a safety deposit box, or boxes, or maybe even a storage unit?" Suel asked.

"God, for all we know, he could be living the life in a five-star hotel."

Suel laughed. "Gee, maybe we should check the list of people registered here."

"Yeah, wouldn't that just take the cake? Any news on the interview McCabe and friends did on Declan O'Brien?"

"Yeah, and not good, although not really a surprise. Apparently, he's still at St. James Hospital. He's been appointed a solicitor and isn't talking. Right now, he's looking for all charges to be dropped, and if we do that, he'll talk."

"All charges to be dropped?"

Suel shook his head. "You know as well as I do, they're just going through the motions. They'll end up with a slightly lesser charge, he'll agree to talk, and other than confirming whatever we already know, namely that Sullivan was behind the break-in at your home, he won't be telling us anything new."

Dillon nodded. "Sullivan has got to have that stuff somewhere."

"We've gone through his bank and credit card records. Nothing suggested a payment to a storage unit or

even a safety deposit box. There's no record of him owning a second property in the mountains or over in Galway
or somewhere out west. He hasn't traveled outside the
country. We've sent teams through all his pubs, and they
found nothing out of the ordinary."

"Except that we can't find him, and does it seem
logical that he could be wherever all the jewelry is?"

Suel seemed to think for a moment and then nodded.
"Yeah, sure, but where would that be?"

"Maybe the Sunset House? It's empty. I know we
had someone go through it, but did they check it at, say,
2:00 in the morning when he could be sleeping there?"

"Interesting. No, I'm sure they went through the
place during daylight hours. Are you thinking we have
someone go over there?"

"Actually, I was thinking we go over. Maybe 2:00
or 3:00 this morning. The girls will be asleep. We can
check the place out in about fifteen minutes. Either he's
there, or he isn't, and we head back here when we don't
find him. You could sack out here, Paddy. I've got two
beds."

"Two beds would be good because I don't like getting whisker burn," Suel said and laughed.

FORTY-ONE

Dillon had the alarm on his phone set for 2:30 am. He slept fitfully and was wide awake a half-hour before the alarm went off. He laid in bed, checking the time on his phone every five minutes until 2:30 finally came, and he rolled off the bed.

"Not to worry, I don't think I ever went to sleep," Suel groaned.

"Let me just peek into the girl's room," Dillon said. He quietly opened the door leading to the other room. The TV was still on, but the sound was off. The screen illuminated the room. Both women were asleep under the covers in Louisa's bed. Gemma's head was beneath a pillow, but she was snuggled up next to Louisa's back with her arm over Louisa's shoulder.

Dillon quietly closed the door. "They're both sound asleep. Let's head over there. You have your lock kit?"

"It's in my car. I'll drive, and we can check the place out. Hopefully, there isn't an alarm on."

They both took their pistols, slipped on jackets, and rode the elevator down to the ground floor. They walked out the main door and into the parking lot. Once they climbed into the car, Suel reached over, opened the glove box, and pulled out what looked like a brown leather checkbook cover. "Just in case the door is locked," he said and slipped the cover inside his jacket. He started the car, and they headed out of the parking lot.

At this hour of the night, it was just a little more than a five-minute drive to the Sunset House. The pub was attached to the corner of a three-story residential building. There was a traffic light on the corner just outside the Sunset house. It turned red as they approached, and Suel stopped. The three large windows on the ground floor and the entrance to the pub were covered by metal roll-up shutters. Each one of the shutters was embellished with a variety of illegible graffiti. A blue octagonal sign for ADT Business Security was attached to the corner of the building above the front door.

"You think that sign is legit?" Dillon asked just as their light turned green.

"I would think so," Suel said as he pulled across the intersection. Being a residential structure with multiple units, there didn't seem to be any parking spaces available. As they drove past the back of the Sunset House, Dillon glanced over and saw a pickup truck parked at the rear door of the pub.

"Keep driving down the street, Paddy. There's a pickup parked in back of the pub."

"A pickup?" Suel said and continued down the street past two open parking places. He turned at the corner, drove maybe fifty feet, made a U-turn over the curb, and headed back to the corner. He turned off the lights and stopped in the middle of the street, ten feet back from the corner of the building.

"Let me hop out and see if I can spot anyone," Dillon said.

"Wait a minute. Open the glove box. I've got my binoculars in there," Suel said.

Dillon opened the glove box and pulled out the binoculars. "I'll check things out."

Suel reached up and turned off the switch for the inside light. "Okay, good to go."

Dillon slipped out of the car, quietly closed the door, and hurried over to the corner of the building. He brought the binoculars up and studied the back of the Sunset House. The pickup truck was gray and had been backed in perpendicular to the street. It was parked ten feet in front of the rear door. The door was metal, and there wasn't a window, so Dillon couldn't tell if a light was on inside the pub. The windows on the two stories above the pub were dark. He wondered if the pickup had anything to do with the Sunset House. Since the pub had been closed for weeks, it might be a local resident who parked there at night.

He watched and waited and was just about to walk back to the car when the rear door to the pub opened, and a man in a dark jacket and a black stocking cap stepped out pushing a two-wheel dolly. A large wooden barrel was on the dolly. The barrel was probably a whiskey barrel, which was not uncommon in pubs. They were used as tables to set your drinks on and stand around while chatting with people. It was just strange that someone was moving the barrel at almost 3:00 in the morning. Dillon focused on the individual for a long moment before he hurried back to the car.

"You see anything?" Suel asked.

"Yeah, put your lights on, pull up to the building so that pickup can't leave. I can't be sure, but I think it's Jasper Sullivan with that pickup."

"Sullivan," Suel shouted as he switched on his headlights and raced around the corner. Thankfully, no cars were coming. He screeched to a stop in front of the pickup, now boxed into the parking space. Just as Dillon opened the passenger door, a shot rang out, exploding the window on the rear door. Dillon dropped to the ground and rolled behind a parked car.

"You okay?" Suel called just as another shot when off.

"Yeah, I guess that answers any questions. I'm calling for backup," Dillon shouted. Suel fired off two rounds as the figure ran back into the building.

The first squad car arrived a few minutes later and set up a position at the front of the building. Squad cars with sirens blaring were arriving from all over the city. The streets were eventually blocked off a quarter mile in every direction. Forty minutes later, the Emergency Response Unit, in helmets, protective vests, and armed with automatic weapons, were lined up along the side of the Sunset House.

Dillon and Suel were now huddled behind parked cars opposite the back door of the pub. The wooden whiskey barrel was still resting on the two-wheeled dolly just behind the gray pickup. From where Dillon and Suel remained, they had not seen a light come on in any of the windows on the second or third floors. They didn't have a radio, so they were talking to someone named McGinn on Dillon's cell phone.

The Emergency Response Unit moved along the back of the building toward the back door. There were eight members, and they moved as one until they were next to the door. The first member took hold of the doorknob, stepped behind the door, and opened it so the other members could rush in. Dillon, Suel, and two other officers were focused on the windows on the second and third floors, watching for any movement.

After a couple of minutes, lights appeared on the second floor and eventually on the third floor. No shots had been fired, and Dillon and Suel were given the all-clear to enter the Sunset House. They entered through the rear door, which led into a storage room and then into the pub. The shelves on the bar and behind the bar were all empty. There were five whiskey barrels lined up along a back wall where customers would presumably stand and drink. Three walls had large silhouettes where framed paintings or maybe posters had once hung. Other than behind the bar, where two officers now stood, there was no place to hide.

Suel opened a door on the far wall marked 'Private.' A staircase led up to the second floor, and two members of the Emergency Response Unit were just coming down the stairs. "Sorry, lads. I'm afraid it's an empty house," one of them said as they stepped past and headed into the pub.

"What the hell?" Dillon said and headed up to the second floor. The stairs led to a landing with a large room on either side. Lights were on in both rooms. The room that looked out over the back of the building, the parking area, and the pickup truck was empty except for a worn brown leather couch and wooden chest that appeared to serve as a coffee table. A half-empty bottle of Jameson sat on the chest. A rumpled pillow and a wool blanket were tossed on the floor at the end of the couch, suggesting this was probably where Sullivan had been sleeping.

They walked back out to the landing. The other room looked out over the street and the traffic light. It had apparently been the office at one time based on the wooden desk. Three empty paper bags from Bewley's, a coffee shop and lunch establishment on Grafton Street, lay crumpled on the floor next to the desk. Two wooden chairs were in front of the desk, and an antique copy machine was against the far wall.

They stepped out of the office and took the stairs up to the top floor. The stairs went up eight steps to a landing and then six more steps heading back toward the center of the building and up to the third floor. They entered one large, empty room covering the entire third floor. There were windows on three sides of the room. One of the corner windows was open, and two members of the Emergency Response Unit were standing next to it.

"Is he out there?" Dillon asked."

One of them shook his head and said, "He was at some point, but he's gone now. There's a ladder attached to the exterior that leads to the roof. We've two men up there, but there's no sign of him. I'm afraid he's gone."

Dillon shook his head and swore. "Where in the hell could he go?"

"Fire escapes on both sides of the building. Your man was in a hurry, sirens coming from every which way. I'm sure he climbed down and walked away before most of us were even here. He fired at the two of yous?"

Dillon and Suel nodded.

"He was probably on the roof two minutes later, ran to the far corner, climbed down, and walked away. There's nowhere to hide up there. It's just one large empty space. Actually, there's nowhere to hide in the entire building."

"You check the restrooms?" Suel asked.

Both men chuckled. "Yeah, men's and ladies. Believe me, he's gone. You think he was here to steal the whiskey barrels?"

His partner laughed and said, "Plonker probably didn't know they were empty."

The comment prompted a thought. "Thanks, guys. Sorry it didn't work out," Dillon said and hurried toward the stairs.

FORTY-TWO

S uel kept up with Dillon racing down the stairs as he said, "For the love of God, would you ever slow down, Dillon? We're not going to find your man. He's fecking gone. We're liable to break our necks at this speed."

"Stick with me, Paddy. It's at his pickup."

"He didn't hide in his blooming pickup, Dillon," Suel shouted as Dillon jumped off the last two steps and charged into the pub room.

The two Emergency Response members standing behind the empty bar watched as Dillon ran out the door with Suel in hot pursuit.

"Jesus Christ, Dillon," Suel said. He bent over and placed his hands on his knees, gasping and trying to catch a breath. "Go, go ahead and check. Sullivan's not in the bleedin' pickup."

Dillon was leaning against the rear gate on the pickup, staring up into the darkened sky, breathing heavily. "I know he's not in the pickup, Paddy. I want to check this. Listen," he said. He placed his hand on the handle of the two-wheeled dolly, stretched his arm over the front of the whiskey barrel, took hold, and tipped back the dolly and the barrel. A noise suddenly emanated from the barrel, not unlike a bag of coins being jostled.

"What the hell?" Suel said as Dillon lowered the dolly and the barrel.

Dillon studied the top of the barrel and said, "You still have that set of lock-picking tools in your jacket?"

Suel nodded as he reached inside his jacket, took out the brown leather checkbook cover, and handed it to Dillon.

Dillon set the cover on top of the barrel and opened it. Among the items were three tension wrenches, 'L' shaped pieces of metal. Dillon grabbed the largest one and studied the lid on the whiskey barrel. There was a one-inch area that was indented, and he slipped the tension wrench between the lid and the top of the barrel, then carefully pulled the wrench up. The lid slowly rose. Suel quickly wedged his fingers on either side of the wooden lid and lifted it off the barrel.

Dillon looked into the barrel and grinned. "Ha, ha, ha, we fecking did it, Paddy. Look what we found," Dillon half-shouted.

Suel looked into the barrel and saw the pile of silver and gold jewelry glistening and shining from the light above the back door. "Oh my God. I don't believe it. Will you look at that, Dillon? Maybe we should just put the barrel in my car and drive off."

"Yeah, we wouldn't make it through the intersection. At least this night wasn't a total waste."

"You think that's all of it?"

Dillon looked inside the barrel and then approximated the height of the pile on the outside of the barrel. "A pile of jewelry maybe two feet high. Yeah, this could be everything."

"We should probably get the Emergency Response Team to transport this to the Property section at headquarters."

"Stay with this while I find McGinn," Dillon said.

Suel picked up the lid and placed it halfway over the top of the barrel.

Dillon walked back into the pub. He didn't see McGinn and headed back up to the second floor. McGinn was in the office room, sitting on the corner of the desk, talking with one of the Emergency Response members. The man had sergeant stripes on his uniform, suggesting he was probably the second in command.

"What's up?" McGinn said as Dillon entered the room.

"We found something you should see," Dillon said.

"It's not another body, is it? Your man is already suspected of killing four people."

"No, thankfully, it's not a body. But it pretty much ties the four murders together."

McGinn and his sergeant looked at one another, stood, and followed Dillon out of the room and down the stairs. As they hurried through the pub toward the back door, it was obvious something was up, and the three men in the pub followed them out to the pickup.

Suel had lowered the back gate on the pickup and was now sitting in the back of the truck. He slid out as Dillon stepped out the back door, and the five Emergency Response men followed.

As Suel lifted the lid off the barrel, Dillon said, "Go ahead and see for yourself."

McGinn and his sergeant looked in first, stared for a long moment, looked up at each other, and then looked in again. "Where in the hell did this come from?" McGinn asked as he stepped back, and the other three men looked in.

"A robbery back on New Year's Day at the Bell Art Gallery in Darndale. We're pretty sure the four Finglas murders are tied to the robbery, and your man, Jasper Sullivan, was involved."

McGinn shook his head. "Well, this is some rather strong evidence that he was certainly involved in the robbery."

A tow truck eventually arrived and hauled the pickup away. The top was put back on the whiskey barrel, and it was loaded into the Emergency Response van. Suel drove Dillon back to the Croke Park Hotel, dropped him off, and then went on to Special Branch. It was almost 8:00 when Dillon quietly entered his hotel room. He hung a 'Do Not Disturb' sign on the door handle and then peeked into the girl's room. They were both still asleep, and Lucifer was stretched out and snoring on the other bed.

Dillon took off his shoes, laid down on his bed, and was sound asleep in less than 90 seconds. Noise from the girl's room woke him. He checked the time on his cell phone just after 10:00. Lucifer hurried into Dillon's room and stood by the door, suggesting a trip outside would be a good idea.

Dillon stepped into his shoes, grabbed his jacket, and headed out. They walked along the Royal Canal up to Drumcondra Road and then walked back to the room. Just as they stepped in, Louisa popped her head in the door between the rooms and said, "Oh, there you are. We were about to order breakfast. Have you eaten yet?"

"Breakfast? It's almost lunchtime."

"Well then, let me rephrase that. We were about to order a late breakfast. Have you eaten yet?"

"No, I haven't, and if you'd bill that to my room, that would be perfect. I'll have the full Irish breakfast," Dillon said.

"I'll phone it in," Louisa said and closed the door.

Twenty minutes later, they were all eating breakfast in the girls' room. Dillon didn't mention anything about the events at the Sunset House and Jasper Sullivan disappearing. Once they finished, Dillon stacked the breakfast dishes on a tray and set it out in the hallway. The girls settled in on Louisa's bed and brought up another episode of a romantic comedy series Dillon had never heard of.

He headed into his room, shaved, took a long hot shower, and then phoned Suel.

"What's up?" was how Suel answered.

"That's why I'm calling you. Anything happening?"

"Not as far as I know. Actually, I'm in an interview room. I was just grabbing some shuteye, and I—"

"Oh, I'm sorry, Paddy. I grabbed a couple hours and just had breakfast with the girls. They're into another TV series if you can believe—" Dillon heard a phone ring in the other room. "Damn it, that does it. A phone call on one of their phones. No doubt it's Gemma. I told her I was gonna take the damn thing if I caught her using it."

"Maybe calm down, Dillon. She might have just hit the disconnect button or something and didn't answer the call. Dillon, you there?"

"Yeah, just listening. I can hear her talking. She's on the damn phone with someone, probably telling them where she is, and we're footing the fecking bill. Let me call you back," Dillon said and disconnected. He tossed his phone on the bed, took a deep breath, and headed into the other room.

FORTY-THREE

Gemma was on the phone, talking. Louisa was lying next to her, watching with a worried look on her face.

"You're sure it's him? He asked you about me?" Gemma looked up at Dillon, shook her head, and held up her hand to stop him as he approached.

"I told you not to talk on the damn phone. Now give me the fecking—"

"Shut up for a minute. This is important," Louisa said just as Gemma rolled over her and stood in her underwear on the far side of the bed.

"And he's still there?" Gemma said. "Okay, okay. Yes. I will. He's right here in front of me. No. No. Just put some clothes on and get out of there, Nicola. Yes, I'll tell him now. Yes, and hurry," she said and disconnected.

"Gemma, I told you not to—"

"That was my friend, Nicola. Jasper Sullivan is asleep in her bed."

"What?"

"She said he showed up early this morning, pounded on her door, and she let him in. He gave her two hundred euros and then fell sound asleep after, well, after they were finished.”

“He’s there? At her place? Are you sure?”

“Yes, he’s a regular. He sees her almost every week. He drank some whiskeys, and now he’s in her bed, asleep.”

“Jesus Christ. What’s her address?”

“Her address? Umm, I don’t know. I just know how to get there. It’s not too far from here.”

“Do you know what street she lives on?”

Gemma looked about to cry and shook her head no.

“Okay, that’s okay. Take me to her. Come on. Let’s go.”

“Let me just do my hair, and I—”

“Gemma, your friend Nicola needs you. Get some clothes on, and let’s go.”

Dillon ran into his room and grabbed his phone, jacket, handcuffs, and gun. He took hold of Gemma’s hand, told Louisa to stay put, and they hurried to the elevator. Once they were in his car, he called Suel. He put his phone on speaker and handed it to Gemma.

“Now, what do you want?” Suel said after two rings.

“Paddy, we got a location on Jasper Sullivan.”

“What?”

“Gemma got a call from a friend—”

“My friend Nicola,” Gemma added. Dillon shot her a look. “Oh, sorry to interrupt.”

“She knows where this woman lives, but she doesn’t know the street name or the address. We’re headed there now. Stay on the line, and as soon as we're there, I'll give you the address."

"Let me call you back, Dillon. I'll alert DCI McCabe," Suel said and disconnected before Dillon could respond.

Dillon pulled out of the parking lot and headed up Jones Road. Following Gemma's directions, he took a left onto Clonliffe, and another left onto Drumcondra. Two minutes later, Gemma directed him to turn left just a block before the Sunset House pub.

"That's it there, the place with the red door," Gemma said, nodding at one of the dozen two-story at-tached brick units.

Dillon pulled to the curb just as a frightened-looking dark-haired woman opened the red door and hurried out of the house dressed in jeans and a sweater. She ran to-ward the car. Based on her breasts bouncing beneath the sweater, she wasn't wearing a bra, and he figured she just pulled on the jeans and sweater. He pulled the pistol from his belt in case Sullivan suddenly appeared.

"Wait, wait, don't. That's my friend, Nicola," Gemma said, looking down at the pistol. Dillon pushed the button to unlock the doors, and Nicola quickly slid into the back seat. She had tears running down her cheeks and a fresh bruise on the right side of her face.

"Oh, Gemma, thank you, thank you, thank you, for coming so fast. He's still asleep upstairs in my bed, but I just want him out of there."

"I'm so glad you called. I want—"

"Nicola, what's your address here?" Dillon said, cutting off Gemma just as his phone rang. "Suel?"

"Yes, where are you?"

"Hang on, let me get you the address. Tell him your address," Dillon said as he handed his cell phone to Nicola in the back seat.

She grabbed the phone, took a deep breath, and said the address so fast Dillon could barely understand it, even though he was parked right in front of the place. Suel must have said something to her because she repeated the address, this time much slower. She nodded and handed the phone back to Dillon.

"Cars are on the way," Suel said. "You okay?"

"Yeah, we're fine. She's out of the house, and—" Dillon suddenly heard a distant siren. "Oh shit."

"What?" Suel asked.

"I can hear a siren. Gotta go," he said and handed his phone to Gemma. "Talk to him," Dillon said and hopped out of the car. He pressed the fob on his key, locking the car doors, and hurried toward the front door. He stopped on the front stoop, took a deep breath, slowly opened the door, and stepped inside. He listened for a moment and didn't hear anything. The layout appeared to be similar to his place, and he peeked into the sitting room. It was empty, although he made note of the empty whiskey glasses on the coffee table. He tiptoed over to the kitchen door and slowly opened it. The kitchen appeared to be empty. He glanced at the far side of the kitchen counter, looked at the reflection on the oven door, and only saw cabinets. He stepped onto the landing and slowly, cautiously made his way up the stairs.

He took the stairs two at a time, keeping his feet on the outside edge of the steps so they wouldn't creak, all the while holding his pistol in a two-fisted grip pointed at the open bedroom door. Toward the top of the stairs, he heard a noise and stopped, then heard it again. Someone was snoring. He made it to the top of the stairs and slowly entered the bedroom.

Jasper Sullivan was in the middle of the Queen-sized bed, snoring. A red silk scarf was wrapped around each ankle and tied to the bedpost on either corner of the footboard. What appeared to be a dog leash was attached to the bed posts on either side of the headboard, and both were attached to a black leather dog collar around Sullivan's neck. Four chains, about two feet apart from each other hung halfway over the upholstered headboard, and a can of whipped cream was on the bedside table. If he had any doubts, the Celtic tattoo on the right shoulder Gemma had mentioned the other day was clearly visible. For a half-second, Dillon wished he had his cell phone, so he could take a picture.

He could hear sirens, still somewhat distant but growing louder. Sullivan suddenly snorted and wrinkled his nose. He started to roll onto his side, but with his legs tied to the bed posts, he couldn't quite get on his side. He attempted to kick his left leg free and then groaned.

Dillon suddenly slapped a handcuff around Sullivan's right wrist, yanked his arm over his head, and attached the cuff to one of the chains hanging over the headboard. Sullivan's eyes blinked open, and with his free arm, he attempted to grab Dillon.

Dillon slapped Sullivan's arm away, wound up, and delivered a solid fist to Sullivan's nose, twice.

Sullivan groaned and placed his free hand over his nose as blood ran down his cheeks.

"Jasper Sullivan, I'm arresting you on suspicion of participating in the robbery of the Bell Gallery and in the murders of Terry Tebbot, Connor Dunne, Neil Kinan, and Thomas Davy."

Sullivan coughed and groaned as more blood flowed from his nose, just as two sirens pulled up in front of the house.

Dillon yanked on the handcuff clipped to the chain on the headboard. The chain was solidly attached.

"An Garda Síochána," a voice yelled from downstairs as footsteps hurried into the entry.

"Upstairs," Dillon replied.

Four officers thundered up the stairs and entered the bedroom.

"What in God's name?" the first officer said as he shook his head. They all looked at Sullivan tied and handcuffed on the bed and laughed.

"Nice job of securing him," another officer said.

Sullivan turned his bloody face away from the laughing officers and placed his free hand over his crotch.

FORTY-FOUR

When Suel arrived fifteen minutes later, there were five squad cars out in front of the place. Sullivan was still chained to the bed and had been the subject of a number of photos. Nicola was seated downstairs in the sitting room, giving a statement. Gemma was doing the same thing in the kitchen.

Being a rather regular paying customer, Sullivan, after climbing down the fire escape from the roof of the building, hurried over to Nicola's home with the idea of staying there for the better part of the day until the Gardai had given up on their search. A Dublin Drink receipt for an Aer Lingus flight to Spain the next day was found in his wallet, but since all the airlines had been alerted, he never would have been able to board the flight or any other flight for that matter.

Dillon was back in Special Branch, giving his official statement to DCI McCabe and two other officers. Once Gemma was finished with her statement, Suel drove her back to the Croke Park Hotel, where she and Louisa resumed watching the TV nonstop.

It was almost 3:00 by the time Dillon made it back to the Croke Park Hotel. He was tired, hungry, and pleased that it appeared the Finglas murders had been put to rest. When he stepped into his room, Suel was sound asleep on one of the beds. Dillon peeked in on Gemma and Louisa. They were settled in front of the TV with Lucifer between them.

"How are you doing, Gemma?"

"Oh, you're back. Everything go okay?"

"Yeah," Dillon said and nodded. He took a deep breath, and as he exhaled, he actually felt the stress begin to release. "Just a long, crazy day. Fortunately, it seems to have turned out well. I'm guessing, with Sullivan locked up, you ladies are free to go home. Do you want me to call you a cab or have an officer take you home?"

They looked at each other, and Louisa said, "Well, since you've made the arrest and we're going to be safe, could we maybe spend one more night here? It would be nice to eat in that fancy restaurant."

Dillon seemed to think for a brief moment and nodded. "Yeah, I think that would be okay."

"Great," Gemma said. "We've got five more episodes to watch in this final season."

"Oh, well, don't let me interrupt," Dillon said. He flashed a smile and headed back into his room. Suel was still out cold. Dillon settled onto his bed and fell asleep almost immediately.

EPILOGUE

Suel and Dillon woke up around 7:00. They ordered dinner to the room, discussed Sullivan's arrest and the jewelry, and then Suel said good night and left. When Dillon climbed into bed, he could still hear the TV playing in the other room, but he was too tired to care.

The following morning, after a 10:00 breakfast, two officers appeared and escorted Gemma and Louisa home. Dillon checked out and phoned DCI McCabe, who told him in no uncertain terms that he was to take the rest of the day and tomorrow off. He was not to appear in Special Branch for the next forty-eight hours.

Once home, Dillon and Lucifer took an hour-long nap in the middle of the afternoon and then walked around Albert Park three times before heading back home.

It wasn't until the following morning when it dawned on Dillon that he hadn't phoned Shannon Kinan. In fact, he hadn't talked to her in days, so he placed the call.

She answered almost immediately. "Oh, Dillon. I was beginning to wonder. Everything okay?"

"Yes, better than okay," Dillon said and told her about the past few days. He mentioned the whiskey barrel full of jewels, the incident at the Sunset House with Sullivan, and finished up with Sullivan's arrest. He glossed over the specifics of Sullivan tied to the bed and didn't mention the can of whipped cream.

"So, you think Neil was involved with this robbery? I never really heard much about it on the news. These four men who were shot, were they all involved?"

"Yes, unfortunately. They were all together on New Year's Eve. We got images off their phones, and then it appears each one was murdered by Jasper Sullivan. In fact, one of the things that helped put this all together was Neil had given a woman a necklace that was one of the items stolen from the Bell Gallery. The necklace has been identified by the gallery. Its estimated value is over a hundred thousand euros. I doubt Neil was aware of that." It was quiet for a long moment on the other end of the line. "Are you still there, Shannon?"

"Oh…umm…yes. It's just, well, a lot of information to absorb. God, Neil, in a way, it's not surprising. I don't think I'm going to tell our mother about the necklace."

"I think that might be a good idea," Dillon said. He was about to ask if she wanted to get together for dinner when he suddenly heard a male voice in the background.

"Everything okay, honey?"

"Oh, well, umm, thank you for the call," she said and hung up.

Dillon stood there thinking for a couple of minutes and then dialed a number. Suel answered after a couple of rings. "Now what?"

"Wondering if you might have time for dinner later today?"

"Does this have anything to do with Shannon Kinan coming to her senses?"

"She must have talked to Kira," Dillon said, and they both laughed.

THE END

Thanks for taking the time to read <u>Jewels to Kill For</u>. If you enjoyed the read please consider leaving a review, it really helps.

Check out the sample of <u>Retirement Scheme</u>, the next book in the Jack Dillon Dublin Tales series.

RETIREMENT SCHEME

PROLOGUE

AIB, Allied Irish Banks, is one of the big four commercial banks in Ireland, with over a hundred and seventy branches in the Republic. The Grand Canal Dock Branch is located at 2 Hanover Quay, between the South Dock Steak House and a bar called Boojum, a Mexican Burrito Bar. At 3:54 on Friday afternoon, the bank was due to close in six minutes. Two men approached the bank from opposite directions. Both men wore faded caps, disposable face masks, wigs, and latex gloves beneath their dark brown cotton gloves.

The older of the two held the door for his partner. The partner nodded and whispered, "Four minutes," as he stepped inside and headed toward the bank's teller counter. The older man stepped over to the table in the center of the lobby. A rack filled with blank deposit and withdrawal slips was in the center of the table. He stood with his back to the teller counter, facing the desks of two bank officers.

The older woman in front of the man at the teller's window thanked the teller, arranged her cash in her billfold, set the billfold in a pocket of her purse, zipped the purse closed, thanked the teller again, and stepped to the side.

The man took a deep breath, stepped forward, and said, "I'd like to make a withdrawal." He handed the bank teller his note and a shopping bag. The note read, 'Empty your drawer. I have a gun.' In case the teller had any questions, he pulled back his windbreaker, revealing the pistol in his belt. Her eyes grew wide, and he politely said, "Do it now, please."

She nodded and began to quickly pull the stacks of euro notes from her cash drawer. As she did so, the teller four feet to the left, a woman named Tierney, asked, "Megan, what are you doing? Megan?" She glanced over at Tierney.

"Megan, give her the shopping bag. Fill it up, be quiet, and nothing will happen," the robber said.

"What do you think—" She stopped and stared as he pulled back his windbreaker.

"Better just do it," Megan said. She quickly handed the shopping bag over to Tierney just as an elderly woman stepped up to the counter and slid a deposit slip and two twenty euro notes toward the teller.

"Pardon me, ma'am, I was just finishing a transaction here," the robber said as he stepped over and gently moved her aside.

"Excuse me. I think you might want to consider waiting your turn. Good heavens, where did you learn your manners?" She made a move to step back in place, but he held his ground and gave her a not-so-gentle shove. "Oh, what in the name of—"

The man at the table pulled a pistol out, fired toward the ceiling, and shouted, "Everyone on the floor, now. Come on, move, get down on the floor. Don't even think of pressing a button, you stupid slapper. Move away from your desk and get down on the floor. Everyone follows directions, and no one gets hurt. Let's go, do it now," he shouted and waved his pistol at a wide-eyed woman still seated at her desk staring at him. She suddenly moved from her chair and onto the floor. "Face down on the floor. Move. Now."

The robber reached over the teller counter, took hold of the shopping bag, glanced around for any additional currency, and headed for the door. He nodded as he passed his partner, who quickly followed.

As they stepped out of the bank, the older man took an olive drab canister from his windbreaker, pulled a pin, and tossed it into a distant, empty corner. The canister exploded a few seconds later, immediately filling the bank with a gray-white smoke. The smoke was too thick to allow anyone to make it to the door, so everyone remained on the floor, coughing and crying.

A few minutes later, a couple stepped out of Boojum, the Mexican Burrito Bar. They noticed the smoke in the bank lobby, and the man held the door open, gradually releasing the smoke outside, while his girlfriend called 999, the Irish Emergency Response number. The first Garda vehicle arrived four minutes later.

ONE

US Marshal Jack Dillon, assigned to Dublin's An Garda Síochána, Special Branch, got the call as he settled onto the couch next to his dog, Lucifer. He had just turned on the 6:00 news, where the leading story was a bank robbery on Hanover Quay, when his phone rang. He checked the screen on his phone, Emergency Response and answered, "Dillon."

"Sir, Emergency Response calling, requesting your presence at 2 Hanover Quay. An AIB bank has been robbed."

It figures, Dillon thought. "Have you contacted DI Suel?"

"Yes, he is en route, sir."

"Mark me as on my way."

"Thank you, sir," the caller said and disconnected. Dillon repeated the address to himself as he entered it into his cellphone's GPS. He turned off the TV, let Lucifer out into the front garden, and hurried up to his bedroom. He strapped on his shoulder holster, pulled a jacket from his closet, and coaxed Lucifer back inside with a biscuit.

He cautiously approached his car, careful not to step in Lucifer's recent deposit, and headed to Hanover Quay. The squad cars, double-parked in front of the AIB bank, identified the location from two blocks away. The building was a seven-story structure. The upper six stories featured all glass housing units with large balconies that were probably going for a million euros each. As he approached, a taxi was just driving away from the South Dock Steak House. Dillon pulled into the spot, took the An Garda Síochána identification sheet from his glove box, and set it on the dashboard. He climbed out of the car, draped the lanyard with his ID around his neck, and headed toward the bank. The building's ground floor units were dark gray concrete with the name of the various businesses, South Dock Steakhouse, AIB Bank, and Boojum, in steel letters above the windows. The bank had a nondescript entrance except for the fact that, right now, the area was taped off by white tape with blue letters that read '**An Garda Síochána**.'

All the lights were on inside the bank, but there was a substance on the windows that limited the view. As he approached, Dillon ran a finger across the exterior of the window but didn't get any residue. Apparently, whatever was on the windows was on the inside. A uniformed officer was standing at the door. As Dillon stepped beneath the An Garda Síochána tape. He held up his ID. The officer nodded and moved aside so Dillon could enter.

At this hour, it was largely An Garda Síochána on the premises. He nodded at a couple of familiar faces and glanced around. He saw three security cameras mounted in different corners. Hopefully, they had been able to record the incident. He headed over to his partner, DI Paddy Suel, who was talking to two individuals at the teller counter.

"Oh, here he is now, finally," Suel said as Dillon approached.

"I literally just got the call not twenty minutes ago. How long have you been here?"

"Five, maybe ten minutes. That's all it took for me to proclaim that a robbery had taken place."

Everyone chuckled. Dillon wrinkled his nose. "I'm guessing they set off a smoke device on the way out. I can smell it, and it's all over the windows."

"And over everything else in here," Suel said and nodded at all the footprints on the floor in what appeared to be very fine dust. "Fortunately, no one was hurt. Two senior individuals were taken to Mater Hospital just to double-check. They were having difficulty breathing after lying in that cloud for ten or fifteen minutes. There's a security tape, not quite four minutes long. We can check it out in the Operations office. It's already been sent to Special Branch. Come on, it's back this way," Suel said and led the way past the teller counter and through a door. There was a short hallway with four doors. They walked past an open office with two officers Dillon recognized. They were speaking with a white-haired man, maybe fifty years old, seated behind a desk.

The nameplate next to the door read Thomas Mullen, President.

The door further down was labeled Operations. Suel knocked on the door as he opened it. Two men were inside. Dillon recognized one of them, Jim Burke, from the Tech Department in the headquarters building. Burke's specialty was facial recognition. They were seated at a desk with three screens mounted on the wall in front of them.

As they stepped in, Burke turned around and said, "Good evening. This is Dermot Casey."

Casey looked up and nodded at Dillon and Suel.

"Dermot has been kind enough to send files to Special Branch and a number of other units. Derm, you want to run that tape for these gentlemen? They're with Special Branch."

Casey nodded but still didn't say anything. His hands flew across the keyboard, and a moment later, three frozen images came up on the screens. One screen focused on the entrance, one focused on the lobby, and the third screen focused on the teller counter. Each image had a twenty-four-hour time in the upper right-hand corner of the screen. At the moment, all three screens displayed the time as 15:54:21. Dillon and Suel stepped behind the two men, and Burke said, "Okay, Derm, play it at normal speed first, then we'll show them the focused version."

Casey ran his fingers across the keyboard, and things began to move on the screen covering the teller counter and the screen covering the lobby. At 15:54:37, the entrance door opened, and two men stepped in. They had long hair that hung over their ears, and they were wearing faded caps, disposable masks, sunglasses, jeans, and what appeared to be navy-blue windbreakers. There were no identifying characteristics on the caps or the windbreakers. One man headed for the teller counter and stood in line behind an older woman. The other man stepped to the counter in the center of the lobby.

As the woman in front of the man stepped aside, he moved forward and handed a note to the teller along with a brown paper bag. They watched as the teller said something, and the man pulled his windbreaker back, exposing the pistol tucked into his belt. As this was going on, the man standing at the counter in the middle of the lobby appeared to be focused on something or someone out of camera range.

The man at the teller counter suddenly moved in front of the woman in the line next to him and said something to the teller. The woman he moved in front of did not appear to be happy and said something to him. Suddenly, the man at the lobby table drew his pistol, fired a shot over his head, and shouted something.

The shot apparently got the attention of everyone, and they began to stretch out on the floor. The teller quickly filled the shopping bag with cash from her drawer. Both tellers disappeared from the screen as they crouched down below the counter. Three individuals could be seen on the lobby screen. All three were lying face down on the floor. One of them, a gray-haired woman, had her hands placed on either side of her head. Both robbers appeared on the lobby screen for a brief moment and then at the door. The man with the shopping bag stepped out of the bank while the other man paused at the door. He took a canister from his windbreaker, pulled a pin, and tossed it into a corner behind him. A moment later, all three screens fogged up. The time in the upper right corners of the screens read 15:58:43. The entire episode took just a few seconds over four minutes.

"There you have it, lads. A few seconds longer than four minutes, probably due to your wan telling your man to mind his manners. They're in and out and disappear."

"What's with the smoke bomb? They're almost out of the place, and no one's going to stop them."

"I'd guess just a precaution," Burke said. "Delay any emergency phone calls or someone following. Teams are in the process of gathering CCTV tapes from surrounding businesses. Anything stand out to you two?"

"That smoke bomb your man sets off. It looked like there was an ID number on the thing. I think his hand was covering up some of it, but I could see L83 in white letters on the canister."

"It's a British military training device," Burke glanced over at a sheet of paper on the desk in front of him. "The actual number is L83A1. A smoke bomb for training purposes in the army."

"They didn't appear to be current members in the Army," Suel said. "You think they came down from the north?"

"Bring up the images of them stepping in the door, if you would, please, Derm."

Casey typed again, and the clocks on all three screens reverted back to 15:54:21. Only the screen focused on the front door began to count the seconds off. Casey froze the image once both men were present on the screen.

"A few things. As we review the tape, you'll notice these are the only two people wearing face masks. Also, I can't prove it, but my sense is at this early stage that both men are wearing wigs beneath those caps. The windbreakers are nondescript, as are the hats, and I would suggest that both have probably been discarded if not destroyed."

Dillon and Suel studied the image on the screen. Casey's comments made sense.

"With the masks, the sunglasses, and the caps, what chance do you have at facial recognition?"

Burke shook his head. "Almost none. I might be able to narrow it down to a few hundred individuals, but there's almost no chance of coming up with a specific person."

"Do you think this was their first dance?" Suel asked.

"It's quite possible, but if it is, they've studied up on what to do and not to do. If I had to guess, I would say they're students looking to get an advanced degree."

"Students?" Suel asked.

"Not someone attending a university. I meant they're learning as they go along. This may well be their first dance but be prepared to see them again."

TWO

They watched the tape at least a half-dozen times and didn't come up with anything new. Dillon and Suel went back out to the lobby. Dillon walked over to the lobby counter and gazed up at the ceiling, studying.

"What are you looking for?" Suel asked.

"On the security tape, your man pulled out his pistol and fired into the ceiling to get everyone's attention, and he yelled at them to get on the floor."

"Yeah, shooting the gun is certainly one way to get folks to pay attention."

"Take a look and tell me when you can see a bullet hole. I certainly can't find one. He was standing just about here," Dillon said, moving to his right about half a foot. "This rack of deposit and withdrawal slips was centered on his chest on the tape. He raised his arm over his head, pointed at the ceiling, and fired, but I don't see a bullet hole."

Suel looked up and stared at the ceiling, searching. "You think he fired a blank?"

"Right now, I'd say that's entirely possible. I can't see where it hit, and it should have been almost straight upward if it was a live round."

Suel studied the ceiling. "I'm not finding anything. So if they're loaded with blanks, and they've gone to a lot of trouble to get a reasonably small amount of cash, what does that mean?"

"I think it means they've got a lot to learn."

"Did we learn anything from the witnesses?"

Suel shrugged. "The woman that your man jumped in front of was positive he had a Dublin accent. He told her he wasn't finished with his transaction. She told him he should wait his turn and then asked him where he learned his manners. I don't know. It's just not adding up."

"And they've no one working security?" Dillon asked.

"Only before holidays, the last two days, and the first two days of any month. Those would naturally seem to be their busiest times. Dermot Casey is the only employee still here, and he was locked in the room with his security cameras during the robbery. There's Mullen, the president, but he's currently being interviewed, and I suspect they'd take an awfully dim view if we stepped in. You want to wait around until they're finished?"

Dillon shook his head. "I'm thinking we head out, maybe grab a pint. Casey sent us the four-minute tape. It would be interesting to check it out. See if, indeed, they were wearing wigs, for starters. I don't know, Paddy.

You think they might have gone online and just gotten information on how to pull off a robbery? There are all sorts of sites that would have that information. Tell you to wear a disguise. I'm guessing that with the cotton gloves they had on, they probably were wearing latex gloves beneath the cotton to eliminate any DNA trace. No mention of a vehicle parked out front."

"There's a parking ramp around the corner, Dillon. How about this? They park in the ramp. Pull off the robbery and remove the wigs, sunglasses, and windbreakers. One of them hides in the back seat, and the other one drives them out of the garage to someplace where they change. Maybe the car is stolen, they set it on fire, drive off in their own cars, and pretty much vanish into thin air."

"Not so far-fetched. Hopefully, we can trace them on CCTV tapes tomorrow. It's just…I don't know…it doesn't seem to be adding up."

"Yeah, I'm with you. You want to check out the parking ramp around the corner?"

"It couldn't hurt," Dillon said.

"I was afraid you'd say that. Come on, let's do it, but you're buying the pints when we're finished."

The parking ramp was a four-story concrete structure. Payments were all made with credit cards, no cash was accepted, Which meant that the operator's office set between the entrance and exit was empty, and the lights were off.

Dillon and Suel split up, with Suel taking the even levels and Dillon the odd ones. The ramp was only a third full. Lots of open parking places and nothing like windbreakers or wigs lying around. Dillon lifted the lids on the trash bins next to the elevators and found exactly what he expected to find, cups, wrappers, newspapers, junk mail, and three different empty half-pints. He also found a black bra, which was not what he had expected. He had taken the elevator up to the fourth level and worked his way down. It barely took a half-hour. Suel was waiting for him at the exit gate.

"Find anything?" Dillon asked.

"Absolutely nothing. You?"

"Nothing unusual other than a black bra, but I figured you already had one, so I left it in the trash bin."

"Probably a good idea. Hell, we don't even know if they parked in here," Suel said.

"Yeah, although this would be the closest place to disappear from sight. Change to another quick disguise, and one of you hides in the back or even inside the boot, and off you go. With that smoke bomb, even if the Garda arrived in a minute or two, they'd be involved in getting people out of that mess, and the robbers would have all the time in the world to casually exit and drive out of town."

Suel nodded and said, "You aware of a car set on fire anywhere?"

"You mean destroying the evidence? No, I haven't seen anything come across on my phone. Of course, once they're out of the immediate area, hell, they could drive up to Meath or down to Wicklow County and destroy the vehicle or just leave it on the street with the keys in the ignition for some idiot to make off with the thing thinking he'd made a big score."

"I think the best thing we could do would be to adjourn to the Autobahn pub, where you can buy me a pint, and we can discuss what our next move is going to be."

"I can't believe you're starting to make sense, Paddy. Let's go."

THREE

Dillon glanced around the pub and asked, "What do you think?"

Suel took a deep breath and exhaled. "I still think we're going to see these two again. Unfortunately, I believe Burke was right. They're using this as a learning experience. How much money do you think they got from today's effort? One, maybe two thousand euros? It strikes me as an awfully big risk to take for that small amount. Given the sense of planning they seem to have put into the operation, wouldn't they have realized, at some point, that there was a finite amount of cash?"

A waitress approached, and Dillon raised his hand, signaling for two more Guinness. "If what you say is true, Paddy, and I'm not suggesting you're wrong. But if that is the case, my thought is we'll see them again sooner rather than later. And if that's the deal, where is their next target? A larger bank? A busier bank? It's not rocket science to realize that today's robbery occurred at a small neighborhood bank for a couple thousand euros. Even if they want to move up the ladder, a larger bank isn't going to work because the place will be too big for two individuals to rob. Plus, a larger bank will have security people who would be armed. That's an entirely new problem that they would have to deal with."

Suel nodded. "Yeah, you're right. But I just can't see them continuing at this level, a couple thousand, and if you're caught, you'll be spending six to ten or maybe even twelve years behind bars."

"But these guys, I don't know. Maybe the ultimate target isn't a bank. Maybe it's a business, someone's office, a jeweler, or even some kind of warehouse."

"It will be interesting to see what, if anything, we're able to get on CCTV footage. Maybe if we—"

The waitress suddenly appeared with two pints of Guinness. She set one in front of Suel and the other in front of Dillon. "Fifteen euros," she said.

"My dad told me he'd buy both pints," Suel grinned and nodded at Dillon.

She looked at Dillon, glanced back at Suel for a brief moment, and joked, "No doubt hoping to get his wayward son back on track."

Dillon laughed, pulled out a twenty euro note, and set it on her tray. "Keep the change. Your comment was worth it."

They clinked glasses and both took a hearty sip.

"You're not aware of these two showing up anywhere in the past, are you?" Suel asked.

Dillon shook his head. "No. If I were, I would have mentioned it. I think it will be interesting to see what comes up on CCTV. My guess is we're going to be looking at next to nothing. At no surprise, the note your man passed to the teller was printed off, so there is no handwriting to compare. A total of seven words, short and to the point."

"Looking at the tapes, what do you think they did wrong?" Suel asked and took another sip.

"In all honesty, not much. Were it not for your wan, giving the man a hard time, they may have been able to walk out of there, and no one would have been the wiser. Only firing the pistol, apparently, a blank, is what got everyone's attention and got them on the ground. I find it interesting they didn't collect wallets and purses. It's not unusual to gather all that up."

Suel nodded. "Yeah, but in the instances where it's been done, there's usually a group large enough to have one or two people in charge of that. Just the two of them? It would have put them on the security cameras for another minute, maybe two. The fact that they didn't do that suggests they had at least a rudimentary plan going in. It seems obvious they wanted to get out of there as quickly as possible."

"Yeah, and it seemed to work. I still like the idea of the smoke bomb being used to get the Gardai focused on moving people out of the lobby and not looking for the robbers, or at least giving them time to casually disappear and not attract any attention. Hopefully, we'll get a car and license number on CCTV, and that will be the end of it. I'm still coming back to why in the hell anyone would do this. They've got about a ten percent chance of not getting caught, and for what? Two thousand euros? It's crazy."

"Yeah, that's the bottom line." Suel drained his glass. "Hey, thanks for the pint. I'll catch you in the morning."

They walked out together and headed home. Dillon drove past Tara's house, just across the lane and up a couple of doors from his place. There was a gray Volkswagen Golf parked out front, and the drapes in the sitting room were drawn, meaning she was entertaining someone or being entertained. He pulled into the front garden, let Lucifer out, and made himself a grilled cheese sandwich. Once he finished eating, he let Lucifer back in. He scanned the TV for a movie, but nothing caught his interest. He watched the tail end of the late evening news and headed up to bed.

FOUR

Since it was Saturday morning, Dillon woke up forty-five minutes before his alarm would normally go off. He hadn't set the alarm, so, of course, he didn't sleep in. He crawled out of bed, pulled on a sweat suit, and headed downstairs. He put the coffee on and turned on his laptop. He had eleven emails waiting, not one of any interest. He didn't need a new mattress, he was happy with his car and home insurance, and then there were the three political emails from people he would never vote for. He deleted one after another and cleared his emails in about ten seconds. He logged into YouTube, brought up last night's US evening news, and listened to that while he prepared his breakfast.

Halfway through breakfast, Lucifer appeared, and Dillon let him out into the front garden. He finished breakfast, filled Lucifer's food and water dishes, and let him back inside. He checked the local Dublin news, nothing really of interest and only a brief mention of the AIB robbery yesterday afternoon. He went upstairs, shaved, grabbed a shower, and hopped in the car. As he backed out of his drive, it wasn't lost on him that whoever belonged to the gray Volkswagen Golf at Tara's house across the lane was still there this morning. He drove to his office in the An Garda Síochána Headquarters building located alongside Phoenix Park.

He parked close to the main door and entered the building. Once in the Special Branch section, he settled in at his desk and opened the first of a half-dozen files regarding yesterday's AIB robbery. He examined the images of the two individuals as they entered the bank. He focused on the faces, enlarging the images and examining the little he could see of the hairlines on the two individuals. Burke had suggested that both men were wearing long-haired wigs beneath their caps, and Dillon was inclined to agree.

The two men had on disposable masks, but Dillon noted that the suspect with the blonde hair had what appeared to be maybe a half-day's beard growth in the area of his sideburn and hairs in his ear that appeared brown or possibly auburn. If he'd shaved first thing in the morning, the beard growth Dillon was studying would make sense at almost four in the afternoon.

The sunglasses on both men were reflective, and for a half moment, Dillon recalled snapshots of his father as a young man in a US Army uniform wearing mirrored sunglasses upon his arrival home from Viet Nam.

He studied the wrists on both individuals looking for a hint of latex gloves underneath the brown cotton work gloves. The gloves were tucked into the elastic-reinforced sleeves of the nylon windbreakers, and he was unable to detect any latex. Examining other images, he noted the remnants from labels that had been cut off from the rear of both pairs of blue jeans.

He couldn't be sure, but the pistol that the one suspect held and fired appeared to have a black carbon fiber finish. He enlarged the image, but it blurred what he thought might be the manufacturer's name to the point that he couldn't make it out.

He made a list of questions and suggestions regarding the wigs, actual hair color, and the type of weapon and sent them to Emily down in the Tech Lab. That done, he headed out of the office, made a quick stop at his local Aldi grocery store, and drove home. This time, the Volkswagen Golf was gone from Tara's house.

Lucifer met him at the door and hurried out into the front garden. Dillon put the groceries away, grabbed the leash, and took Lucifer on a walk. They did three laps around Albert Park just outside of DCU, Dublin City University. Each lap was 1.2 miles, and when they'd finished the third lap, both Dillon and Lucifer were ready to head home.

Dillon placed a call to Aiofe McDonald, a woman he'd dated off and on, and ended up leaving a message. "Hi Aiofe, Jack Dillon calling. It's been too long since we went out. Just wondering if you'd like to join me for dinner this evening. Nowhere in particular, but I'm in the mood to eat in a restaurant for a change. Just let me know, and I'll gladly pick you up."

He disconnected, then went upstairs, changed the sheets on his bed, vacuumed the bedroom, and cleaned the bathroom sink and the glass in the shower. He had dozed off on the couch in front of the TV when his phone rang. He cleared his throat and answered in what he hoped was a sexy voice, "Jack Dillon."

"Are you okay, Dillon? You sound like shite," Suel said.

"Oh, you, I was hoping it was a woman I'd called and left a message asking her to dinner."

"Oh, for lord's sake, forget it. If she has any brains, she won't be calling the likes of you back. Hey, listen. I'm going to be watching the rugby match on the telly tonight. We're playing the All Blacks, New Zealand's team. If you're not too busy, why don't you pick up some beer and come over."

"Yeah, I suppose I can do that. If I don't hear from that woman in the next thirty minutes, I'll give you a call and—"

"Dillon, it's almost 5:00. You're not going to hear from her. Come on over. Oh, and don't forget the beer," Suel said and disconnected.

Dillon walked into the kitchen. Suel was right. It was almost 5:00. He'd apparently been asleep for an hour and a half. Aiofe hadn't returned his call, and whether he liked it or not, he knew he probably wouldn't hear from her. He let Lucifer out into the front garden, then went upstairs, showered, and changed. On the way to Suel's, he stopped at a local shop and grabbed a twelve-pack of Smithwick's Blonde Ale. He parked in front of Suel's place ten minutes later.

Given Suel's character, you'd expect a place with overgrown grass, gardens filled with weeds, and maybe two or three newspapers on the front steps. Just the opposite was the case. The lawn was always neatly trimmed, and the gardens, edged with stones painted white, had a number of different flowers, not to mention a half-dozen rose bushes and two rose trees. The two front windows had flower boxes with a lovely array of red and yellow flowers.

Dillon stepped into the front garden. Just as he closed the gate behind him, Suel opened the front door wearing jeans, a long sleeve Irish rugby jersey, dark green with a white collar, and a black apron. "Aww, Paddy, how nice of you to get all dressed up for me."

Suel shook his head, took the twelve-pack of beer from Dillon, and said, "Believe me, I didn't dress up for the likes of you. Come on in. You're the first one here."

Dillon stepped inside and followed Suel into the kitchen. He could see three roast chickens through the window on the oven door. "The first one here? You've got other folks coming?"

"Not to worry, the two of us plus my friend Sean and three others."

"Three others? You should have told me. I would have picked up a case of beer instead of just the twelve-pack."

"We've plenty of beer and wine, and if things get desperate, I have a half-dozen whiskeys. Here make yourself useful and toss this," Suel said as he slid a wooden salad bowl across the counter to Dillon. A salad fork and spoon were already in the bowl.

Dillon began tossing the salad as Suel opened a bag of green beans and dumped them into a frying pan. A moment later, the doorbell rang.

"Oh, that should be Sean. Would you mind letting him in?"

"I'm on it," Dillon said as he hopped off the stool and stepped into the entryway. He opened the door and was about to say, 'Hi, Sean,' until he focused on the red-haired woman holding what looked like a white bakery box.

She was maybe six inches shorter than Dillon. Dressed in tight white shorts, with a black belt and a red and white striped off-the-shoulder top. She smiled and said, "Oh dear. I hope I'm in the right place. Does Paddy Suel live here?"

"He does, and he's cooking in the kitchen at the moment. I work with him. My name is Jack Dillon," he said as he held out his hand.

"Noreen Rooney, nice to meet you," she said as they shook hands.

"Let me take this for you," Dillon said and took hold of the bakery box.

"Dessert," she said. "Thank you. So you work with Paddy? Are you the American he's always talking about?"

"Probably, but don't believe whatever he said. I'm really a very nice guy."

She laughed as Dillon closed the door behind her. "He only says nice things about you."

"Then he's one of the few," Dillon said, and she laughed again as they headed into the kitchen.

"Oh, Noreen, thanks for coming. The other girls should be here shortly. Can I get you a beer or a glass of wine?"

"A glass of wine would be wonderful. White, if you have it."

"Coming right up. You met my partner, Dillon? Hopefully, he didn't say anything too rude or insulting."

"No, he was very polite. Oh, I baked all day and made a dessert, then placed it in that box."

"How very thoughtful," Suel said as he filled a wine glass and handed it across the counter to her.

"Thoughtful? You told me I had to bring it, or you weren't going to let me in."

The doorbell rang, and Suel said, "There's trouble. You mind letting them in, Noreen?"

She took a sip of her wine, set the glass on the counter, and said, "Watch this for me, and don't let Paddy drink any, please." The doorbell rang again as she stepped into the entry.

They heard the door open, and then a male voice said, "Oh, Noreen, here to keep us all in line?"

"Come on. We're all in the kitchen. How you keeping, Sean?"

"Good, thanks for asking. Not a bother."

Everyone chatted, sipped their drinks, and Suel eventually took the chickens out of the oven. "We shouldn't wait any longer for the Mahoney sisters. They'll simply have to catch up," Suel said just as the doorbell rang.

Noreen hurried out of the kitchen, and a moment later, the three men heard shrieks and laughter. "Oh God, prepare yourselves, gentlemen. With the three of them we'll be lucky to get a word in."

TO BE CONTINUED . . .

Thank you for taking the time to check out <u>Retirement Scheme</u>, the next book in the Jack Dillon Dublin Tales series. Things are about to get rather complicated and nasty, better grab a copy. Enjoy!

BOOKS BY MIKE FARICY

CRIME FICTION FIRSTS

A boxset of the first four books in four crime fiction series:
Russian Roulette; Dev Haskell series
Welcome; Jack Dillon Dublin Tales series
Corridor Man; Corridor Man series
Reduced Ransom! Hot Shot series

The following titles comprise the Dev Haskell series:
Russian Roulette: Case 1
Mr. Swirlee: Case 2
Bite Me: Case 3
Bombshell: Case 4
Tutti Frutti: Case 5
Last Shot: Case 6
Ting-A-Ling: Case 7
Crickett: Case 8
Bulldog: Case 9
Double Trouble: Case 10
Yellow Ribbon: Case 11
Dog Gone: Case 12
Scam Man: Case 13
Foiled: Case 14
What Happens in Vegas… Case 15
Art Hound: Case 16

The Office: Case 17
Star Struck: Case 18
International Incident: Case 19
Guest From Hell: Case 20
Art Attack: Case 21
Mystery Man: Case 22
Bow-Wow Rescue: Case 23
Cold Case: Case 24
Cash Up Front: Case 25
Dream House: Case 26
Alley Katz: Case 27
The Big Gamble: Case 28
Bad to the Bone: Case 29
Silencio!: Case 30
Surprise, Surprise: Case 31
Hit & Run: Case 32
Suspect Santa: Case 33
P.I. Apprentice: Case 34
Rebel Without a Clue: Case 35
Puppy Love: Case 36

The following titles are Dev Haskell novellas:
Dollhouse
The Dance
Pixie
Fore!
Twinkle Toes
(*a Dev Haskell short story*)

The following are Dev Haskell Boxsets:

Dev Haskell Boxset 1-3
Dev Haskell Boxset 4-6
Dev Haskell Boxset 7-9
Dev Haskell Boxset 10-12
Dev Haskell Boxset 13-15
Dev Haskell Boxset 16-18
Dev Haskell Boxset 19-21
Dev Haskell Boxset 22-24
Dev Haskell Boxset 25-27
Dev Haskell Boxset 28-30
Dev Haskell Boxset 1-7
Dev Haskell Boxset 8-14
Dev Haskell Boxset 15-19
Dev Haskell Boxset 20-24
Dev Haskell Boxset 25-29

The following titles comprise the Jack Dillon Dublin Tales series:

Welcome
Jack Dillon Dublin Tale 1
Sweet Dreams
Jack Dillon Dublin Tale 2
Mirror Mirror
Jack Dillon Dublin Tale 3
Silver Bullet
Jack Dillon Dublin Tale 4
Fair City Blues
Jack Dillon Dublin Tale 5

Spade Work
Jack Dillon Dublin Tale 6
Madeline Missing
Jack Dillon Dublin Tale 7
Mistaken Identity
Jack Dillon Dublin Tale 8
Picture Perfect
Jack Dillon Dublin Tale 9
Dublin Moon
Jack Dillon Dublin Tale 10
Mystery Woman
Jack Dillon Dublin Tale 11
Second Chance
Jack Dillon Dublin Tale 12
Payback Brother
Jack Dillon Dublin Tale 13
The Heist
Jack Dillon Dublin Tale 14
Jewels To Kill For
Jack Dillon Dublin Tale 15
Retirement Scheme
Jack Dillon Dublin Tale 16
The Collector
Jack Dillon Dublin Tale 17

Jack Dillon Dublin Tales Boxsets:
Jack Dillon Dublin Tales 1-3
Jack Dillon Dublin Tales 4-6
Jack Dillon Dublin Tales 1-5

Jack Dillon Dublin Tales 1-7
Jack Dillon Dublin Tales 6-10

The following titles comprise the Hotshot series;
Reduced Ransom! Second Edition
Finders Keepers! Second Edition
Bankers Hours Second Edition
Chow Down Second Edition
Moonlight Dance Academy Second Edition
Irish Dukes (Fight Card Series)
written under the pseudonym Jack Tunney

The following titles comprise the Corridor Man series:
Corridor Man
Corridor Man 2: Opportunity knocks
Corridor Man 3: The Dungeon
Corridor Man 4: Dead End
Corridor Man 5: Finger
Corridor Man 6: Exit Strategy
Corridor Man 7: Trunk Music
Corridor Man 8: Birthday Boy
Corridor Man 9: Boss Man
Corridor Man 10: Bye Bye Bobby

Corridor Man novellas:
Corridor Man: Valentine
Corridor Man: Auditor
Corridor Man: Howling

Corridor Man: Spa Day

The following are Corridor Man Boxsets:
Corridor Man Boxset 1-3
Corridor Man Boxset 1-5
Corridor Man Boxset 6-9

THANK YOU!

Contact the author:
- Email: mikefaricyauthor@gmail.com
- Twitter: @Mikefaricybooks
- Facebook: Mike Faricy Author
- Website: http://www.mikefaricybooks.com

Published by

MJF Publishing